WHAT IS LOVE?

"One cannot imagine living a lifetime without true love, while passion, which burns so very brightly, may be snuffed as quickly as a candle in the wind," Richard said.

Patience had never heard Richard address another topic with such intensity and conviction. It was as if the darkness had taken away the Richard she knew and given them back an intriguing stranger. The black sleeve beneath her gloved hand, the brush of his domino upon her own, seemed suddenly more interesting than usual.

Pip sighed and set off without them. "Come along," he coaxed impatiently.

"Yes. Enough of love." Richard straightened, his face returning to its customary calm, the mask hiding his emotions almost as much as the darkness had.

Patience fell into step without demur. And as they walked she stole furtive glances at her friend, observing as if for the first time the way the lamplight touched upon Richard's chin and throat, gilding jawline and lips. She could not help wondering what lucky female had captured those lips to stir such passion.

A Game of Patience

Elisabeth Fairchild

A SIGNET BOOK

SIGNET
Published by New American Library, a division of
Penguin Putnam Inc., 375 Hudson Street,
New York, New York 10014, U.S.A.
Penguin Books Ltd, 80 Strand,
London WC2R 0RL, England
Penguin Books Australia Ltd, Ringwood,
Victoria, Australia
Penguin Books Canada Ltd, 10 Alcorn Avenue,
Toronto, Ontario, Canada M4V 3B2
Penguin Books (N.Z.) Ltd, 182–190 Wairau Road,
Auckland 10, New Zealand

Penguin Books Ltd, Registered Offices:
Harmondsworth, Middlesex, England

First published by Signet, an imprint of New American Library,
a division of Penguin Putnam Inc.

First Printing, May 2002
10 9 8 7 6 5 4 3 2 1

Copyright © Donna Gimarc, 2002

PUBLISHER'S NOTE
This is a work of fiction. Names, characters, places, and incidents either are
the product of the author's imagination or are used fictitiously, and any
resemblance to actual persons, living or dead, business establishments, events,
or locales is entirely coincidental.

*To all who have patiently waited
in playing the games of life and love*

Author's Note

The game we call Solitaire in the United States has been known in England for many years as Patience, the virtue most required for successful play.

Chapter One

Eight-year-old Patience Ballard waited.

Seated in the tufted leather window seat in the yellow drawing room, she sat playing the game that bore her name, feeling quite contrary to both. The ormolu clock on the mantel served as her only companion, its languid ticking echoed by the gentle slap of her cards against the dark and light polished wood of a small, Italian inlay card table: the eight of spades, the queen of lozenges, not the face she was looking for.

She drummed the fingers of her right hand upon the table and pounced upon another card. Still no king of hearts.

What she waited for she could not name, but like the missing heart it tingled in her bones, her fingertips, her toes. It poised just ahead of her, just out of reach, in the periphery of her vision, waiting for her to catch up to it. Something intangible and wonderful. Life-changing.

She did not want to wait. She longed to throw herself into the anticipated mystery, that wonderful unknown, but knew that was not how this game was played. She must wait, as a clever player of Patience waits for kings and queens, knaves and aces to show their faces, one by one.

No one had noticed her new ruby red dress.

Her mother had assured her they would, that she would be rewarded for the pains of holding still for innumerable fittings, for the stays she must wear to fit into it. Unending compliments and attention Mama had promised.

But it was not true. Lady Royston had murmured something about how pretty she looked, and Lady Cavendish had smiled and nodded in agreement, but that was all that had happened. No one else cared how she looked. Certainly the one she had hoped might give her a compliment had said nothing.

Above her, songbirds in cages had been painted on the ceiling, and in the canary yellow damask that lined the walls, birds flew. In her stupid, pinching stays she sat equally caged, while the clock chimed the death of her childhood—her freedom—and the cards were trapped facedown against the table.

"One ought not run and tumble in such a dress like any common hoyden," her mother had admonished her firmly.

Run and tumble? Indeed, one could not. She could barely sit calmly, stiff as a playing card, without groaning in discomfort.

Added to her general state of breathlessness, the cards her mother insisted she play, rather than traipsing about with the lads like some mannerless hoyden, seemed bent on hiding from her. She needed a king—the king of hearts—and she had the strongest feeling he was buried beneath her face cards, where it began to look as if he would remain unavailable.

Patience was not quite clear just what a hoyden was, only that it was undesirable to be one, but she would much rather be playing the part, if that was what she had been doing these many years, with the boys, Richard and Pip.

Of the two boys Patience's mother liked Richard best. He was, she told Patience, a very smart lad, clever at his studies, not given to pranks, neat and tidy with his belongings, and impeccably polite. A tall, dark, serious lad, Richard was the blackbird to Pip's canary. He was the much younger of two sons, and he and his brother, Chase, did not get along.

"A dependable lad," her mother called him. "No worries over that one." Unlike his brother Chase, she meant. And unlike Pip. Dear, darling Pip.

Patience was in love with Pip. She meant to marry him one day, she had informed her mother, if marry she must.

Her mother had nodded, brows arched, and said, "You will tell me when the viscount asks for your hand?"

"You would not say no to him, would you?" she had asked.

Her mother had barked a laugh. "Say no to the Earl of Royston's eldest son? I should think not, my dear."

Patience was not surprised to be met with such a reply.

Pip's real name was Philip Yorke, Viscount Royston, for he was firstborn, and would one day inherit his father, the earl's, title and fortune, but everyone called him Pip because he was bright and quick, and small for his age. Philip seemed far too serious a name for a fellow always laughing and jesting and playing clever pranks. Pip suited him perfectly.

Everyone loved Pip. He was the golden apple of his father's eye, a favorite of his younger brothers, Charles and Geoffrey, the bosom bow of Richard Cavendish, second son to Lord William Cavendish, the third Marquess of Cavendish.

No one denied Pip anything. Not his father. Not his mother. Certainly none of the servants dared question his wishes, and so when he ran into the room as she sat grumbling at the ten of spades she had just unearthed, and raced at once to where she sat, and dove to the floor, where he skidded on the polished parquet to a position beneath the table, shaking her neat rows of cards completely out of alignment, she was not entirely amazed that he should shout up at her, "Need a place to hide!"

She did not question his right to bump against her knees, wrinkling the sumptuous, ruby red riches of her new, very grown-up Christmas gown, only remarked crossly, "Watch it. You upset my cards."

"Sorry." He peeped up at her from beneath the lip of the table, his eyes the blue of forget-me-nots, thickly fringed in golden lashes, long and curling like a girl's.

"Such a pretty boy," her mother had once said of him.

He was pretty, in the same way her sister's buff-colored spaniel was pretty, all silky hair and big eyes.

"Why do you not play with us?" he whispered, the big eyes narrowing. "Do you not like us anymore? Or have you come to care for cards more than games?"

Patience sighed, and would have responded at length had she not heard footsteps in the hall. "He's coming," she hissed. "Are you sure he cannot see you?"

Pip chortled and lifted the hem of her skirt, then plunged beneath the folds of fabric with a muffled, "Now he can't."

Before she could insist that he had no business beneath her new skirt, breathing hotly into the thin muslin of her petticoat, his hand hot and sweaty upon her stockinged ankle, Richard strode into the room, his long legs making short work of the distance between them. "There you are, Ballard," he said. "Haven't seen Pip, have you?"

Pip gave her leg a suggestive nudge.

"I have not set foot outside of this room for the past three-quarters of an hour," she said truthfully.

"Playing Patience, are you? How goes the game?"

"Miserably," she said. "I would much rather be playing hide-and-seek with the two of you."

"How did you know we were playing—" He stopped and glanced about the room, his gaze falling at last on the table where the black and white zigzagged backs of her cards staggered in uneven rows.

Beneath her skirt, Pip sat very still, his fingers tightening a trifle, caging her ankle.

Richard's head tilted. A tight little smile touched his lips. His gaze slid away from the cards, a quick glance. Had he looked beneath the table?

Patience was certain he had found them out. A flush of heat rose to her cheeks, embarrassment surfacing. She could hear her mother's voice in her head: *How does a young lady explain a lad hiding under her dress? It is most unseemly.*

She opened her mouth, searching for the right words.

"Pretty dress," Richard said carefully.

She clapped her mouth shut in surprise. A compliment was not at all what she had expected.

His eyes, a dark moss agate green, framed by blackbird-winged brows, searched hers most intently. The smile was completely missing from his lips. "Is it new?"

She blushed, not so much because he had noticed, and she was pleased that at last someone should notice, but because Pip was pinching at her calf.

"Yes. Do you like it?"

"Bright," he said, and then a little shyly, lashes fanning darkly against the pallor of his cheek, "Looks soft."

"Yes." She stroked the sleeve, and gave Pip a kick. Did he mean to bruise her? "Velvet. I love the feel of it."

Richard's hand lifted, as if he meant to touch the fabric. Halfway there he froze, face flushing.

"Go on," she said, holding out her arm. "It's lovely."

Beneath her skirt Pip shifted, both hands ringing her ankle, giving her leg a little cat-clawed shake.

Richard, his face gone almost as scarlet as the dress, leaned close enough that he might brush the tips of his fingers across the sleeve, fleet as a bird on the wing. "Nice," he murmured.

She shrugged. "I begin to dislike it."

"Oh?" His brows rose.

"Because of the dress I cannot play as I usually do. Mama is afraid I will get it dirty, or tear the hem."

"Ah," he said, using the exact same tone, the same nod his father sometimes used, as if he understood entirely. He clasped his hands in the small of his back—a blackbird with wings folded. The color in his cheeks subsided. "Perhaps we could join you in a hand of cards, and save hide-and-seek for another day, when you are more suitably attired."

The idea, even his unusually formal language, pleased her, and yet she was all too conscious of Pip crouched catlike against her knee, his head making a tent of her velvet skirt, a breeze wafting up under the heavy fabric, chilling her everywhere but those places he touched. His hands, the bulk of him leaning into her thigh, were too hot.

Her cheeks warmed. Her mother would faint at once if she ever found out her daughter had allowed a lad freedom to tuck himself beneath her nether limbs.

"That would be lovely," Patience said, and gathered up the deck with a sweep of her hands. "But perhaps you had best find Pip first."

Richard nodded, stepping back from the card table. "No telling where he's gotten off to," he said quietly, and with a quick glance, a shy, smiling glance, he strode from the room as swiftly as he had entered it.

"Gad!" Pip cried out when his footsteps had faded, and he crawled out from under the table. "I thought he would never leave. Why ever did you engage him in conversation? Did you not realize I was suffocating down here?" Giving the hem of her skirt a little kick he said, "Bloody velvet was devilish hot."

His hair did look a bit disheveled, a trifle damp at the nape of his neck.

"I did not ask you to jump under my dress," she said sharply. "It was dreadfully improper of you to do so. I think he knew."

"Richard? Don't be daft. He's not that clever. He would have said something if he knew."

Of course. He would have. It would have meant his winning the game, wouldn't it? And yet she could not stop playing the moment in her mind, the moment he had looked down at the table, at the crooked rows of cards. Something in his eyes had been so watchful, so intently watchful. Deep within her she was filled with the conviction: He knew.

He knew, and had chosen not to embarrass her.

"Pretty dress," he had said. The compliment meant more to her than those of anyone else who had noticed the dress. Certainly Pip had not said a word in praise.

She smiled, and wondered if mother was right after all: It was time for her to behave like a young lady, not a hoyden.

Chapter Two

Seventeen-year-old Patience remembered.

Memory gathered about her like the colors of the evening, fragile as the petals of a delicate flower: rose and violet, the walls on one side of the street touched with gold, the other side fallen into darkness, a visual echo of past and present, one so clear to her, the other cloaked in shadow.

A warm breath of a breeze caressed her curls, played with the heavy satin of her new scarlet domino, lifting it like wings, kicking the hem across Richard's thigh as she took the cast-iron step into his brother's canary yellow coach. Nine years had passed. Nine years in which she had depended upon the unshakable support of his gray-gloved hand.

She had kept the memory of that afternoon—with all its potential—close through the passage of the years. She had relived the promise of it, the pulse-racing sense of the forbidden, the heat of Pip's breath at her knee, the cat's-paw warmth of his hand at her ankle. Her secret, like a caged bird, freed for no one, trusted to no one. Not even Richard.

She had imagined—oh, how much she had imagined, heart fluttering, thoughts atwitter—what every following encounter with Pip would be like.

And tonight she would find out again. Richard meant to take her to him. To her dear, beloved Pip.

Tonight would be a magical night—she knew it. The thrill of possibilities, of potential, gathered along her spine, the base of her neck, in the tips of her fingers and toes. It stirred butterflies in her stomach and rib cage.

"Pretty domino," Richard said quietly, with the same observant intensity he had possessed since childhood, with the same ageless moss agate eyes.

"Thank you." Patience gathered the luxurious folds of material around her, smoothing the satin that draped her knees as she settled against the squabs. She was so much older, so much wiser than she had been that long-ago afternoon.

A better player, she thought.

He followed her in, the coach dipping and swaying until he settled, the sun catching him full in the face, revealing in harsh detail features she knew as well as her own. He smelled of cedar and lime, tangy and crisp, the scent he always wore.

"Color suits you," he said.

Trust Richard to notice. Dear Richard. Dependable Richard. He was still her mother's favorite.

The domino was a costly wealth of deep scarlet, fully lined in black. Red brought out the roses in her cheeks, and deepened the rather ordinary brown of her hair. Patience loved to wear red whenever she could, though her mother considered it far too flamboyant a color for a young woman of taste. Quite proper for a young girl's Christmas dress, not at all the thing for a young woman's masquerade domino. And yet Patience had held out for it, and at last Mama had relented despite Papa's protest that it was a foolhardy expense, that she could just as easily wear her sister, Pru's, hand-me-down yellow.

But Mama knew canary yellow did not suit Patience's complexion. The domino had never looked good on Pru. Papa had relented.

Richard's compliment was well appreciated, therefore, but it was not Richard's compliments Patience sought. He was too ready with them. Whenever they encountered one another he made a point of saying something politely complimentary. It was his way.

She would much rather hear compliments from another who was less generous with pretty words.

"Are you sure he will be there?" she asked, sitting forward. She bounced a little in anticipation, which was not at all ladylike, but Patience had never found it easy to be ladylike every single moment of the day.

"I am absolutely sure." Richard turned to look out the window at the dark and light shuffle of houses, like a great deck of brick-faced cards. Shadow and sunlight played across his features, making a mystery of the familiar. Dark and light colored his voice as he said, "Pip never misses an opportunity to impress."

Pip. Dearest Pip. She had not seen him—how long had it been?—could it be more than four years? Thirteen she had been the last time they had climbed trees together, and played backgammon and chess. Thirteen, and still not as ladylike as her mother had wished. Indeed, she had felt completely green in that last encounter, awkward and spotty. Pip and Richard had seemed so much older at sixteen. Beyond her touch. Especially Pip, who seemed to avoid all awkwardness as he grew, the years so very kind to him in every way but one.

His father had died at an early age, as had Richard's. She could not fathom such a painful loss. Her own father was a picture of health and happiness, ruddy cheeked and clear eyed. She could not imagine life without him.

She had heard much of Pip, of course. His bereavement had vaulted him to fresh position and wealth. Everyone in London spoke well of him. Handsome Philip Yorke, recent heir to the Royston title and fortune, able guardian of his younger brothers' futures. He was an earl now. Clever Pip. Lucky Pip. The *ton*'s darling. Catch of the Season. Rumor flew he was soon to be snared. That a certain wealthy young lady had captured his heart.

Patience had so long imagined herself in such a role that she had been startled and pained to discover her opportunity lost.

"Is he in love with her, do you think?"

If anyone would know it would be Richard—dark, quiet, sensible Richard, who had stood by Pip through the pranks he had been famous for at Eton, who had convinced him not to gamble away all of his fortune on the horses, who reminded him often that he set an example for his younger brothers.

Too bad, really, that Richard held no such sway with his elder brother, Chase, heir to the Cavendish fortune. Chase was very like Pip. He liked to gamble. He was often to be seen in the company of low women. He drank to excess. Rumor had it he ran through the family fortune with unseemly haste, no thought for the future—no example for his younger brother, who did his level best, as his brother's bookkeeper, to salvage the family's waning fortune.

Richard turned from the window. His lips thinned as he said carefully, "Pip has always possessed a great capacity for falling in love."

Generally with the most unsuitable women, Patience had heard her mother complain. There had been a dreadful rumor that Pip had run away to Gretna Green with a beautiful ballet dancer the week before his father died—that Richard had gone after him, that he had hushed up the whole affair. When she had asked Richard if it was true he had said, "You must not believe every mean-spirited bit of gossip you hear, Patience."

"Will she make him a suitable wife?" she asked with trepidation as they turned a corner, wheels rumbling.

Richard nodded, frowning against a sudden onslaught of sunlight. It bathed his face in gold, made his features seem suddenly masked. "Completely unobjectionable," he said. "He breaks pattern. But then, Pip is always full of surprises."

Patience did not know whether to take heart from such a remark or to fall prey to despair. "Do you think he will be glad to see me?" she asked wistfully as the coach crossed Westminster Bridge, the Thames agleam with brassy light, the sound of flowing water soothing.

Richard looked at her without speaking, his eyes like polished agate, the sun gilding his lashes, jaundicing his complexion. It glared too starkly upon his Roman nose, a king's nose, such bright emphasis not at all flattering. But then his mouth twisted in a most winsome smile— the smile of their youth—an expression she saw far too infrequently these days. In that fleeting moment his features were transformed, shifting from blatantly unattractive to compellingly handsome, as if he were clay, remolded by a hand of light.

They rumbled away from the bridge, into the sudden shadow of narrow lanes and tall warehouses. For a moment his shape was indeterminate, swallowed by the darkness.

"Pip will be thrilled to see you, Patience." When he spoke, nothing but light in his tone, the sun found him as if drawn, and he was Richard again, just plain Richard. "How could it be otherwise, my dear? Is that scent of jasmine I smell? Quite captivating, I assure you." A faint flush stained his cheeks, as it had when they were children and he was in some way flustered.

Blinded by a sudden shaft of sunlight, she smiled with the idea that Pip might find her equally flustering now that she was grown. She was not a beauty, as her mother was all too ready to tell her, but Papa had said on more than one occasion, "Patience is pretty with youth, my dear, and a dab hand at choosing colors that suit, holding a proud posture, and arranging her hair."

She liked her hair. It was thick and lustrous, and while it had not much natural curl, one might, with the assistance of a curling iron, coax it into whatever shape one desired.

It dangled in ringlets now, gathered in a dark knot above her right ear, with crimped bangs to soften the height of her forehead. She had taken pains. It was a flattering style. Richard had approved. He glanced at the cluster of curls once again as they turned onto Kennington Lane.

"Time to don your mask," he said. "Shall I help you in tying it so you do not crush your curls?"

"Please do." She turned her back to him, pressing the beribboned bit of scarlet silk and pasteboard to her face.

He fumbled for the ribbon, fingers grazing the edge of her ear, the sensation sending a thrill down her spine. She wondered, with a deep sigh, what it would feel like to be touched so by Pip.

"I must say I am surprised your parents agreed to your coming to Vauxhall." Richard drew the ribbons tight, his touch gentle and sure. "It is a more dangerous haunt than in their youth."

Behind her mask Patience flushed, ashamed. Her cheeks felt hot to the touch. "I did not precisely tell them, Richard."

"Oh?" He sat forward abruptly and gently turned her so that he might look into her eyes, his expression, as was his custom, all too serious. "What exactly did you tell them?"

She hoped that the mask overshadowed her guilt; She could not look long into that delving green gaze, could not bear the disappointment that pulled down the corners of his mouth and gave flight to blackbird brows.

"Only that you had asked me to accompany you to a ridotto alfresco, and that you promised to have me home before midnight. Mama never questions where I am going when you have agreed to escort me, for she says you would never allow me to fall into bad company."

He exhaled heavily, stirring the curls over her ear. "And what will she do if she discovers I am the bad company?"

"You?" She was startled he should say so, that he should think so. Mama was always singing Richard's praises: *Dear, dependable Richard*, she called him. *A credit to his mother.*

"How are you bad company?"

Richard patted impatiently at the brocade pockets that lined the door. "In agreeing to this foolish whim of yours to go to Vauxhall for no more reason than to surprise Pip with your presence in London." His expression, even the tone of his voice, was distastefully serious as he plucked forth his mask, satin over pasteboard, like hers. "I am touched by your parents' trust in me, and in honoring that trust you must promise to stay close the entire time we are here, for there are pickpockets and scalawags aplenty in the gardens."

Patience nodded, curls bouncing, lower lip thrown out rather mulishly. She did not like it when Richard took such a scolding tone, when he treated her as if she were a little girl. Could he not see she was a woman grown? Old enough for marriage and children was surely old enough to decide she wished to go to Vauxhall for an evening.

Her petulant gloom was of momentary duration. Through the window, as Richard quietly donned his mask, she saw the little porched doorway he had described—in the midst of a redbrick wall, the entrance to Vauxhall—and streaming into it through the double Dutch doors, in the brilliant glow of the sunset, a line of similarly masked and dominoed guests.

In a sudden rush of crushed satin she pressed her nose to the window and cried out with irrepressible anticipation, "That's it, isn't it?"

Richard nodded and tapped his silver-topped ebony wood cane against the roof of the coach, which drew to a halt as he threw open the door and leapt out, extending his hand to help her descend.

"Make haste," he said when she paused in the doorway to gape, anticipation rising, leaving her giddy with impending possibilities. "We must not hold up traffic."

"Catch me," she called lightheartedly, and flung herself out, knowing he would catch her as he had always caught her in her leaps from the oak tree they had climbed as children. Dear, dependable Richard.

Pip had been too small to catch her then, a head shorter than she, while Richard towered above the two of them, lanky and lean, broad of shoulder and strong of arm—stronger than she and Pip put together.

He had always caught her, swinging her as he did, so that her skirts belled about her ankles, and she felt as if she were flying.

He did not disappoint her. His arms were ready and waiting, the sturdy brace they had always been, a warm well of cedar and lime. He lifted her, whirling, cloak belling, so that it seemed she flew on scarlet wings, as if it were yesterday, as if they were children again. Dizzied, laughing, she fell against his chest, and he laughed as well—but not a carefree laugh. It was a nervous chuckle, and he wore an undeniably shocked look in the instant that he clasped her to him, preventing a certain fall. Before he could scold her for her unladylike behavior, she whirled away laughing, pulling him out of the street, tucking one demurely gloved hand into the crook of his elbow. "That was fun! Been back to the tree of late?"

"Right before I set out for London," he said, as he patted his pockets for his change purse. "Took the dogs for a long walk, visited all our old haunts."

She smiled and twirled giddily toward the entrance, domino flapping at her heels. She would make it fly again. She was ready for adventure, ready for the reuniting of their threesome—no more caged feelings, no more waiting for things to happen.

"And have our initials survived the years?"

"As if it were yesterday," he said evenly.

She smiled, pleased. "Too many years since I have climbed our benevolent old oak."

"Do you think you could still manage it?"

Was it skepticism that glittered in his eyes? It was difficult to tell behind the mask.

She drew the domino demurely about her and dipped a formal curtsy. "Now that I am the hoyden no more?"

His brows rose. His mouth took a displeased downward turn. "Surely hoyden is too strong a term? I would have said now that you are so much the lady."

She laughed, unwilling to be serious this evening, this wonderful, forbidden evening. "Fooled you, have I? I shall tell Mama you said as much. She values your opinion." She slid a mischievous glance his way. "As for the tree, I am sure I could scramble into it, given a boost."

He laughed aloud, a true laugh, not the anemic chuckle he had given before. This heartfelt noise made her laugh as well. It was not often she could make Richard laugh. He had always been harder to amuse than Pip, who laughed at everything. The whole world seemed made for no more reason than to amuse Pip.

"I should be happy to oblige," Richard said as he handed several shillings to the gatekeeper and pocketed their tickets. She might have thought he was flirting with her most outrageously had he been any other young man, but this was Richard—staid, reliable Richard. He would never say anything the least bit suggestive or off-color.

They stepped through the portal into a vista of broad walkways and trees, the walkways crowded with gaily dressed visitors. And along the walkway, through the tree branches, ran strings of lamps that, even as she watched, sprang to glowing life all at once, twinkling like a thousand fairies, wings aflutter, illuminating a curving row of painted dinner boxes to their left, a stilted pavilion to their right further illuminated by oil lamps on posts.

An orchestra sat in staggered rows above the mill of the crowd, white wigged and black coated, tricornered hats perched amidst carefully powdered curls. Brass horns caught the light, sounding a fanfare. Chins were propped upon gleaming wood; dark elbows took pointed position, jerking in unison as the violinists drew plaintive wails by dip and saw of the bow.

Music swept toward them, sweet and lively. It made her long to dance, and as she was not one to deny herself, especially standing in a place she ought not to have come to, wearing a mask that hid her identity from all who might disapprove, she caught up both Richard's hands and whirled him about in time with the music, the red domino belling about both of them.

"Patience," he chided gently. "You make a spectacle of yourself."

"Yes," she agreed. "But as I am masked, no one knows except you." She pinched his cheek, hoping to provoke a smile, and when he did not soften threw her head back to take it all in, mouth falling open on a sigh. "This is splendid!"

Richard took her hand and pulled her out of the way of a loud group of revelers who followed them through the gate. "Actually, it is rather tawdry, but I am glad if it makes you happy." He gave her fingers a brotherly squeeze.

"Deliriously so." She beamed at him, and knew this night was to be all and more than she had imagined.

Someone bumped her elbow as they passed. She

clutched Richard's fingers a little tighter and leaned into his arm, remembering his warning of pickpockets.

"I am pleased to hear you say so," he said earnestly, and gave the corner of her mask a tweak. "You have seemed a trifle despondent these past few weeks."

She could not tell him it was all Pip's fault, that she had fallen into a bit of a pet because he made no effort to call on her. Pip, whom she had been most curious of all to see again, especially after his name was mentioned by several of their guests, and always in such interesting terms, and always in connection with the name of Sophie Defoe, beautiful, wealthy, well-liked Sophie Defoe.

Her nemesis. The woman who had stolen her future.

Dear Richard gazed down at her, rather striking, even a little mysterious in black domino and tall, black beaver hat. His eyes were too dark behind his mask to read, but she heard concern in the question: "Are you melancholy, Patience?"

"Me? Melancholy? Don't be silly." She flapped her hand at him and made every effort not to let her true feelings show in response to such a delving question. Was she still as transparent as a child? How did he read her so accurately, even in the midst of a public display of giddy glee? No one else did. She had become quite artful at hiding her feelings and schooling her features.

"Now"—she lifted her chin as she drew her domino about her like a satin shield—"however shall we find him in such a crush?"

Richard's mouth pulled down a little at the corners as he turned to scan the dinner boxes, dozens of them, one after another, fronted by white columns, the crenellated roofline sweeping ahead of them through a low grove of trees. Each box was painted with allegorical figures or striking scenes from well-known plays, each contained a linen-draped table. Richard's mouth always quirked in just such a fashion when he was tired or disappointed.

She wondered if such a look had anything to do with Chase. She had overheard her mother complain to father, "Poor Richard will soon go begging, if that brother of his continues to throw good money after bad."

Surely things were not as bad as all that! Richard dressed well, and his brother's coach, while not of the latest fashion, was richly appointed, and drawn by a fine pair of horses.

"Never fear," Richard said, and indeed, Patience could see no sign of fear in her friend's steady gaze. "I know exactly where Pip will be. But have you no wish to see the beauties of the park first before we chase down the scamp? There is a transparency of a mill, and the tin cascade, and a gilded Aurora, and two Apollos. The light is just right to enjoy all of it."

She shook her head and tucked her hand more completely into the crook of his arm, then adjusted her mask that she might see better. "No, no. If you please, dearest Richard, take me straight to our Pip," she said. "It is too many years since we have said a word to one another, and I would see how he has changed. You did tell him we were in London?"

"I did."

She looked down at her shoes, very special red-heeled shoes. She had chosen them especially to go with the domino. They had been dear, those shoes. She felt very daring in them, like the night, and the chance to see Pip. "I must own I am disappointed that he made no effort to call upon us, as you did."

"Yes. Well . . ." Richard never seemed comfortable with compliments. "Social niceties are not Pip's strong suit. I cannot say when he last saw fit to call upon anyone formally."

"Has he become a mannerless brute, then?"

Richard tugged at his mask. "Not at all. It is only that his company is in such demand. Come. You shall see firsthand."

He set off at once, as if he knew the gardens well. It was a pretty walk along the wide promenade toward the curve in the gallery of empty dinner boxes toward something that peeped above the trees, a false sun, and three false stars shining above the aged copper of the roofline, promising greater beauties. Glass-globed lamps strung through the trees underlit the leafy bowers. Music swelled from the trees to their left, strings and horns and reedy flutes.

"There is a leaden statue of Handel," Richard said, "in the opposite direction."

She was in no mood to turn around, to delay her first sight of Pip.

She asked him about the empty dinner boxes.

"No one eats much until after the cascade at nine," Richard explained.

They passed a kiosk where chickens roasted on spits, and an enormous ham sliced paper-thin gleamed pinkly. The smells stirred Patience's stomach to a most unlady-like growl.

Richard tilted his head to look at her, amused. "We can, of course, make an exception. Would you care for something?"

She laughed and shook her head. "You were not supposed to hear that."

"Hear what?" he inquired with mock innocence.

She gave her tummy a pat. "The hoyden. Now and again she tries to speak."

"You will not say no to a Shrewsbury cake, a glass of wine or champagne?" He pulled a worn leather purse that bore his initials from his pocket. It had once been dyed bright red, his initials picked out in yellow, and yet so many times had it been shoved in and out of his pockets that almost all of the dye was worn away from the raised grape-leaf pattern that circled the initials. He jingled the purse merrily.

So enthusiastic his offer. She could not tell him she hungered for sight of Pip far more than for Shrewsbury cake. It would be impolite to refuse, however, and Richard had taught her nothing so much as the importance of manners.

She chuckled and reached for her reticule. "Sounds lovely."

He led her to the kiosk, where a chalkboard listed available wines, port, and arrack, and bottles were stacked in great wooden cases. He refused the coins she held out to him, and would not listen to her protests that

Father had given her money for just such occasions, but counted out the necessary amount with care from his sad leather purse, then tucked it away again in his pocket.

"You cosset me," she said as they carried away their glasses, sipping and nibbling as they strolled. "It is very good of you, Richard."

"It is nothing." He brushed away her praise, and asked after her family, as he always did, though it had been but two days since he had seen them in person, and she would much rather speak of other topics, other persons— like Pip, whom Richard saw frequently, and yet he never seemed anxious to speak of him.

"Mother suffers occasional megrims," she said. "I do not think she cares much for London. Too noisy, too smelly, she claims. Too much to see and do. She is ever so appreciative that you make time to show me about." She watched him as she said it, searching for some sign that what her mother had said about Richard's financial situation might be just as true. "Care for half of the cake?" She broke off a large bite and held the rest out to him. He had not bought a piece for himself, which she thought odd, for Richard had always loved cake.

"You do not want it?"

She nodded. "I am too excited to eat. Unlike Mama, I love London, and I am delighted there is so much to do and see."

He polished off the confection in short order, and asked as he brushed away crumbs, "Did you finish the painting?"

The painting? He wished to speak of her paltry painting, when she would paint her eyes with sight of Pip?

"No," she had to admit. "I am not at all happy with the water in the Serpentine."

"Very difficult, water," he sympathized. "For it is never just water."

"Exactly. One must take into account all that it reflects. But beyond that, I do not think I am gifted when it comes to artistic endeavors."

"You have only to apply yourself, and you can do anything, Patience."

Anything but insist we go see Pip now, no more waiting, no more chitchat.

"You sound like Father," she complained. "But I am right. You must trust me. I am very good with numbers and geography and stitching and cards, but the true arts of a lady—music, poetry, and painting—I cannot seem to conquer." *Any more than I can close the distance between Pip and myself.*

"Must you?"

Trust Richard to question the obvious. "Mama seems to think I shall never win a husband without such talents," she said with a sad little laugh. "Or at the very least, some deep appreciation of them."

Lord knew she would never win Pip now that he was promised.

Richard's masked face seemed cast in even more serious lines than usual.

"Is that why you have come to London?"

"Husband hunting," she said with a nod. "Mama hates it when I put it so bluntly, but"—she patted her tummy—"I was never one to mince words."

The green of his eyes caught the light of an overhead lamp. "I rather like that in you. I think you will not mind too much if I am equally blunt."

She adjusted the mask, peering at him over the rim of her glass through the eyeholes. The bubbles from the champagne tickled her nose, which made her long to laugh again, but Richard did not sound in the least amused.

"Sounds like a lecture coming." She lifted her glass and made every effort to look back at him as seriously as he regarded her. "I would warn you, if it starts with the words, 'You are too young for marriage,' I will thank you to hold tongue, my friend."

He tugged uneasily at his neckcloth, unblinking. "You think yourself ready for marriage, then?"

Patience sighed, not at all patient with such a remark, or their dawdling pace. She wanted to see Pip. "*Some* people think I am."

He said nothing.

"I have had offers, you know."

He snorted his disbelief. "Who?"

Not at all flattering, his response. She sipped the last of her champagne, considering her answer, and then she lifted her chin and regarded him coyly from the corner of her eyes. "Did I not tell you?"

"No, you did not." He frowned and took the empty glass from her hand and, shaking the dregs from it, demanded, "Who?"

"Such a worried look, Richard," she scolded playfully, wishing to tease him. "It does not matter who, for neither of them was suitable."

"There were two? And you only now mention it to me?"

"I did not think it would interest you terribly. They were, as I said, unsuitable."

"No prospects?"

"One of them is quite well-to-do."

"A rogue, then?"

She laughed. "No. That would have been far more interesting."

His frown deepened. "What then?"

"No prospect of my ever feeling affection for them."

"Ah. A very good reason, that."

She expected the pucker between his brows to ease. To the contrary, it deepened.

She tugged at his arm and teased, as she had always teased away his dark looks: "I thought so, though Papa grumbled, and Mama says I throw away opportunity, that good men do not grow on trees."

"No, but neither would they see you miserable."

"Of course not. They wish me happiness, as they have known happiness."

"I wish it, too," he murmured.

"Most kind of you, Richard. I promise not to turn down any other suitors without informing you, and not to marry anyone without your wholehearted approval."

He nodded, the pinched look leaving his mouth. "I shall hold you to your promises."

Chapter Three

Patience expected magic.

Hints of it dangled glowing from the trees, fairy lights to light the path as they followed the row of dinner boxes that curved in a deep horseshoe framed on either side by pinnacled turrets, domed niches in which Patience caught a glimpse of the promised statues of Apollo. Ahead, in the deepest curve of the shoe, loomed a larger pavilion, triple tiered and balconied, with a stone arch at the top fancifully aglow with light, gay with color and noise.

Magical. Yes, this evening promised magic.

Richard wore his serious expression again.

Patience gave his arm a playful nudge. "Anyone among your acquaintance you can recommend to me? Someone who will not mind a wife without artistic talents?"

He took the question seriously, as she had known he would. "Tell me, Patience, what faults would you indulge in a husband?"

"Faults?" She arched her brows and tried, for the moment, to look just as serious as he, while in her mind's eye all she could picture was Pip—wonderful Pip. "Why, none. I expect perfection."

Half serious, half in jest these words were said.

His brow furrowed above the black silk of his mask. He looked for a moment like a confused bandit.

She wanted to laugh at seeing his dear features so

perplexed. To control the amused quiver of her lips she
pursed them. "Do I set my sights too high?"

He smiled, knowing she teased him. She always teased
him. "For mortal man, perhaps. But there have been
Greek gods who took mortal wives. Perhaps you can find
an English one."

She laughed. "Wife?"

He laughed as well. How she loved the sound of it.
"You know that is not what I meant."

It was her turn to be serious. "Well, if there are no
English gods, and I am forced to settle for mere, flawed
mortal, if I were fond of him, I think I should have to
accept him as he was."

"Good."

"I may not be ready for marriage, but I quite think I
am ready to fall in love."

He tilted his head to regard her most intently. "Are
you really? Well, if that is the case . . ." He drew a deep
breath and let it out with a sigh. "There is one."

Did he mean to tease her now? She studied his features carefully—what she could see of them beneath the
mask. "Only one English god? I thought as much. Will
he have me, do you think? Shall I retreat to a nunnery?"

He tried not to laugh, and failed, which made her
smile. She loved to make Richard laugh.

"If you are very good," he teased.

"Oh, dear," she said. "Do you think he will recognize
me in this mask, and know that I have been up to mischief in Vauxhall Gardens?"

"I think he might forgive you if you promise not to
tease me into bringing you here again."

Too serious he sounded again. Too serious the look in
his eyes. Patience was in no mood to be serious. "This
one you mentioned?" She waggled her brows at him.

"Yes?" he asked warily.

"Tell me more."

"Well." He closed his eyes a moment, and then turned
to look away before he said, "Rare is the man you
could love."

He left her speechless a moment with such a remark.

And then he looked at her, the mask hiding what she needed to see in his eyes. She could not tell by way of his mouth if he still teased her, until he went on, saying, ever so seriously, "Rarer still the man I would entrust you to."

He took her breath away, so unexpected was the compliment, the depth of feeling in his voice.

"I am touched," she said at last, and reached out to touch his arm.

He started back, leaving her hand poised in midair. She did not quite know what to make of her friend when he spoke with such intensity and then shied away.

"I would not have just any man," she said, her voice matching his in intensity. "I knew I could count on you. Who is this *one?*"

He pursed his lips. Such a serious mouth. So seriously he took their conversation, when she had not intended to be at all serious this evening.

He sighed and turned to watch the orchestra a moment, and when he turned back to her the almost overwhelming sense of focus and intensity had vanished. "Do you mind waiting for his name? He is not currently in a position to make a serious attachment."

She laughed, rather relieved he should say so, definitely relieved he took a lighter tone. "Perfect. Neither am I. All I want this evening is to have some fun with old friends."

"And so you shall, for here we are."

Their destination proved to be one of the Turkish alcoves of the pavilion, fancifully shaped cast-iron braces girding the inner aisle of the gallery. Here a crowd clustered around a circle of card tables, masked ladies and gentlemen peering intently at backgammon and chessboards. A gentleman walked among them in a peacock blue coat, white-figured waistcoat, and chalk white small clothes. An eye-catching white cockatoo perched on his shoulder. An emerald, amethyst, and gold paisley scarf had been tied across his eyes and nose as blindfold. Leading him from table to table, just as eye-catching, perhaps a bit more so, a bright-eyed blackamoor lad clad in an exact match of his master's coat and waistcoat also boasted a splendid emerald and amethyst turban edged in gold bullion.

Patience gasped. "Oh, my!"

He had grown taller, little Pip. This dashing young gentleman was a good head taller than she, slender of build, his limbs well formed, his posture proud. He was all that she had imagined and more—much more. She might not have recognized him at once had it not been for the unchanged and irrepressible cheeky grin, the tip-tilted nose, those carefully pomaded golden locks.

She remembered how his hair had curled against the humid dampness of his neck—the humid dampness of his hand about her ankle.

The cockatoo squawked and preened, crest rising. "Pay me a penny! Pay me a penny!"

A richly clothed woman at one of the tables obliged the bird in holding out a coin.

As it took the copper in its beak, Pip scolded in a voice far deeper than she recalled, his tone familiar, as was the jaunty tilt of his head, "A penny, Pippet? Silly bird. The duchess could as easily afford to give you pounds."

"Silly bird," the bird agreed with a piercing whistle.

The crowd laughed.

"Pippet?" Patience chuckled, joy bubbling in her chest like champagne. "How long has Pip carried a bird about on his shoulder?"

"A fortnight. Perhaps two." Richard's voice seemed singularly unenthusiastic. "Since he tired of the monkey that used to cling to his hair."

Patience tried to imagine Pip with a monkey perched on his shoulder instead of the bird. She had imagined him in many ways, but never with a monkey or a bird.

"Shall I give him a shout?" Richard asked flatly.

Her heart lurched into her throat.

"Wait." She stopped him with a touch, unprepared to face this flamboyant creature she had so long dreamed of seeing again.

Richard looked down at her hand. "I thought you wanted to speak to him." He sounded faintly . . . was it resentful? Perhaps it was only the mask that made him sound different.

"What is he doing?"

"Making a spectacle of himself. It is his favorite pastime." Again the flatness of voice, as if he were put out by the question. His gaze fell. His tone changed. "Pip plays chess and backgammon, blindfolded, a dozen games at a time, at least once a week here."

Patience could not prevent admiration from infusing her voice. "He always was clever at games."

"Yes," Richard agreed evenly. "Even more so now."

Was he jealous?

She could not be certain, could not read his expression as he stood masked beside her, his gaze following Pip's movement, but it made sense that any ordinary young man would be jealous of the head-turning creature before them.

"Does he win?" she asked.

"More often than not. You know Pip's way with games. The two of you were alike in that way. He walks away with a fistful of sovereigns whenever he does one of these garden gambles."

A trace of wistfulness—definitely a trace of wistfulness was to be heard in those words, and for the first time Patience considered how it must have been for Richard, always the loser, always polite in complimenting them on their skill. She and Pip had, from the start, been a challenge to one another; she better than he at backgammon—he the usual winner when they played chess. Neither of them liked to lose.

Richard had always been the good sport, a gentlemanly loser. Even when his father died. Even as his brother squandered the family fortune. He would not speak of such things to her, no matter that she always asked after his family. Such a quiet, uncomplaining soul.

She smiled at him. "Can anyone play?"

He nodded. "If there is an opening. Do you wish to play?"

"I want to beat him."

"At backgammon? There is a board coming open now."

One of the players rose from a table as he spoke. The chair, once emptied, was as quickly filled.

"Sorry," Richard said, taking her hand, and leading her closer to the games. "We must make a push to the front in order to take a chair."

"I would prefer a chessboard," she said. "If one comes open."

"I thought you were better at backgammon?"

She waggled her brows at him. She had imagined this moment, prepared for it. "I've been practicing."

He considered the tables afresh. "Ah! Well then, perhaps Lady Wilmington will give up her place."

He pushed forward and bent his sleek, dark head to address a pretty young woman with beautifully coiffured honey-colored curls.

Patience found herself wondering who this Lady Wilmington might be to Richard. She knew him well enough to touch his hand, to bat at his cheek with her closed fan.

And Richard smiled, as if he were in no way offended!

Lady Wilmington turned to look at Patience through a glittering silver mask. She beckoned elegantly with gray-gloved hand, her every movement and gesture a source of fascination. As she rose from her chair, a look of intense interest in her eyes, her gaze slid from Richard to Patience and back again.

"Richard tells me you can beat Philip." She leaned closer to whisper. "Is it true? I have never had the pleasure."

Deep was her voice, and throaty. How did she manage to sound at the same time breathlessly seductive and stay-your-distance standoffish?

Patience smiled uncertainly. "I—I always beat Pip at backgammon. Chess, never." She shrugged. "But I love a challenge."

"Pip, is it you call him? So that is the mystery of the bird's name." Lady Wilmington gestured toward the cockatoo with a graceful sweep of her fan, a mischievous smile taking possession of her lips. "Naughty Philip. How he did tease when I asked him."

Her words were suggestive. Patience was unsure how to respond. She glanced at Richard, only to find all of his interest focused on Lady Wilmington as she rose, gracefully relinquishing the chair with a playful wink behind her fan and the suggestion, "Your move, my dear. It is endgame and I am afraid I leave you with few options. My king is in check."

Chapter Four

Patience studied first the board, and then her opponent.

Only four players were left in the game: Her white king and a pawn that must be queened, the black king and his rook.

As she sank into the chair, eyes flitting from the chessboard to Pip and the boy and back again, she calculated her next move and how much time she had to make it.

Richard leaned down to say, "I shall be just behind you, talking to Lady Wilmington."

"Mmm-hm," Patience murmured, her mind already focused on the game. She was rather good at narrowing her attention. One must be to succeed at chess, at backgammon, at cards.

Pip approached, his every gesture flamboyant, designed to catch eyes. The tails of his coat whirled as he turned from chessboard to backgammon. The lad who followed like an obedient and adoring pup called out each move made by Pip's opponents. Pip nodded, smiled brightly, directed the lad where he wished his men moved, and told a joke while the lad did his bidding.

A gasp, a groan, a smattering of applause from those who looked on, and the backgammon player sank back, his men blocked from further play.

"How does he do it?" she heard a woman murmur, and shut out the gentleman's reply as she turned all her attention to the board, to the battle before her.

Lady Wilmington's king was in peril. Patience moved him from knight five to knight four.

And suddenly Pip was before her, in a whirl of pomade and cologne, the odor unfamiliar, exotic, loudly spicy, pinching at her nose, forcing her to look at him, to stare at him, to forget everything but Pip.

He took her breath away.

Pip. Dear Pip. Glorious Pip. Handsome Pip. His chiseled chin, missing all baby fat, jutted firmly, more pronounced than before. The spare, agile force of his stature seemed more intense, mature. Every tight-knit muscle in his compact frame pronounced him alive, so very alive, and virile, and male.

All of the longing she had kept buried within herself these many years surfaced, overwhelming her, setting heart and pulse to fluttering. Her mouth went dry. All words, all coherent thought flew from her head, a flock of squawking birds, like the one who eyed her, head cocked, from his shoulder.

This fine young man had once slid beneath her skirts! He had grasped her ankle and breathed humidly upon her knee. She had imagined this encounter so many times, so many ways, none of her imaginings anything like the reality of the moment. Pip was so very large and colorful and devastatingly real! He was a stranger to her, an unknown, which conflicted completely with her sense of having thought of him, of having known him in her mind and imaginings every day since their last conversation.

Intimidated, she flinched backward as Pip and the cockatoo swooped close. "Hmm," Pip murmured as he leaned in to sniff her hair.

She had never imagined this.

"New player," he announced as he stood tall. "Female. A young female. Am I right? Come to rescue an imperiled king?"

"Yes." The lad at his heels leaned against her table, his eyes as bright as the bird's, adoring, acknowledging his master a clever fellow.

"Yes," the crowd called out to him, echoing that sense of adoration.

"A young female set on besting you." She guarded

her voice, throwing it deeper than usual, trying to sound self-assured and throaty, like Lady Wilmington.

The lad announced to him her move. "King to knight four."

Pip smiled and ruffled the boy's hair, and leaned in over the chessboard as if he could see through the blindfold. He said with a seductive drawl, "You cannot best me, my dear. Your poor pawn is hopelessly outmanned." And with that he announced his move—"Rook to queen five. Check"—and went on to the next player while the lad saw to it that the rook threatened her king once again.

Patience eyed the boy with interest, wondering who he was that Pip should use him thus.

The lad gave her no more than a glance. He was the firefly darting brightly from game to game, his posture and stance mimicking that of his master, the cheeky grin that possessed his mouth exuding confidence and superiority.

She focused on the board again, the cheers as Pip rousted another opponent fading in her mind as she studied how she might yet queen her pawn. She would not be distracted by the sudden heated rush of memory. She must not think of the moment this handsome young man had crawled beneath her velvet skirt so long ago, so very long ago, and both of them changed enormously since then.

She must narrow all thought and feeling to the limitations of the chessboard. She sharply studied all possible variations of movement across the field of dark and bright squares.

It was obvious what she must do next. She moved her king out of immediate danger, and Pip was upon her again, in a whirl of coattails and the spicy riches of liberally applied cologne. It was clever of him, really, to assault the senses so completely. Pip the dazzler. Pip the whirlwind of energy. He overwhelmed and conquered—as he always had. He was not, after all, a complete stranger.

"White king to knight three!" the lad cried out.

Pip leaned in close again to say, "We have met before, my pretty, yes?"

"Yes," she admitted, low-voiced. "On more than one occasion." Her manner was flirtatious, as Lady Wilmington had been flirtatious.

Head cocked, Pip smiled the dazzling, heart-catching smile she remembered, the smile that had won him what he wanted so many times as a child. He had always wielded it like the sharpest of swords, straight to the heart. Men and women fell prey to the power of such a smile. It made her knees weak. Her heart thudded loudly in her ears.

"Rook to queen six," he instructed the lad. Again the smile flashed. "Check again, my dear. Your king is on the run, and soon to be mated."

He whirled away, her eyes fixed on the board, and she saw at once the possibility for her pawn.

She moved her king and sat back to watch his next approach. Another player fell under his spell, another cheer from the crowd, and then he was teasing and laughing with a gentleman at the backgammon board next to hers, the fellow flushing as scarlet as her cloak when the dice favored Pip.

Glowing with his exertions, even more handsome than before, the tails of his coat, and blindfold aflutter, Pip and the exotic cockatoo swooped down on her.

"What have you for me, my lovely?" he asked.

"White king to bishop two," the lad cried.

Pip cocked his head, as if surprised. "And so you would force a stalemate, would you, in queening your little pawn?"

"I do not give up without a fight," she said, amazed that he remembered the board so clearly.

He smiled, shrugged, and made the move she had anticipated: rook to queen five.

He meant her to queen her pawn, sacrifice his rook, and end the game in a draw, but she had a surprise waiting for him upon his return to the board.

"Pawn to bishop eight," the lad cried.

"And so"—Pip yawned, as if her move bored him—"your pawn becomes a queen."

"Not queen," she said, and watched him swallow the yawn with a dawning frown.

"No?"

"No, my pawn becomes a rook."

He pondered this development a moment before, with a shrug, he said, "Rook to queen's rook five."

He might have whirled off again as the lad moved his rook, had she not swiftly made her own move and said quietly, "King to knight three. Check."

The crowd flocking about the tables chirped in surprise.

"He is trapped," someone murmured.

Pip stopped, head cocked, more birdlike than ever, the faintest of disappointed expressions tugging at his lower lip.

"Beaten me, has she?" he asked.

"Indeed she has," someone called. Was it Richard?

Pip bowed with an elaborate flourish. "And thus it is demonstrated that it can be done with nothing but a clever pawn."

Patience smiled. "As long as that pawn is in the hands of a clever woman."

Behind her, Lady Wilmington laughed.

Beneath the blindfold Pip's lips thinned, and then he smiled his most seductive smile. He leaned over her chessboard so that they were, for a moment, face-to-face, so close that she was swallowed up by his cologne. His pomade overpowered her. The virile, unfamiliar undercurrent of the man her childhood companion had become took her breath away. "So, Mistress Confident," he said, his breath a caress against her cheek, "do you dare to play another game with me? A different game?"

Heat flooded her cheeks. She found she could not look at him. He loomed too close. She thought again of the day he had slipped under cover of her skirts.

The crowd's comments grew bawdy.

Patience blushed, unused to being noticed, much less applauded in so public a fashion.

Pip had always possessed flash, and the right words, and an attitude of superior strength. He used it to help him win. She had watched him rattle Richard with it for years.

Richard. She turned her head to look for him. But Lady Wilmington stood alone. Patience gripped the chessboard to steady herself, to reclaim her equilibrium.

Where had Richard gone?

Pip meant to unnerve her. It would give him an edge in the game. And she was unnerved without Richard at her back, dear, dependable Richard.

"Tell me how I know you, my pretty," Pip whispered, his breath dizzyingly warm against her ear, his lips a breath away, as she had imagined. *Oh, my!* This was much better than she had imagined. This very real and very virile Pip shook her far more than any Pip of her imaginings.

She inhaled sharply, then caught sight of movement in the crowd ahead of her, the movement Richard taking fresh position, that he might observe her play from better vantage, that she might observe him. He smiled reassuringly.

It bolstered her courage. This was only Pip, after all.

"Come, come, my dear. Tell me, where have we met?"

Her voice clear enough to carry to the edges of the throng, she said, "Telling too much, my lord, would spoil the game. But I would warn you I am much better at backgammon than chess."

The crowd applauded.

Pip barked out a laugh as he rose, posture proud, the paisley silk that bound his eyes whipping in the breeze, his expression as cocksure as the cockatoo, who thrust out its chest and unfurled its topknot of feathers with a cry of, "It's a game. It's a game."

Pip was amused. He was always amused. "Oho!" He threw back his head to laugh. "A worthy foe!"

Beyond him, with the slightest of nods, Richard pointed to the abandoned backgammon board closest to where he stood.

Spirits high, laughter bubbling in her throat, Patience

rose, situated herself behind the board, and swiftly arranged both sets of men to begin the game. Around her, new players filled the empty tables.

How did he do it? she wondered, impressed afresh. Twelve games at once, while blindfolded. Could it be he memorized all twelve games as he went? Pip had always demonstrated a remarkable gift for remembering things.

She thought again of the moment in which he had slid under the table, under her skirts. Heat flared in her cheeks—and lower, a heat, a need he stirred in her. It left her as damp as the nape of his neck had been that day. He would remember as clearly as she did. She was sure of it.

He took them on again, a dozen players. He flitted between like a jovial, clever-witted butterfly. The crowd loved him, the players, too, even as he beat them. He had a special word, the gleam of that heart-stopping smile for each and every one of them.

The outcome was no different than expected. He beat them, one after another, except for her. She had always bested Pip at backgammon. To best him blindfolded hardly seemed sporting.

The dice favored her from the start with double aces, which brought a smile to her face, a chortle to her lips every time she let them fly from the cup. She played a running game, her back men hitting or jumping the bar early due to a series of doubles, Pip's lad calling out the play with a glee that matched her own.

Pip did his best to catch up, but the numbers were not fortuitous.

"Quatre ace!" the lad cried out. And *"Trois deuce!* Bad luck again, my lord, for you are left open for a hit."

And with the next throw, as luck would have it, hit him she did, trapping his man for the better part of the play. She had him from the start. She knew it. She could feel it in her bones. It sang in her veins almost as loudly as did her pleasure in seeing him, in watching him make his moves without his knowing it was she who blocked his play.

He frowned on his next throw when *deuce ace* fell to

his lot, opening up another man for another hit. He pursed his lips unhappily on the fifth cast, tossing aside the cup in frustration when the lad announced low numbers yet again.

He had no choice but to play a blocking game, his manner growing more intent with every pass. The brilliance of his smiles faded; his teasing manner grew more ascerbic when she trapped two of his men on the bar.

He knew he was losing.

She knew she would win, and reveled in it—even teased him a bit. It was not altogether kind of her, but it was Pip, and she had always enjoyed teasing him, besting him. She was sure he would eventually recognize her voice, or the manner in which she moved her pieces. She waited for discovery.

Perhaps it was unfair of her. He was, after all, distracted.

Her sense of elation at the idea of a double victory soured as their play progressed, as Pip's remarks became more biting, as his forehead knitted in a frown above the paisley blindfold, as his sparkling smile and unending wit faltered. Pip had always hated to lose. On occasion, as a child, he had been known to throw tantrums. She had almost forgotten. It was so long ago. He was now a man grown. She had never imagined he still fell prey to any ill-mannered sensibilities. And he had met her first win with good-natured jests and a keen sense of competition.

He had changed, but not completely.

She began to think he would not lose twice to her with the same mature humor and sportsmanship. She hated to think he might revert to childish petulance. He had once gone four days without speaking to her when she beat him too soundly at whist.

Was it wise of her to publicly humiliate him before they had so much as said, "How do you do?"

She wanted to impress him, to astound him with how much she had changed, not alienate him from the start. She wanted him to see her as a beautiful and clever young lady, not a public annoyance.

Beating him had seemed so appropriate just a moment

ago, so perfect. Now, as double sixes carried all but one of her men off the board while he struggled with two laggards, she was anxious to be gone.

And so, with the final throw, to the crowd's cry of "Backgammon!" before Pip and his diminutive shadow could ascertain his defeat, before Pip could tear the blindfold from his eyes and recognize her, she rose in a rustling flurry of red and black satin and abandoned the game.

Chapter Five

Patience ran. A crimson bird given wing, she flew through the gathering crowd, no clear idea where she was going.

Behind her she heard sudden commotion. A thumping clatter, a cry, the flap of wings, a screeching squawk. She turned to see Pip wrenching the blindfold from his face as he vaulted the table, the cockatoo, clipped wings flapping awkwardly, trying to fly from his shoulder.

"You!" Pip cried out, the word meant for her. "Yes, you, in the red!"

His cry spurred her onward, through a sea of masked faces turned to look.

"Stop!"

The thump of running footsteps gained on her. The cockatoo screeched in earnest. The lad wailed, "My lord. The bird!"

Half of Patience's mind urged her to stop; the other half railed, *This is worse than before!* He must not catch up to her, must not know who created such a scene.

She lifted her skirts and ran—away from the pavilion, into the darkness. Trees loomed ahead, a block of shrubbery and trees, surrounded by a head-high fence to keep one on the main promenade. She did not turn to look, simply ran, afraid she had ruined her chances with Pip, ashamed of her own pride, far too conspicuous at the moment in her red domino.

The bird's screeching faded; the lad's cries died away. Only the thump of Pip's heels pursued her from the pathway into the grass, toward a spot where the fence staggered drunkenly. She was not the first to skirt the hedge and take cover in the trees. A path had been beaten down by the passage of feet.

Breathless, he called, "Wait!"

Too close. He was too close. She darted behind a holly, racing between tree trunks, branches catching at her hair, her mask.

"Patience, please!"

That he used her name brought her up short, took her breath away. From the shadows, beneath one of the trees, came a grunt, a sultry moan. Two pair of legs were startlingly visible, one pair male, alarmingly hairy, half-clad in hunter's green breeches lowered to the knee, exposing canary yellow stockings, pale thighs, and a breathtaking moon of pale buttocks that thrust itself in rhythmic motion between the second pair of legs, clearly female, clad in rumpled white-on-white striped stockings.

Patience might have assumed the woman in trouble but for the crooning noises made, and the fact that the white-stockinged legs moved as she watched to wrap around the man's pale torso, drawing him closer.

All of this was witnessed in the blink of an eye. Patience's mouth fell open in a gasp.

Fornicating! The two were fornicating in a public park!

Astounded, gasping, anxious to flee, she whirled in her tracks, mask slipping to her chin. Blindly she set off back the way she had come, struggling to right the eyeholes that she might see again. No more than a few strides, and she plowed into the all-too-solid form of a man.

He knocked her to the ground in a scarlet sprawl, landing on top of her in much the same scandalous position she had just witnessed. Mask blinding her, arms and legs entangled, her heart thudded like a runaway horse's hooves. His thundered in her ear in the brief moment her cheek pressed against his chest.

She was about to let loose a bloodcurdling scream when Richard asked in the most reasonable of voices, "Where in heaven's name are you going?"

Not Pip. Not some stranger who meant to assault her. He smelled of cedar and lime.

Richard's arms clasped her. Dear Richard. Dependable Richard.

"Oh, Richard!" She shoved free from his grip, righting the troublesome mask, feeling doubly foolish as she struggled to rise to her knees, to right her gown.

She could not look at him as he stood, not with the memories, the odd emotions she currently carried. She could not disconnect her mind entirely from the terrifyingly provocative image of a man's naked buttocks thrust between a woman's welcoming legs.

His breath came hard and fast as he jumped up and held out his hands. The look on his face was one of shock and growing anger. "What possessed you to run away like that, without so much as a word? Into the trees, of all places. You've no idea how dangerous this place can be for a young woman alone."

She could not tell him, could not argue that she was far more aware than he realized. Richard would be horrified. He would insist upon taking her home.

No more groans came from the trees—not so much as a rustling noise in the shrubbery. Had Richard seen what she had seen? Did the lovers watch them from the cover of the trees?

"I am sorry," she said at once, hoping he had not, hoping he would never know. She laced her fingers through his and leaned into the support of his arm as she stood. "You are right, of course."

He batted a leaf from her skirt. She shook away a flurry of grass and dirt, and led him back toward the staggered section of fencing. Pausing in the cover of the holly she shook her skirts one last time and eyed the seams of her dress for damage from her fall. "It was very foolish of me to run."

His features gentled, the worried pucker of dark brows overriding the pinch of his lips as he plucked a twig from her hair. "Why did you?"

She darted a glance over her shoulder, unable to remember now. The distraction of two sets of legs—and the action they had been engaged in—was mind numbing.

"I ran because . . ."

"Yes?" Richard's gloved thumb stroked a lump of dirt from the side of her glove. He gave her fingers a friendly squeeze, and yet in that moment the motions seemed much more than friendly. His every touch seemed in some way connected to the squeeze of stocking-clad knees, to the thrust of bare buttocks. Her body ached down low, in a manner she had never felt it ache before, as if she had been the woman in rumpled stockings, as if she had borne the weight of a naked man cradled against her thighs.

She jerked her hand from Richard's, folding her arms across her chest.

"I ran because . . ."

She could not imagine behaving so shamefully with any man, not even Pip. Pip! The card game. She flung out her hands in a frustrated gesture. "Because I was winning. You know how Pip hates to lose." She hoped he would understand, that he would not find her enormously foolish. "It is not terribly mature to long to best one's friend at games, is it?"

He reached the edge of the trees before her, ducked behind a nearby bush, and barred her from moving forward.

"What are you—"

He pressed a silencing finger to her lips, the kid leather pleasantly scented with his cologne.

She wondered for a wild moment if he meant to kiss her, here in the shadow of the trees, if dear, dependable Richard would ever dream of taking liberties, legs bare, buttocks thrusting.

He leaned closer.

She leaned back in disbelief.

"Wait," he whispered, "until the path is clear. I would not wish your reputation ruined by . . . a misunderstanding. This place . . . these trees . . . are used for . . ."

"Illicit dalliance," she hissed. "I know."

He studied her a moment, tight-lipped.

"I mean, I've never—"

"Of course not," he said, and turned his attention to the promenade.

She closed her eyes, curious what it would be like to participate in illicit dalliances, to be kissed, held, to lie naked with a man.

Her cheeks fired. The ache between her thighs intensified, went liquid. What was this strange desire? Was she a hoyden after all?

"Quickly now." Richard beckoned.

She stumbled in skirting the edge of the fencing, felt completely self-conscious when Richard steadied her elbow, when he guided her billowing domino past the raw edges. His touch felt different, provocative. His glance, too, as if it kindled more heat in her.

They had done nothing in the least untoward, and yet she felt they took part in scandalous acts.

He cradled her hand in the crook of his arm, as was his habit, and she found herself no longer comfortable there, skin tingling, aware of his every movement, her nerves on edge.

"There," he said, and gave her hand a pat. "That's better. And in answer to your question, I have always believed that the point to games is to enjoy another's company in a pleasant pastime."

Pleasant pastime? Like lying naked with a man beneath a tree?

She shook her head. She must erase the vision of what she had seen from her mind. She must focus on what Richard was saying, on what had been happening before her mad dash for the woods.

"You do not agree?" he asked.

Pip. The game. She had run from the game.

"Certainly it was not ladylike," she smiled, amused by her own unintentional double entendre. The remark applied equally well to her desire to beat Pip at games, and the desires expressed in the game she had just witnessed played out beneath the trees.

"What? Running?" Richard raised another aspect of what might be considered unladylike.

"All of it," she said impatiently—impatient with herself. "I did so want to be ladylike when he saw me for the first time."

She did not know what else to say, how to make him understand without sounding the complete idiot. "I was winning, and inwardly gloating, and it seemed suddenly most impolite of me to . . . to . . ."

"Disgrace Pip publicly?"

He knew the workings of her mind too well, dear Richard. She wondered if he would understand her mixed feelings about what she had seen.

"Pip is not one to hold a grudge," he reminded her.

She let loose a breath. It seemed she had been holding it in for some time. She was the complete idiot! Sheepishly she studied her expensive red-heeled shoes, now muddied.

"But . . . I would not have him regard me . . . I would prefer not to have to try to explain . . ."

"What you cannot fully explain to me?"

"Yes."

"We need not tell him it was you."

She felt shamefacedly grateful that he should say so, but could not be content. "He knows it was a woman in red."

He looked her up and down, his attention on her body, on her clothing, bringing heat to her cheeks. He laughed and stepped closer. She backed away, heat thrumming between her thighs again. She was not at all accustomed to Richard staring at her person.

"You need not be the woman in red," he suggested, brows raised. "Lift your chin."

She had no idea what he was about, but this was Richard, after all. Warily, but obediently, she lifted her chin.

His breath was warm on her face, his gaze serious as, fingers fumbling, brushing her throat, he undid the domino's clasp and lifted the warm weight of satin from her shoulders. She blinked, the sensation surprisingly sensuous. Turning the cloak inside out, he draped her again, in evening-chilled satin.

Of course. How simple!

So painless Richard made the thorniest of problems.

"It now appears you wear a black domino with red trim," he said, smoothing the seam across her shoulders.

"Brilliant!" She clapped her gloved hands with such enthusiasm he blushed and grew even clumsier than before. But perhaps it was only that he must now fix the clasp from the inside out, his fingers warm and hard against her throat, little room for maneuvering. It required dexterity. He could not manage it with his gloves on, and so he bit down impatiently on an immaculate kid fingertip and tugged his hand free. How warm his bare fingers at her neck! She had not realized the evening air had grown so chill.

She shivered and then blushed, her mind on two sets of legs. Her eyes were drawn to Richard's legs, the muscular bulge of his thighs. She forced herself to look away, then to look him in the eyes. How warm his expression, how affectionate. It pleased her to think he was no longer mad at her.

"How do I look? Will Pip know?" She patted the billowing folds when he was done.

He yanked the glove on again as he looked her over with a curt nod. Behind him, from the pavilion, the voice of Mr. Charles Dignum rang out sweet and true.

Not so sweet Richard's voice. "Gave me a devil of a scare, running away as you did. Do not ever do that again while you are in my care."

Patience did not like to see him frown at her. It ruined the moment, her pleasure in his clever idea. It reminded her she was younger and more foolish than he.

He thrust his elbow in her direction as sharply as he said, "Come along, then."

She obeyed, the moment spoiled.

Pip's audience proved too thick for the two of them to continue abreast of one another the closer they got to the game tables. Patience let go of Richard's arm as they approached. At least that was the reason she convinced herself she dropped his arm. She could not admit to herself that she felt suddenly awkward and self-aware

with his every touch. She could not even begin to admit
a more selfish reason, a reason that might remind her
yet again that she was a foolish young female. Had she
been completely honest, she would have had to admit
she did not want Pip's first view to be of her clutching
Richard's arm. She had never imagined it thus.

Richard looked back when her fingers slid away, concern in his eyes, a return of that panic he had met her
with when she had run away. It bothered her to provoke
such a look.

"I am right behind you," she assured him.

He nodded, mouth pinched, and now and then glanced
back to see that she still followed.

The peacock-coated lad passed among the final round
of beaten players, turban in hand, into which he gathered
the coins his master had won.

Pip had removed his blindfold, and stood talking to
the pretty Lady Wilmington, dimples flashing, a coy smile
tugging at his lips. He seemed to be trying to coax her
into something.

She thought the words his lips formed were, "Tell
me, who . . . ?"

The cockatoo unfurled the snow white feathers at its
crest, and shrieked, "Dickey-boy's here. Dickey-boy.
Dickey-boy."

Pip turned. "Richard!" he called cheerily. "How good
to see you."

The cockatoo bobbed its head and repeated, "Good
to see you. Good to see you."

Lady Wilmington turned her head with exquisite grace.

"Yes, Pippet. I am here," Richard agreed, and reached
out, finger crooked, to stroke the bird's breast.

The bird leaned into his hand as if it knew and enjoyed
the gesture.

Patience hung back, unwilling to intrude, for Lady Wilmington gazed upon the two with something akin to
adoration.

"Ah, Richard." She held out a graceful hand. "You
are just the gentleman to tell Philip . . ." Her gaze
strayed over Richard's shoulder. Her brows rose ele-

gantly as she spotted Patience. ". . . about the young woman in red."

Patience blushed.

Pip grabbed at Richard's arm, sending the cockatoo scrabbling for higher purchase. "You know her?"

"I do," Richard said quietly.

Patience dawdled on the edge of the group, now gossiping, who had been observing Pip's games.

The lad handed over the turban now heavy with coin.

"Mr. Trumps!" Pip called.

Pip put a hand up for the bird, who stepped onto his finger, and as quickly onto the lad's shoulder.

"How did we do?" Pip asked.

"Well enough," the lad allowed.

"Pieces of eight, pieces of eight." The bird cackled.

Lady Wilmington gave Richard's arm a familiar squeeze, and leaned her head back so that not only did her throat show to advantage, but she might cast a coy glance in Patience's direction. "And does the clever girl captivate your heart as much as Philip claims she captures his?"

She had captured Pip's heart? Had he really said so? Patience could not hear properly above the applause for the singing Howell sisters, who stepped to the edge of the performance balcony and curtsied to the audience.

Richard said something she could not make out at all. His posture seemed more rigid than usual.

Pip laughed and flung his blindfold at him, then ruffled the tight curls of the lad who went about collecting the backgammon boards and game pieces.

"Completely infatuated," she heard Pip say, and inched closer. "Head over heels."

Who was infatuated? Did Pip mean his fiancée?

Then Pip insisted, "Tell me her name. I simply must meet any young woman clever enough to best me."

Patience wanted to laugh. A sense of elation welled up within her. She wished she were a cockatoo, that she might sit upon Pip's shoulder and make noises in his ear and rub her beak against his cheek.

Richard was not so pleased. "I would do her better

service in warning her away from you, who are soon to be married."

Dear Richard, ever protective, even when she had no wish for protection.

Lady Wilmington laughed, eyes narrowing to the shape of crescent moons. Though she could not be certain, Patience thought the lovely young woman looked her way and winked.

"Unfair, Dickey-boy." Pip chuckled as he swung the bag of coins like a jingling pendulum. "I am not yet leg-shackled."

Richard frowned. "Would you throw over your betrothed for a complete stranger?"

Patience frowned. That was unfair. She was not a complete stranger.

"Would you call off the wedding?" Richard persisted. "Renege on your promise? Rescind one of the most sensible decisions you have made in a long time?"

"Is it sensible?" Pip muttered to the cockatoo. "If I am so easily distracted from it? I begin to wonder."

Richard tilted his head, lips pressed together, and shot a glance at Patience. He did not look at all happy with Pip—with Pip's responses.

And Patience? How did she feel about Pip's sudden infatuation? Was it not what she had dreamed of? Wished for? Yes. No denying it, but—there was always a but—Patience knew how changeable Pip's mind was. He blew like the wind, always in a new direction.

She reveled in the possibilities his words opened up for her; she even dared to hope her dreams might yet come true, but she had presence of mind enough to shake her head at Richard, hoping he would understand. She did not want him to reveal her as the woman in red. She did not want to read disappointment in Pip's eyes in realizing his mystery woman was no mystery at all, only paltry Patience, his childhood playmate.

And yet neither did she wish these two dear friends of hers to continue brangling. "Richard tells me I shall like your betrothed. Will I, Pip?"

Pip whirled in a flash of peacock-colored tails.

He stared at Patience for an instant in openmouthed curiosity, and then in dawning recognition, the light in his eyes, the brilliance of his smile thrilling her to the bone.

"Patience!" he cried, grasping her hands and whirled her about in a little dance, so that the cockatoo on his shoulder spread wing and arched high its crest with a disgruntled squawk. "Is it our Patience you have brought me, Dickey? And a Patience all grown-up, just as you did say."

"So you do remember me?"

"Remember you?" Pip stopped his jig and held her at arm's length, his gaze raking over her, head to toe. "Look at you, my dear. How could I forget? Surely you must know I will never forget. Do you comprehend how much I have been longing to see you?"

Flattered, breathless, blushing, Patience scolded him lightly: "Not enough to come and visit me, it would seem, old friend."

Pip had never been one to suffer feelings of guilt. "Oh, but I have been meaning to. Tell her, Dickey-lad. Have you not told our dear Patience how many a time we have discussed coming to see her?"

Richard stood quietly watching, his expression neutral. "Many a time," he agreed.

Beside him, Lady Wilmington eyed them with guarded curiosity, amusement playing about her lips.

"You must tell me all about your wedding plans," Patience coaxed. "When shall I meet your fiancée? Will she be here tonight?"

"Sophie Defoe does not come to Vauxhall." He looked at her as if she suggested the ridiculous.

"Ever?"

"No." His upper lip quirked. "Did you not know, my dear Patience? Vauxhall is not an altogether proper place for an unmarried young lady to be seen. Certainly not in her first Season."

"As I am?"

He waggled his brows mischievously. "Precisely."

"Am I ruined, then?"

"Are you?" he asked with genuine curiosity. "You must tell me."

He was teasing her, as he always had.

"You are not at all nice to question it."

"And in so saying would you label yourself 'not at all nice' as well?"

"You mean to confuse me. To play games."

He chuckled. "Always."

"I have no patience for it. Never did."

"Ah, but Patience itself is a game, is it not? So you cannot ever completely extricate yourself from play, now, can you?"

"That's different."

"Feminine logic."

"Masculine posturing."

He laughed. "Do you know, Patience, you are the only female of my acquaintance I never tire of conversing with?"

She blushed, thrilled, and looked away, saying, "You mean to flatter me, as you make a practice of flattering every female you encounter."

"I am quite serious in my flattery."

"Then I will politely thank you, and question such a remark in but one way."

"Yes?"

"Does this mean you tire easily of your fiancée's conversation? Or does she conveniently slip your mind when you flirt with other women?"

"Sophie's conversation? Is completely unobjectionable." He winked at her, and then at Lady Wilmington. "And thus, very tedious."

"And yet you would marry her?"

He nodded. "Must do. No other course open to me."

"And so he will tell you, again and again if you are not careful, my dear," Lady Wilmington warned her.

"I do not understand," Patience said.

"Nor should you," Pip said, with a wink for Lady Wilmington, who chortled behind the cover of her fan. So musical the sound of her amusement.

Deliciously circuitous, Patience found their conversation. She felt they might go on for hours thus, without ever tiring, without ever revealing the truths that dangled tantalizingly from such veiled remarks—as though two conversations went on at once, neither of them very forthcoming.

Their interaction intrigued her, set her pulse to racing.

Pip watched her with a most compelling intensity as he spoke, a vibrant, bright-eyed focus that made her feel clever and witty, daring and pretty. It never occurred to her that he meant to be less than forthcoming when he tucked her hand in the crook of his elbow, saying, "My dear Patience, I would much rather hear about you than rattle on about myself."

Chapter Six

Patience was flattered, pleased. Her heart skipped a beat.

Here was the magic she had been looking for, the attention she craved.

"Come!" Pip suggested. "While Mr. Trumps clears away the games we shall go and observe Madame Saqui." As if in afterthought he threw the question over his shoulder. "Do you come with us, Lady Wilmington?"

"How kind you are to ask," she responded with something akin to sarcasm, tipping her head coquettishly. Then she spread her fan and wafted it before her face in a languid manner. "But I fear not. Walking a fine line has never really interested me."

"It is one of the reasons I cherish your company," Pip said, and bowed over the hand she extended.

"So nice to be appreciated," she said, and, turning, dipped a curtsy to Richard. *"Au revoir,"* she murmured, and with a smile for Patience, took her leave.

"And now you must tell me everything, Patience." Pip gave her hand a pat.

"Everything?" She laughed, the laughter as breathless and bubbly as she felt. "That would prove far too tedious."

Pip laughed, his laughter far deeper than she remembered—a sound that stirred a flock of butterflies in her heart and stomach. How handsome Pip was in the lamplight when he laughed, curls hazed in a golden sheen, cheek gilded, eyes agleam. He had always been so in her imaginings—her golden darling.

"Everything interesting," he amended, as he advised her not to walk too fast, for Pippet did not care to be jostled.

Patience had heard the bird complain and so she slowed her step, and, surprised to find Richard did not go with them, turned and asked, "Are you coming?"

Richard looked up from the chessmen he and the lad stashed neatly into a carrying case. "Go ahead. I will catch up."

"Dickey-boy has seen the tightrope walker many times," Pip explained.

Patience felt a pang that Richard could so easily abandon her, but, caught up in the gleam of Pip's eyes, she soon forgot her disappointment.

"You are much taller than when last we met," she said.

"Indeed." He grinned mischievously, his gaze darting to the neckline of her dress. "We have both of us grown to advantage."

She blushed, secretly proud he should notice, and yet she knew it was not at all gentlemanly of him to suggest such a thing. She wondered if perhaps her décolletage was a trifle too low.

Ahead of them the lamplight doubled around a small pavilion, and in the trees above, a rope stretched across an open space, a thin dark line in the golden glow.

A woman seriously intended to walk across such a slender thing? It seemed an impossible feat.

"How many hearts have you broken?" Pip asked, slowing.

"What?" Patience turned her thoughts from broken bones to broken hearts. "Me? None."

"I cannot believe it," he teased. "No offers?"

"Offers. Yes. Two," she said proudly, and as if to accentuate her pleasure in announcing as much, a blue rocket soared into the sky above their heads with a high shriek and a shower of blue sparks.

The cockatoo spread its wings and squawked at the sky.

Pip's brows arched. "Then you lie to say you break no hearts."

"Hearts were not engaged," Patience assured him, distracted by the shower of blue sparks from which a woman in a filmy costume emerged, yellow parasol in hand. Contradicting gravity and science, she stepped into the air between the trees, a bower of leaves and starlit sky her backdrop.

"How can you be sure?"

Patience tore her gaze from the spectacle. "Of what?"

"How did you know hearts were not engaged?"

How fascinated he seemed to be in her answer, for Pip did not so much as glance in the tightrope walker's direction. His eyes, reflecting a fresh shower of blue light, gazed fixedly at her.

Unused to such focus, Patience found it most gratifying. It fired within her the sense that she was special, her perspective important, valued.

How had she known? No one had asked her such a question before. Not her father, nor her mother. Neither of her suitors had questioned the matter. She had never really posed the question to herself, and yet here stood Pip, insisting she do so rather than enjoy Madame Saqui's swaying progress.

"They rushed to ask for my hand," she explained. "Before they had taken time to know me. And . . ." She hesitated. Her attention wavered. She could not resist turning her eyes again to the spectacle above.

"And?" he prodded.

How brave the young woman was, she thought. How confident. She grew dizzy looking up at her. How could a woman calmly step onto so flimsy a thread?

"Oh, one of them seemed more interested in impressing Father than in impressing me, and spoke of me, in my presence, in the third person, as if I were not there. I could not think why I should love him."

Madame Saqui's parasol swayed. The crowd below her perch gasped their concern.

"What a fool!" Pip said.

He did not mean the tightrope walker. When Patience turned to face him again as the woman safely reached the platform at the end of her rope, he watched her, not the performance.

"And the other fellow? How did he reveal his true feelings?"

His persistence was flattering—indeed, invigorating. She smiled and tried to calm her pulse, to subdue the rise of sheer joy that left her feeling as if, like Madam Saqui, she walked on air.

"Mmm." She had to think back. It seemed so long ago, and she had left it completely behind her. "I suppose it was because he talked of nothing but land and funds and inheritances, and how much his mother was sure to like me. Most disconcerting. I felt always as if she stood between us—as if he regarded me through her eyes rather than his own. I think both of these gentlemen were more in love with the idea of marriage than with me."

Madame Saqui curtsied from her platform, and as the crowd applauded she ran nimbly across her wire once again.

Pip studied Patience, brows knitted, as she laughed and gasped and applauded.

"How wonderful!" she said.

"Wonderful, indeed, to see you laugh again. How long has it been since we have seen one another?"

"Four years, seven months," she said, surprised he must ask, and yet unwilling to reveal her disappointment. She concentrated on Madame Saqui. "I wonder how long it takes to learn such a thing. She does not look in the least afraid, does she?"

From the corner of her eye she watched him, saw him flash the heart-stopping smile. He said with a seductive note of mischief in his voice, "Are you not at all afraid of being labeled a fusty old maid?"

She laughed. "At seventeen? I think not."

He laughed as well, teasing her, as he had always teased her. "And was not your heart engaged even a little, Patience?"

"No," she admitted. "I liked them both well enough, and was flattered they should offer for me, but in truth I am no better versed in love than they."

"And did you not think you might grow to love either of them?" He nudged her in the ribs, such contact quite thrilling, if not at all appropriate for a young lady. Here was Pip as she remembered him. Pip the tease. Pip the creature of insatiable curiosity. Her darling Pip. The warmth of his gaze, his touch, his voice, fired within her an unexpected glow, an unexpected intensity of need that he should smile at her again, that he should approve of her, perhaps grow to love her.

How interested in her every word he seemed. How exhilarating his attention.

"Love them?" She shook her head. "Impossible."

The cockatoo screeched in his ear.

He calmed the bird, his hands gentle and sure. Patience wondered what it would feel like to be stroked so, to be addressed so affectionately, despite the words chosen.

I love you, she wanted to screech in his ear.

"I mean to give you back to the one-legged pirate from whom I bought you if you do not behave in a more mannerly fashion," he promised the cockatoo, who bobbed its head and let loose a piercing whistle.

"Your heart has never been touched?" he asked.

He stole Patience's away with such a question, with his refusal to be distracted from their intimate topic. She drew a deep breath. Their conversation teetered far more dangerously than Madame Saqui had. She could not respond unequivocally in the negative. Her heart had been touched, after all, by him. Since they were children she had loved him, yearned for him, dreamed of him. She longed to tell him as much, here in the moonlight where a woman had bravely walked a fine line among the stars, but she hesitated, unsure of herself, of him, swaying on the tightrope of her feelings.

She thought of Sophie Defoe.

The air smelled of fizzled gunpowder.

When she responded, her voice, too thin, tripped in her throat. "My heart was touched. Once. Long ago. But tell me what it is like to be truly in love, Pip. And loved enough that you would ask for a young woman's hand. I must learn from your example."

Chapter Seven

Patience braced her heart for a mortal blow.

Pip laughed, a deep-throated, explosive laughter that turned heads and stirred answering smiles on the faces of those who heard it. Pip's laughter had always had that effect on people. She must smile as well, though she was unsure just what it was she had said to stir such a boisterous reaction.

"You assume I marry for love, my dear Patience," he teased, his voice low, his brows waggling.

But of course she had. A most provocative remark. What did he mean by it?

"Mistakenly so?" she asked with a deep thrill of curiosity, wings of hope lifting her heart.

In a flash of colored satin the lad, Mr. Trumps, dragged Richard into the light of one of the lamps. "Here they are!" he cried.

Their intimate conversation came to an end.

"What did you think of Madame Saqui?" Richard asked.

Before Pip could reply, trumpet fanfare and the patter of gloved applause marked the end of the tightrope walker's performance.

"We paid her no mind," Pip said, and, leaning closer to Patience, added with a conspiratorial smile, "Did we, my dear?"

Patience knew Pip meant to make Richard feel he had missed out on something. He had used the same ploy as a child. She had always considered it a cruelty in him.

"Pip was just about to tell me—"

"A lesson in love," Pip said with a wink.

Richard hid all expression behind cover of his mask.

The cockatoo screeched in Pip's ear again, as if in protest.

"I asked Pip to tell me what it is like to be in love," Patience clarified.

"Did you indeed?" The dark, winged brows rose. "And how did Pip answer?"

"I didn't," Pip said. "You interrupted us."

The bird squawked.

"Like this bird interrupts us," Pip complained. "Tiresome thing."

"Forgive me," Richard said evenly. "Please proceed."

"What? Looking for lessons in love, yourself, Dickey-boy?"

"No. Wondering if you have any real understanding of such a state."

Pip laughed. "Far more than you, I should think. Certainly far more experience."

Pipette threw out his chest, feathers fluffed, ruffling Pip's hair in the process.

Pip handed the bird to the boy. "Here, take him away. He grows restive."

Patience found herself staring at Richard rather than the transfer of the bird. "Have you fallen in love, too?" she could not resist asking. She could not imagine Richard in love. She could not imagine what he was thinking with his eyes overshadowed by his mask.

Richard stood motionless, a blackbird, wings folded. He took so long to respond that Pip gave him a shove on the arm and blurted, "Gammon. Not even a bout of puppy love?"

At exactly the same moment Richard croaked, "I am in love now."

Patience gasped.

"With whom?" Pip demanded.

Richard turned his back on them, domino swaying, dark as a crow's tail, as he set off, away from the lights and music.

"I would rather not say," he called back over his shoulder.

Pip looked at Patience wide-eyed. "Who?" he mouthed.

Patience shrugged, as surprised as he.

"Oh, tell us," she implored, following him, Pip at her heels. "If there is anyone you might tell, it must be us."

Richard kept walking, gravel spurting from beneath his heels. The treed enclosures closed in on either side of them, gone gray now as dusk fell, and the lighting was not so good in this part of the gardens. Oak and ash swayed in the breeze, leaves whispering. She thought of legs beneath these trees, and tried to imagine Richard in such a position, not beneath trees, of course, but somewhere, anywhere, with the woman he loved. Shocking thought! A hoydenish thought if ever there was one.

"Does she not reciprocate your feelings?" Pip guessed.

Patience wondered if he might be right. She had seen a flicker of emotion in Richard's eyes when he had blurted out his secret. Was it pain? Or embarrassment?

He stopped, allowing them to catch up to him, though he did not look at her as she fell into step beside him. The stars above drew his gaze. Starlight silvered the black satin of his mask.

"I have yet to reveal my feelings," he said quietly, dark wings folded, hands clasped in the small of his back, as he had as a boy, the image of his father.

"Surely she has some sense of your affections?" Pip scoffed.

Richard shook his head. His voice came to them quiet but certain. "I do not think so. I have been careful."

"Why?" Patience tried to imagine who among the women she had met at the half dozen or so balls and routs Richard had escorted her to might be the one he cared for.

Richard studied his shoes a moment before he looked into her eyes, starlight captured there. The silhouette his jaw cut against the stars seemed more rigid than usual. "I've little to offer a woman when it comes to marriage."

Of course, Patience thought, sorry she had asked.

"Nonsense," Pip said.

Richard sighed and, bending, picked up a handful of gravel. As he spoke he tossed a pebble hard at the sky, as if he might in that fashion touch the stars. "You do not understand, Pip, what it is to be second-born." A pebble arced ahead of them into the darkness, found earth again with a distant clatter. "No title." Another pebble followed the first two. It made the stars wink. "No inheritance to speak of. Only one's good name and connections to rely upon."

And his name and connections were currently threatened by his brother's wildness. The truth of it hung between them, unsaid.

Pip frowned, then shrugged. He had always taken for granted his station in life, the ease with which things came to him.

Richard turned his hand so that the remaining pebbles rained onto the path at his feet.

Patience raised her face to the night sky, unsettled by Richard's defeated tone, by the idea that she, too, took her position, her family's riches, for granted. She did not want to think of such things. It spoiled the evening.

"Is love wonderful?" She changed the subject abruptly, surprised at the wistfulness in her own voice.

Richard's head jerked in her direction.

Pip laughed. "My dearest Patience!" His voice fell soft upon the darkness. "Have you never been in love?"

His dearest Patience! She liked the sound of that. It fit the dream she had long carried of him in her heart.

And yet, he was promised to another. To Sophie Defoe.

"I do not think I have ever been in love," she murmured. "Not really. Infatuated, yes." She yearned to cry out to him how long that infatuation had lasted, and for whom. "But love? I do not think so."

They stepped closer, these two, her dearest friends—the better to hear her—and she felt a moment's embarrassment to ask them such a thing, but this place, the darkness, invited confidences.

"I know what it is like to long for a young man's attention." She stole a furtive glance at Pip. Shadows blurred his expression. Richard was staring at his shoes again. Both stood motionless, listening.

"I know what it is like to yearn for a gentleman's good opinion, to feel a clumsy fool in his presence, all thumbs or left feet." Her lips went dry, her mouth all cotton. She cleared her throat. In this small way, if in no other, she might reveal herself to Pip. "I know what it is like to think about a gentleman every day, wondering if he ever thinks of me. To imagine his smile, his kiss, sweet words."

Richard moved, gravel shifting. She glanced in his direction.

"Is this love?"

Pip turned his face to the lights behind them. He was smiling. His eyes, his teeth, caught the light. "Sounds like love to me," he said.

She smiled back at him, wondering if he had any notion she spoke of him.

Richard's voice exploded from the darkness. "I disagree. You speak of desire. Not love."

"Oh?" Pip's response was caustic. "What then is love, Dickey-lad?"

Richard took his time in answering, but when he spoke, the words seemed to well up from the heart of him, moving in their intensity. "Love follows desire. If one is lucky."

Patience looked away, shaken. Was that all she had ever felt? Desire? Without love? Richard sounded as if he understood deeply what she had yet to fathom.

"Are you sure you do not mean lust, Dickey-boy?" Pip was ever skeptical.

"No. You mistake love and passion. There is a difference." Such certainty in Richard's tone. His black-masked, black-cloaked figure had become one with the darkness, so that the words seemed to float, disembodied, in a void.

Pip bowed toward the speaking darkness, in the Turkish fashion, grinning now. She could hear it in his voice, saw the glint of his teeth. "Tell us, then, o wise one. What is this difference?"

"Passion is overwhelming," the shadow within the shadows said.

Patience could not imagine Richard overwhelmed by anything, and yet the darkness had swallowed him whole.

"It crashes over one," he said. "Blinds one. Consumes one. Instills jealousy, defensiveness, a clutching possessiveness. It can be blissful and destructive in the same moment."

"And love?" Patience was most interested in his diatribe, even if Pip yawned with feigned indifference, and called to them, "Come on, you two. Enough of the maudlin. Time to eat."

Darkness loosed its grip on Richard. Starlight found his nose, the flat of his forehead. It fingered his hair as he stepped forward. Stars were trapped in the eyes he fixed on her, a steady gleam behind the mask. He ignored Pip entirely.

"Love is patient, kind, respectful, even dispassionate," he said with equal dispassion. "It is a warmth of feeling, not an onslaught. It creates, and heals, and binds without clinging." So calmly he spoke, his voice low and even, and yet there was that unexpected glimmer in his eyes.

He reached for her hand and tucked it into the crook of his arm, never pausing in his diatribe. "One is filled with a strong sense of knowing love is worth waiting for, fighting for, perhaps even dying for."

Pip snorted his disdain.

Richard went on, unfazed by his friend's contempt, starlight and lamplight reaching for him now with greedy hands, caressing him with their combined glow, a mingling of silver and gold. "One cannot imagine living a lifetime without true love, while passion, which burns so very brightly, may be snuffed as quickly as a candle in the wind."

They met his outburst with a moment's contemplative silence.

Then Pip blurted, his heels spurting gravel as he turned to walk away, "Goodness, Dickey-boy! Preach us a sermon."

Patience ignored this ill-mannered outburst. She had

never heard Richard address another topic with such intensity and conviction. It was as if the darkness had taken away the Richard she knew and given them back an intriguing stranger. The black sleeve beneath her gloved hand, the brush of his domino upon her own, seemed suddenly more interesting than usual.

Pip sighed and set off without them. "Come along," he coaxed impatiently.

"Yes. Enough of love." Richard straightened, his face returning to its customary calm, the mask hiding his emotions almost as much as the darkness had.

Patience fell into step without demur. And as they walked she stole furtive glances at her friend, observing as if for the first time the way the lamplight touched upon Richard's chin and throat, gilding jawline and lips. He had a rather attractive mouth, Richard did, in any light. She could not help wondering what lucky female had captured those lips, to stir such passion.

Chapter Eight

Patience listened to the raspy voice of the gravel beneath their feet. She listened to her heartbeat. And she thought about what Richard had said about love.

Pip walked ahead of them, broad shoulders, bright coattails, and the shapely curve of his calves catching her eyes. His breeches stretched provocatively tight. Legs. She found herself completely distracted by the sight of, the memory of, legs. Pip's legs. A stranger's legs, buttocks pumping. She glanced down at Richard's legs, then looked away. Was she no better than the hoyden beneath the trees, stockings rumpled, skirt shoved high?

She shook her head, shook away the thought.

They walked the length of the gardens along the crunching gravel pathways, through four evenly spaced stone arches. Angels and scrollwork hovered above their heads.

Heaven help her. She was looking at legs again! Richard's thighs, and he would be mortified if he knew.

Dinner boxes. She would look at the dinner boxes. That was safe. They yawned linen-tongued emptiness at her, except for the mythical creatures, the gods and goddesses cavorting along their painted backs. More legs. Painted legs, scantily clad. Some of them naked. Was there no getting away from them?

The lead statue of Handel watched them pass, blank-eyed. Even his hefty sculpted legs fed her fascination.

She must forget legs, especially gentlemen's legs, and focus on what Pip was saying, darling Pip, clever Pip, regaling them with tales of dignitaries and royalty, musicians and macaronis, prizefighters and pranksters, drunken ruffians and daring rogues. All had walked these paths—a long line of legs. She could not help but laugh at the idea.

Richard seemed entertained. He nodded and made just the right noises to encourage such storytelling. Dear Richard. Dependable Richard.

And yet there was more to him than that, more to both young men than she had ever imagined. As she watched one speak and the other listen, she realized she did not know either of them. Not really. Not as well as she had thought.

Pip was in his element. His tales were well voiced, articulately presented, and limited to only that which was sure to amaze or amuse. His enthusiasm for gentlemen long dead with nicknames like "Fighting" Fitzgerald, "Tinman" Hooper, and "Hell-gate" Barrymore fired her imagination.

Such history added luster to the evening—and to the storyteller—a fresh perspective. She had never realized Pip had such a ready tongue, such a knack for the well-turned phrase, the colorful image, and clever quips that had them all laughing until their sides ached. He won her heart all over again.

The cascade, for which practically everyone in the gardens gathered, so that the well-lit site buzzed with voices loud enough to drown out the splashing of the water, was a bit of a disappointment following hard on the heels of such stirring entertainment.

"What think you of our trifling waterfall full of goldfish?" Pip asked sarcastically.

Patience was still thinking about heroes and fighters and troublemakers, and in Pip she saw all three. She thought, too, of what Richard had said, his uncharacteristic show of emotion, the idea that he was in love. It startled her. She had expected Pip to be in love, and he was not, and she had never dreamed Richard's heart might be taken, and it was.

Her world was upside down, as if she had stepped into the reflection in the waters of the cascade.

"The spot where we used to go angling at Hartington Hall is much prettier," she said absently.

"Mmm." Pip laughed. "Do you remember the day Richard thought he had hooked a really big one?"

"We all thought so," Patience reminded Richard with an affectionate shove on the arm. "Before it was done we were all tugging on the line trying to reel the monster in. I remember being sandwiched between the two of you, the line all wet and slippery, stretched taut. We were sure you had a fat brown trout gone under a rock."

"Gudgeoned. The lot of us." Richard smiled.

Pip laughed again, leaning into it, slapping his thigh. "I shall never forget how your stinking fish came flying up out of the water."

"Oh, the smell!" Patience remembered.

"Faugh!" Pip held his nose, which drew the attention of several masked and draped young women, who lifted powdered noses to the wind as if to smell the past.

Pip laughed and winked at them, which set them all to clapping hands to well-rouged cheeks and giggling, an act that proved most unfortunate to their looks, for two of them had missing teeth; the third had more than enough, and all of them crooked.

Patience shook her head. *Hoydens,* she thought. *Professional hoydens.* "Such a horrible reek."

Pip's dimples quivered. His eyes sparkled merrily. And Patience could not tell if it was the attention of three giggling females that brought such brightness to his face—or memory.

"Ah, Dickey-lad." He sighed. "You wore the scent of it for several days, as I recall. I must say I cannot understand why, when you saw the dreadful thing coming straight for your face, you did not think to duck."

Richard chuckled good-naturedly. Dear Richard.

Patience was pleased to see that he could look back on the moment and laugh. He had found no humor in it at all at the time. A great gob of mud and moss-caked leather had hit him smack in the face, and when he had flung it away from him, back into the stream, his line and pole had gone with it.

Scarlet with embarrassment, and then quite green with the smell, Richard had frantically scooped mud from his face with the side of his hand while Patience pinched her nose and told him he had caught a fish after all. A silvery dace wriggled about in his dripping mop of hair. She had squealed and batted it back into the water. Pip, no help at all, had whooped and snorted and fallen into the grass laughing so hard he lost his breath.

He laughed now, almost as hard. They all did.

"I did think to duck." Richard's protest drew a fresh snort from Pip.

"S-s-s-l-l-low thought?" He set them laughing again— the three masked hoydens as well, who seemed to be repeating among themselves every word overheard.

"Have pity on me now," Richard objected, trying to look serious, trying to frown, failing miserably at both. "I had very good reason for what I did. If you will recall we were arranged thus." As he spoke he turned Pip, nudging him into a spot in front of him, and stepped in front of Patience. "Do you remember exactly what we were doing? How we stood?"

"I had just run up with the net," Pip said, and assumed a running stance, hand out, as if he were holding the net.

The hoydens clapped with glee at his odd pose, and proceeded to imitate him.

Patience watched, a bit perturbed by the attention Pip gave the women.

"I was on one knee, holding the rod like so." Richard took the remembered posture, the weight of his body supported by the kneeling leg, his other bent to brace him away from the pull of the current. His thighs, indeed the entire length of his legs, looked much shapelier now than they had then, when he had seemed so very tall and gangly and a bit knobby-kneed.

Coltish, her mother had called him, and like a colt he had outgrown all awkwardness.

The hoydens found nothing to object to in him, indeed

they gave him as many come-hither looks as they bestowed upon Pip. Strange how she had never stopped to consider how other women might regard her friend. Pip had been such a pretty child. He had grown into an extraordinarily handsome young man, but in seeing them side by side, Richard did not suffer by the comparison as much as he once had.

"The line was stretched taut." Richard prodded her arm with his elbow as he pulled back on the imaginary line.

The hoydens were giggling again, but she paid them no mind. She remembered now exactly what had happened, what she had done.

"It bent the pole," Richard said.

She nodded. "It looked as if it might break. I stepped in behind you, like this, and reached around"—her voice dropped—"like this." Well, it had not been exactly like this. He had been so much more the boy then. His neck had smelled of sun and sweat and the worms he had hooked, not of lime soap and cedar-scented cologne and the musky oil of hair pomade. She closed her eyes and leaned her cheek almost to his, and stood a moment swaying, trying to separate past and present. "I braced the upper part of the pole."

He fell perfectly still as she leaned her chin over his shoulder, and stretched her arm beside his, the bulge of his muscle grazing the inner curve of her left arm, her right hand resting gently on his shoulder. Her chest met with the flat solidity of his shoulder blade, just as it had as a girl. Well, not quite the same. She had more bosom than she had then, and it reacted most strangely, as if he were north and she the trembling compass pin. The rise and fall of his back made her breath race like the throb of his pulse in the vein at the base of his neck, a throbbing echoed elsewhere, lower, in a manner she had never before experienced.

She did not remember feeling so very aware of how close they were, of every little move he made. She dared look over his shoulder at Pip, who had abandoned his awkward pose to look back at them.

She wondered for a moment how thrilling it might be to stand thus with Pip's pulse beneath her hand. And in that moment her precious Pip looked her in the eyes and smiled the smile that always took her breath away, and a shudder coursed the length of her spine, lifting the hair at the base of her neck.

Richard's hand rose, sweeping an arc between her and Pip, breaking the spell of that smile, the movement of his shoulder blade so provocative, she felt for a moment as if she engaged in an illicit activity. She shivered again when Richard spoke, his words rumbling from his chest to hers.

"I saw that slimy piece of rotted leather coming straight at my head, and considered for the briefest moment the idea of ducking, and realized I could not, in good conscience."

He ducked and turned, his gloved hand continuing its arc, catching her lightly on the chin, kidskin glancing along her jaw. His fingertips grazed her throat. His hip rotated.

Such an odd sensation—pleasant and dreadful at the same time, as she realized the implication, as it hit her, as it were, full in the face.

Pip no longer netted imaginary fish. He bent over laughing until the air wheezed from his throat like an old set of bagpipes, everyone within hearing distance turning to see what caused such a commotion. "Oh, God!" Pip wheezed. "Patience might have had the face full of rotten leather instead. Oh, lord! That would have been a sight to see."

Richard no longer laughed. His lips pinched down into a tight little smile as he tilted his head to watch from the corner of his eye her frozen reaction.

Her arms were still about him, clutching the imaginary line.

"Thought you might not forgive me," he whispered.

She stepped back suddenly, the truth of his gallantry astounding her.

Pip was lost in the humor of the past, slapping his thigh and chortling. "You saved her such a humiliation, and as I recall she spent the rest of the day pinching her nose whenever you came near."

Humiliating him!

"I remember." The tight smile faded.

"Oh, Richard!" Patience cried, her hand flying out, as if of its own accord, to touch his shoulder. "I am sorry. That was not at all kind of me."

He shrugged. "At the time I wished I might stand back from myself and pinch my nose. Do you know it took three baths to rid me of the smell?"

Patience nodded, while Pip broke into fresh gales of laughter.

"Three baths and rose-scented bath salts!" he shouted, turning heads again. "Which brought fresh humiliation down on your head."

"Oh, dear!" Patience suffered fresh pangs of regret. "How cruel I was to tease you unmercifully for smelling like a garden."

"Like a girl!" Pip crowed. "And so you did. You must admit it was true, Rosy Richard, Dandy Dickey." He was dancing around them now, chanting, turning heads, always the center of attention.

Richard the lad would have flushed scarlet.

Richard, the gentleman grown, laughed. He did not color with embarrassment at all, just threw back his head and let the sound roll up out of his chest. A deep laugh. A contagious laugh. Women's heads turned to see what caused such an openhearted expression of amusement.

Dear Richard was handsome when he laughed, Patience decided. Very handsome indeed.

Chapter Nine

Patience laughed.

In a merry mood they turned their backs on the cascade and traipsed together toward the most brilliant of the lights around the dinner boxes and kiosks, where quite a crowd milled about, purchasing food and competing for a favorable spot to see and be seen.

"Philip!" came a cry. A gentleman waved.

And again, "Philip, my dear," to their right, a woman's voice, an unmistakably flirtatious tone.

"I shall just be a moment," Pip promised. "Why not see about procuring some food, Dickey, my boy? I should like a pullet, if you please, and a glass of wine."

"You must come and join my party, dearest." Lady Wilmington came up behind them in that very instant and linked arms with Patience as if they were old friends.

Patience turned, pleased to see her. She could not be sure for an instant who it was the viscountess addressed—herself or Richard, who smiled such a warm and welcoming smile it made her heart beat a little faster just to see it.

Could this be, she wondered, the one Richard had mentioned? The one he loved? He had never smiled at her in just such a way, had he? And that Lady Wilmington was married would certainly make it awkward to declare one's affections. Would it not?

Richard said, "How very kind of you, my dear Lady Wilmington. I am off to fight the rabble for food. Can I bring you anything?"

"You are a dear to ask," she said. "A bite of ham would be nice, and strawberries, if there are any to be had, and Wilmi does love a glass or two of burgundy if a decent bottle is available."

If there was more to her list of procurements Patience did not hear them. She did not notice either exactly when Richard took his leave. She was too caught up in the sight of Pip snared in the arms of a diminutive young woman with Titian-colored hair, who stood on tiptoe that she might whisper in his ear and stroke the breast of the cockatoo, who seemed to enjoy the attention as much as Pip did.

She had imagined Pip was popular with women, and yet it tore at her heart a little to observe his allure firsthand.

"Beautiful little temptress, is she not?" Lady Wilmington murmured.

Patience gave a guilty start. She had thought her attentions better hidden behind her mask. "It cannot be Pip's Miss Defoe."

"Sophie?" Lady Wilmington laughed, the sound like the trickling of the cascade, a captivating laugh. "What a droll idea, my dear. The gardens are far too rowdy and dowdy a gathering place for a Defoe to soil her slippers."

Patience blinked at her.

"I see I shock you." Lady Wilmington lowered her voice to a conspiratorial whisper. "But you must understand that the Defoes are most particular about the company their daughter keeps before she is married. Ironic, really, that they have agreed to this marriage." She had dimples, like Pip's. They danced quite mischievously as she said, "Pip, as you call him, is not in the least particular about the company he keeps." She gave a nod in the direction of the red-haired beauty.

Patience asked, "Who is she?"

Lady Wilmington's eyes narrowed. Her lips twitched. She looked, Patience thought, like a woman unwilling to reveal her cards. "You must ask Richard," she said with a smile that seemed in some way more calculating than pleased. "I would not have him accuse me of sullying innocent ears. Now come, my dear. Let me introduce you to my husband."

Patience could not say in that instant what captivated her curiosity most: news that Lady Wilmington's husband was with her at Vauxhall, or this mysterious refusal to identify Pip's Titian-haired friend.

Lord Wilmington sat ensconced in a dinner box painted with a scene depicting Paris carrying away a none too unwilling Helen of Troy. He sat like a king, propped on a cushion-covered chair that his lordship's footmen had arranged for him just so. A footstool, also carried into the gardens for his lordship's comfort, propped up a swollen left foot. He and his friends had been playing whist.

"I've a touch of the gout," the old man confessed to Patience, having taken her hand in his for a firm squeeze. She liked him at once, for though he had gone quite bald on top, and the remaining fringe gave no hint of what color hair had once graced his lordship's shiny dome, he was a warm and welcoming fellow. His face tracked a lifetime's worth of smiles. His lips curved in a perpetual upward lift. He might have been Lady Wilmington's father, so great was the difference in their age.

The deference and solicitousness with which she attended to her Wilmi surprised Patience, as did the group of aged souls who kept them company—contemporaries of his lordship—a marquess, a graying viscountess, an Austrian archduke who winked at Patience whenever she looked his way, and a querulous old countess who spoke nothing but French.

The main topic of conversation, in either language, when they were not discussing tricks, trumps, bids, or discards, centered on the decrepitude of age: of nostrums for gout, and tinctures for failing eyesight, of salves for aching joints, and the latest patent medicines for heart palpitations and poor circulation.

Richard had yet to make appearance with the food when Pip joined them, changing completely the mood of their little gathering. The countess, eyes alight, coyly held out gnarled hand for a kiss. She called Pip *chérie,* gave his cheek a gloved caress, and patted the seat of the chair beside her.

Pip greeted her with enthusiasm, flattering her with compliments, patting her arm, but he refrained from accepting the comforts of the chair until he had greeted everyone personally. He bent before the marquess, and at his beckoning, coaxed Pippet to step from his broad shoulder to the old gent's round-humped back.

They beamed at him, called out his name and words of fond greeting—everybody's darling, most especially that of his host, whom he greeted with a hearty, "Wilmington! How goes the gout?"

"Would that it would go," the old man responded with a phlegmy chuckle. "And that you would come to see us more often, young man. Has Defoe laid claim to all of your free time?"

"I have been closeted with him a great deal of late, and well you know why."

Wilmington nodded. "The settlements have been agreed upon, then? A date decided?"

Pip shook his head, his manner and gestures carefree. "We negotiate."

"No sense in rushing into such things, is there now?"

At his side, Lady Wilmington leaned close to her husband's ear to say in the fondest of tones, her eyes sparkling like gems as she regarded Pip, "Quite right, my dear. No sense in it at all."

There was, Patience decided, an undercurrent here, a hint of suggestion and tacit understanding that made no sense to her. These three knew each other well, perhaps better than she knew Pip from childhood. It left her feeling disconnected—an intruder.

And yet Pip would not allow her to feel that way for long. "Come, come." He beckoned, his smile dazzling. "You must sit here, Patience." He indicated the chair Lady Wilmington vacated at Lord Wilmington's elbow. "Do tell his lordship of our fish tale, my dear. Most amusing, I do assure you, my lord. Quickly now, Patience." He gave her shoulder a fond squeeze. "Before Richard returns."

She obliged him, of course. People always obliged the charming Pip. Their little flock of graying nobility readily obliged him in rearranging themselves, and in gathering up their cards to make room at the table for Richard and food. She watched Pip as she retold the childhood tale, as he wound his way among the others, a golden guinea amidst a handful of old silver.

He and Lady Wilmington seemed very friendly. She took a place beside him, and they spoke to one another in low voices, and she smiled and touched his arm in just such a way as he looked into her eyes that Patience suffered a moment's pang of jealousy, until she remembered that it was this woman's balding husband who laughed at her fishing tale, swollen foot propped on the stool beside her own. And while there was no denying that Lord Wilmington was a kind and generous old man, she found all of her jealousy turned to pity that a young woman of such grace and beauty should be tied in marriage to a gentleman so disparate in age and appearance.

That Lady Wilmington should flirt with Pip, with Richard, seemed only fair, if such flirtation caused her aging spouse no heartache.

"Miss Ballard is very good at games, my dear," Lady Wilmington made a point of telling her husband as their conversation wore thin. "Perhaps you can coax her into a hand of cards."

"Good at games, are you, my dear? Just like our friend Philip?"

"I do love games," she agreed.

"Used to beat him at backgammon," Lady Wilmington went on, her manner teasing, her eyes fixed on Pip, whose curls she tweaked when he demanded, "How do you know that?"

Patience felt guilty that she should have been at all suspicious of Lady Wilmington, who went on, her manner teasing, "I know a great many things, Philip, if you will but pay attention. Have you heard, Wilmi, that a very clever young woman beat our friend twice this evening, first at chess, and then at backgammon?"

Lady Wilmington arched a brow at Patience, and smiled in her husband's direction as she pinched at Pip's sleeve.

"You need not gloat," Pip scolded.

"Twice, you say?" Wilmington tapped Patience on the shoulder with his fanned hand of cards. "Is it possible?"

"Yes, indeed," Pip admitted gallantly. "A clever young thing in a red domino. She ran away before I could congratulate her for the second thrashing she gave me. I've no idea who she was." He cocked his head and batted his lashes at Lady Wilmington. "Did you happen to catch a glimpse of her? I am quite convinced she took over your game of chess, my lady, and do not tell me I am wrong in recognizing your laughter sounding from her vicinity when she checked my king with that bloody pawn."

"I did see her," Lady Wilmington admitted, a teasing light in her eyes. "A pretty thing. Dark hair. Dark eyes. A trim little figure."

Patience blushed, and believed her secret revealed, for surely in such a description, Pip must recognize her at once.

But Pip was not looking at her at all. He had eyes only for the charming Lady Wilmington.

"Will you not tell me her name?" he coaxed as he smiled winningly. "Of all women, I must meet one who can best me."

"Must you?" Lady Wilmington's brows arched coyly.

"She cannot honorably do so, you know." Richard's voice spoke from behind them.

In turning they were met with sight of Richard bearing two baskets of food, while at his heels came Pip's Mr. Trumps, bearing a third basket, from which several wine bottles protruded.

"Food at last!" Lord Wilmington crowed. "You are a godsend, my boy. We are all half-starved."

Patience let loose a great sigh of relief, thinking the matter of her identity must now be dropped by way of distraction, but Pip was persistent. As the baskets were opened, and plates of chicken and ham and rolls and strawberries were handed about, he pressed for an answer. "Whatever do you mean, cannot honorably do so?"

Richard gave a little bow to Lady Wilmington. "She gave her word to the gentleman who brought the girl. Or am I mistaken?"

Their hostess, who had risen to see to the pouring of wine, glanced mischievously over her shoulder. "You do think of everything, Richard."

Richard passed the packet of rolls.

"But you must tell me who she is, Melanie," Pip wheedled. "Or do you mean to drive me mad with curiosity?"

"If you are half as clever as you like to think you are, my dear, you will soon divine who she was without my spoon-feeding it to you, Philip. Now please uncork this bottle. Be a dear."

"Did you see her?" he asked Patience as he filled her glass.

Patience looked to Richard.

Beyond the faint lifting of one brow, he offered no response other than to ask her if she would care for a slice of ham.

"A glimpse," she admitted, which made Lady Wilmington laugh and Richard smiled as he inquired, "Mustard?"

"Yes, please." Patience smiled back at him as he spooned a dollop onto her plate.

"Tell me," Pip crowded close, insistent. "What did you think of her? I know I can trust you to give me the truth."

Patience drew a deep breath, letting it out slowly before she answered. "She looked as if she did not want you to know who she was."

Pip plucked a strawberry from her plate. "Go on. Describe her."

Oh, dear, Patience thought.

Richard bit his lower lip and looked away.

What might she tell Pip? What must she say? How did one go about describing oneself? "She seemed sure of

herself when it came to the games," she said. *There.* That
was true. "Not so sure of herself in her surroundings."

Pip's eyes lit up. "She had not been to Vauxhall before? I knew it. I should have remembered such a player
had I encountered her before. What of the gentleman
who ran after her?"

Patience dared not look at Richard, dared not respond
with any sign of humor to Lady Wilmington's sudden
peal of laughter.

"What of him?"

"How did he appear to you?"

She risked a quick glance at Richard. He looked stead-
ily back at her. *How did Richard appear to her?* She had
never really given it much thought. Richard was always
just Richard—dear, dependable Richard. But she could
not describe him as such, now, could she?

"The gentleman was tall," she said carefully. *There!*
That was safe. "Tall," she went on. "Dark hair."

Richard watched her, unblinking.

"Handsome?" Pip asked.

She hesitated.

Richard's gaze slid away.

"Distinguished," she said.

"Most decidedly distinguished," Lady Wilmington
agreed, shooting her a sly wink.

"You will make me a jealous old man, my dear," Wilmington said.

Richard stared at the plate he filled for the countess.
The tips of his ears had gone as pink as the ham.

Patience smiled and went on. "He had an air about
him of intelligence, and dependability."

Lady Wilmington made a strangled noise behind cover
of her fan.

"Her brother, perhaps?" Lord Wilmington suggested.

Patience shook her head. "I do not think so. Their
features were not at all similar."

Pip listened attentively. "She was pretty, yes? I am
sure she was pretty."

Lady Wilmington's smile faded as she folded her fan.

Richard's head rose. Patience could feel the weight of his gaze upon her without even looking at him.

"Surely any woman's perceived beauty is a matter of taste," she said carefully.

"Well, she was most definitely to mine. Smelled nice, too. Lily of the valley, if I am not mistaken." Pip's enthusiasm was irrepressible. For a moment it buoyed Patience.

"I wear Lily of the valley," she reminded him, sure he must know her now, sure it would take only a good whiff of her to jog his memory.

"Is it you who smells so sweet?" Pip asked. "And all this time I thought it her."

The remark struck at her pride, dagger sharp.

"Sorry to disappoint," she said. Her own sense of disappointment swamped her, dragging down the point of her chin.

They were looking at her, all of them, and that Richard and Lady Wilmington knew the truth of it made their examination harder to bear.

"No, no, now, pet," Pip tried to soothe her. "Do not look downcast. You do not disappoint me. Not in the least."

She looked up at him, hopeful, wanting him to make it right again.

"You have been far more forthcoming than these two." He looked pointedly at Richard and Lady Wilmington. "Whom I thought my dearest friends. Now tell me more of my mystery woman."

Patience tossed her head, shrugging aside her melancholy, looking first at Lady Wilmington, who gazed back with a tight-lipped smile—an expression of pity.

She did not wish to be pitied.

Richard's head tilted. His eyes narrowed, as if he would read her feelings without a word said. Patience licked dry lips and, forcing a smile, looked Pip directly in the eyes. "I think she enjoyed herself," she said.

"Did she?" Lady Wilmington sounded a trifle surprised.

"Yes." Patience lifted her chin. "Would you not

agree? It looked as if she enjoyed beating him. She was laughing as she ran away."

"Laughing? Was she really laughing?" Pip asked.

"Exhibiting very strong emotion, yes," Richard said.

Patience smiled at him.

"Is it so very impossible to imagine someone might find you amusing on occasion?" Lady Wilmington teased.

"That tears it," Pip cried. "We must track down this elusive sylph. I must know who she is." He stood and, leaning over the table, reached for Patience's hand. "And you are going to help me."

She thrilled to the touch of his hand. "Am I? How?"

He leaned closer and whispered, "Our little secret."

A secret shared with everyone at the table, she thought, and yet he managed to make it sound magical—intimate.

"I shall call on you soon to hatch my plot," he promised. "You have my word."

Chapter Ten

Patience daydreamed as she walked.

"Our little secret," Pip had whispered. "I shall call on you soon."

How warm his hand to hers, how electric the brush of fingertips. She had thrilled to the same illicit, breath-held feeling of guilty anticipation earlier, at the sight of naked legs.

His breath had tickled her cheek.

His promise gilded the evening. Lamplight painted laughing faces. Candlelight upon the tables gave every eye a bright twinkle. The stars strove to match that light.

"I do not cut short our evening too soon, do I?" Gloved hand at her elbow, Richard steered her through orderly rows of columns that separated them from dinner boxes crowded with revelers.

Patience started. A drunken fellow reeled out in front of them, muttering something incomprehensible. Richard took a firmer grip upon her elbow to smoothly skirt the man's staggering progress.

Under a canopy of leaves they went, she and dear, reliable Richard, who would see her safely home before the revelry grew too rowdy, his arm steady beneath her gloved hand, while her head swam with music and memory and imaginings of the future.

Patience sighed and gave her head a shake, her mind still firmly rooted in the pulse-tingling sensation of Pip's lips grazing her fingertips, his voice provocatively low.

He would come soon—on his honor. She could not doubt such a vow.

"Did you ask me something?"

"Do I spoil your evening in cutting it short?"

"Oh, no. It has been a lovely evening." She twirled to the music, pulling him into the magic of flute and strings, so that they danced instead of walking, and still made progress in the direction he would lead her. And then she fell into demure step beside him, and flung back her head to gaze at the stars that had so fascinated him earlier, and said, "Do you know I have enjoyed nothing so exciting since we have come to London as this trip to Vauxhall?"

"This illicit trip?" he chided. "You did not enjoy our afternoon in Hyde Park?"

"Of course I did. And very kind of you to think to take me there for a lunch alfresco."

"But?"

Patience bit her lower lip and looked up at him through her lashes. "But there is something very exciting about coming here without Mama, knowing she and Papa would not approve, wearing a mask so that no one will know to tell them I have been naughty." She could no longer suppress her smiles, and so gave up the effort. "The hoyden revived," she said with a mischievous sideways glance.

And then she blushed, for with mention of the word resurfaced the image of a true hoyden, her legs at any rate, and suddenly Patience took the word and all its connotations deeply to heart, and felt ashamed to so lightly associate herself with the term.

Richard stopped to look into her eyes as well as one might from behind a mask in an outdoor park under shadow of the row of trees that would lead them through the gatehouse. He tilted his head in remarking, "I do not care to hear you use that word in describing yourself."

Neither did she, at this point, and so she agreed at once.

"As you wish." And knowing why it mattered to her,

she wondered why it mattered to him, and if he had, after all, seen the same legs she had.

"You arouse my curiosity," he said slowly, and she wondered anew if he chose the word *aroused* by chance or by design.

"Do you find this evening more exciting than the ball at Percy's?"

Percy's? Oh, dear. The ball had been, in her estimation, incredibly boring.

She nodded without hesitation. "Much more so."

"Really?" He sounded so very serious in asking, as though her answer surprised him.

Richard was always so very grave in his conversation. Even as a child he had been thus—there was seldom anything light or carefree in his manner.

She gave his hand a squeeze, and hoped to bring a smile to his lips in saying, "I enjoyed meeting your friends, of course."

He nodded gravely. "I am glad."

"This friend you mean me to marry?"

He turned his head, lamplight gleaming in his eyes. "Yes?"

"Was he among them? Did we dance? I loved the dancing."

His jaw tensed. "Was there no one there you were particularly drawn to?"

"Not really. I enjoyed our dance more than any other."

He fell to studying his shoes. "I enjoyed dancing as well," he said. "But?" He looked up, lips pressed together.

It was her turn to frown. "What do you mean, but?" Why should there be a *but* when it came to their dancing?

"There is a *but* inherent in what you were saying," he prodded.

She let go her hold on his arm and turned to observe the last row of dinner boxes. So many people to see here, so many beautiful hats and dresses, so many glittering satin masks. It had been a wonderful evening, a dazzling garden to visit. "Well, there was no chance of seeing Pip at Percy's, was there?" she said.

"Ah! And was that so very important?"

"But of course. The three of us together again. Like tonight. It is my fondest childhood memory. I should have been dreadfully lonely without the two of you to play cards and catch fish and climb trees with."

"I cherish those times as well."

She whirled and, looking back the way they had come, wrapped her arms across her chest and said fervently, "I shall cherish this evening always. Thank you for it. For bringing me to the forbidden garden where proper young ladies dare not roam, and costumed women walk among the stars, and—"

"Pickpockets lurk," he said wryly.

"So you say," she said, and patted the little bulge beneath her skirt that was her reticule. "But I have not been preyed upon, as you so dourly predicted."

"That's a relief, for somewhere along the path from the food kiosks to the Wilmingtons' dinner box"—he patted at his pocket—"my purse was snatched, and I very much regret to admit that we must depend upon your allowance to tip the coachman this evening."

"But of course. And very sorry I am to hear that your evening was so troubled. You said nothing when it happened."

"No sense in upsetting our gay party. I shall repay you, of course."

"Never mind that. It is what the money is for, and I owe you for my dinner, which had to have come from your pocket, as you were the one who fetched it. Indeed, did you pay for everyone's dinner? And the wine? Your pickpocket could not have had much leavings after such an outlay."

"No. He was left with next to nothing." Richard sighed and tipped his hat to the gatekeeper as the man swung wide the Dutch door for them.

It occurred to her that it was rather odd that he should sigh for a pickpocket's losses. Pip would have laughed, as would she. But Richard sighed.

Dear Richard.

Chapter Eleven

Patience delved into her skirt pocket for her purse.

As they stood beneath the stars at the street's edge, waiting while a lad ran to tell the coachman they were ready, she discreetly handed over her reticule and said, "You will need a coin or two for the lad as well, will you not?"

Richard nodded as he struggled with the knotted string, his hands strangely awkward. "Cannot see to do anything through this blasted mask," he complained, and wrenched it from his face.

She said, "Here, let me," and had it open in a trice while he, tight-lipped, head down, shoulders hunched, looked in the direction the lad had run and whirled the mask by its string, around his finger first one way, and then the other.

"Thank you," he said, and took the handful of coins she handed him, far more than he would need, and yet he did not argue with her, did not insist she take any of them back again, simply looked her in the eyes with a most profound expression of gratitude.

"I should thank you," she said, a trifle uneasy that he regarded her so.

He blinked, pocketed the coins, looked away a moment, mask dangling limply, before he said in much more his usual tone, "Whatever for?"

"You did not tell him I was the woman in red," she said.

"Nor will I," he said calmly as he carefully looped the strings about the nose bridge of the mask.

"You knew I did not wish it?" She reached up to untie the strings of her own mask.

He frowned, and paused in answering her, for the coach arrived, and there was the footman opening the door and letting down the step, and Richard held out a hand to her, that she might more easily climb up.

Patience settled into the coach and waited for Richard to seat himself beside her. The door was slammed shut, and the footman's jump onto his station at the back gave the coach its final sway before the horses were bidden "Walk on" by the coachman above.

Richard spoke then, his voice low, that he might not be overheard, so low Patience had to lean forward to hear above the rumble of the wheels. "In all honesty, dear Patience . . ." He twisted to look her directly in the eyes as he spoke, each word enunciated carefully. "I did not tell Pip you were the woman he found so fascinating because I am loath to be the one to put anything in the way of what I consider an excellent match for our friend."

She leaned back abruptly, cheeks burning, as if he had slapped them both, her jaw very tight as she restrained the torrent of words she longed to fling at him. "I see," she said coolly, when she did not see at all. "And why is it such a good match?"

He sighed and rubbed at the bridge of his brows. "Good breeding. A spotless reputation. She has the head for finance that Pip has not, and from all signs she cares for him."

She closed her eyes to him, to the moonlit lines of tension in his forehead, to the rigidity of his posture. She felt betrayed. "And do you see signs that he loves her?"

"Would you suggest otherwise?"

She listened to the wheels' thunder, felt it rumble from the seat she rested her head against, as his breath, his words, had earlier rumbled against her breast. She could not see his face in the darkness, only now and then a glimpse of the curve of his cheek, the movement of his hand, the gleam of his eyes.

I've a headache brewing, she thought. "Something he said made me wonder."

Richard's lips pursed. "If he does not, more's the pity. Of all those he has shown an infatuation for, she would make him the best wife."

She watched for him, in glimpses, surprised to find in the occasional flare of lamplight that he had turned to do the same, his eyes seeking hers from the darkness.

"And the woman in red?"

"What of her?"

"Is he infatuated with her?"

"Of course he is—for the moment. Pip is a man in love with the idea of being in love."

There he was, and there. The familiar nose loomed from the darkness, the steadfast calm regard. His eyes narrowed. "Do you wish him to be infatuated?"

"No, of course not. Don't be silly," she lied as she rubbed the fabric of her sleeve where his hand had rested as he promised to call on her, and soon. Richard was gone again, the coach drenched in darkness deep as a lake, and just as still, and she wondered if she had imagined the hint of concern in his question.

When he said nothing in response and the silence gathered thick as the shadows between them, she asked nonchalantly, "Would it be such a bad thing? Would we not make as good a match as he and Miss Sophie . . . what is her name? I have forgotten." Her head, the clarity of thought, felt as if it were being swallowed by darkness as surely as his face had been.

"Defoe." His voice rose quietly from the gloom.

Defoe! Her foe. She could not read his expression—there was not enough light—but she could see from the occasional gleam of his eyes that he still pinned her with his gaze in an attempt to delve the darkness as much as she. "I cannot see you happy with him."

He could not see much of anything at the moment, could he?

She opened her mouth to object, but his voice cut hers short. "Not just for the moment. I know how incomparably entertaining and absorbed Pip can be. What I mean is that I cannot see you happy beyond the moment. Can you see yourself content with him as an old man? When you are an old woman?"

So seriously he asked the question, so intense the tenor of his voice. She heard him lean forward in the seat, read the gleam of heartfelt concern in the sudden glow of a street lamp. She resisted her first impulse to blurt out a defense, and seriously considered her answer.

He leaned back as she pondered, his features lost to her, and yet she could feel the urgency of that concern even in the darkness.

So long had she imagined Pip as her only happiness that Richard's doubts seemed at first ridiculous. Of course she would be content with him beyond the moment. Had she not been content with thoughts of him for most of her youth?

And yet Richard was not one to waste time with the ridiculous. Would she be happy with Pip an old man, perhaps plump and gouty like Lord Wilmington? How difficult to think so far into the future, to imagine Pip no longer young and virile. Would she love him any less for it? Surely he would cling to his wit, his sharpness of mind. He would not lose his love of games, would he?

She said at last, quietly, with conviction, "I could not, would not love anyone dear to me less for no more reason than that they had aged as much as I."

He said nothing. The darkness cloaked all hint of reaction.

She sighed.

"What of you? And this mysterious love of yours? Could you love her less merely because she grew wrinkled and bent with age?"

Silence from the shadows. She watched his hands stir, restless in their grip upon starlit thighs. Such long legs he had—they had always seemed long to her, especially as a girl.

He uttered a heartfelt, "No."

She thought of Lady Wilmington and wondered if he found her all the more admirable for her affections for the old man she had wed. "And if she loved another?"

He started, leaned forward. Again she caught glimpse of his features. He looked as if she had struck him hard across the cheek with the question. "Why do you ask?"

And so it would seem, whoever she was, she did love another.

"Would you still love her?"

He hovered a moment, unmoving in the darkness as if imprisoned by her question, and she knew for a certainty her suspicions were well-founded. She would lay money on it. He was in love with Lady Wilmington. *Poor Richard.*

"Yes," he said at last, his voice weak, but growing stronger in repeating the word a second time. "Yes, I would still love her!"

"You would wait for her?"

He took a deep breath. "What do you mean?"

"I know who you are in love with," she said quietly.

His head tipped at a fresh angle, the gleam in his eyes reflecting all the light the night had to offer. "You do?"

"It is . . ." She smiled into the darkness, confident she saw quite clearly where love was concerned. "It's obvious to me."

He drew a deep breath and turned to gaze out the window, his hands restless on his knees, the dark sheen of his hair gone silver in the starlight. So tense the dark bulk of him looked, as if he would spring from the moving carriage in an instant.

"You surprise me." He shook his head. In a sudden flash of light she saw that he had closed his eyes. "I thought myself so very careful—discreet. You do not know how many times I have longed to tell you, to reveal all that I feel, to profess my undying affections."

"For Lady Wilmington," she murmured.

The dark shape of him went very still against the backdrop of moving darkness.

She nodded, pitying him. "I like her very well, Richard, after only one encounter. And it is clear she holds you in very high regard. I can see why you would fall in love with her."

His brows shot upward, into the dark shadow the fore-lock of his hair painted briefly on his forehead. "Can you, indeed?" He released the clutch on his knees, flex-ing his fingers as he did so. Was he frowning?

"Yes. Also why you have not revealed—indeed, can-not reveal—your feelings for her." She reached forward to give his poorly illuminated hand an affectionate pat.

His flinch surprised her.

"I promise not to tell anyone," she assured him.

"That would be best," he said, voice low. He retreated into the shadows again, withdrawing his gloved hand from hers.

It pained her that the gesture of affection should be rebuffed. "Quite right," she said with asperity. "I am not one to start a scandal."

"It would be a falsehood," he said flatly.

"What?" she chided. "You would tell me it is not Lady Wilmington?"

"I would. I do." He sounded put out with her.

"I do not believe you."

"Do you call me a liar then?" So angry he sounded, and sad. She could not imagine why he should sound sad if it was not Lady Wilmington.

"No. Never that, but . . . ." She was mightily confused. "If not Lady Wilmington, then who?"

Silence from the shadows. His hands told her nothing.

She made an impatient noise. "But you just said you had been longing to tell me."

He laughed, and yet it was not a sound of amusement so much as chagrin. "And now I've no desire at all. In-deed, I shall lose all patience with you if you persist in asking."

Light at last, revealing what she would rather not see, his features severe, unhappy with her, and then the dark-ness returned, as colorless and empty as her heart.

"You would lose all patience with your Patience?" Her laughter sounded flat and false, and yet she must try to stir his humor, must scan the darkness for some small sign that he relented. "That is not at all like you, Richard. I begin to dislike this phantom woman, whoever she may be, if she puts you out of sorts."

He held tongue, refusing to look her way, seemingly engrossed in the flashes of light and shadow to be seen through the window, irritation trapped in bursts upon his features.

Patience found herself undeniably cross with him as the carriage delivered her in silence to the town house her parents had taken. It was so unlike Richard to sulk—to cease all conversation. So ill-mannered. She did not know what to make of it. Indeed, she did not.

Chapter Twelve

Patience pondered her evening at Vauxhall.

She thought of Pip and promises, and the husky suggestion of his voice, and wondered how soon he would come to her with plots and schemes to chase down a woman of his own imaginings. How was she to tell him that he would ask her to find herself?

She remembered a mindless dash into dark woods, a guilty glimpse at naked legs. She paused, near sleep, curled like a snail in its shell, a caterpillar in a warm cocoon, poised on the edge of a butterfly dream, and could not escape the vision of thrusting buttocks and pale, splayed legs.

Who was it Richard loved? Why did he refuse to tell her?

Her mind's answer—that it was Lady Wilmington—seemed to hang on the edge of truth, a tightrope walker standing tiptoe among the stars. She tossed about in bed for upward of an hour as light and shadow played across the memory of Richard's face, as truth gleamed in moss agate eyes like fairy lanterns, and he took her hand in his and led her out of the path of a drunken nightmare.

She fell deeply into sleep at dawn from pure exhaustion, and woke with a feeling that in her dreams all questions had found answers that slipped away again with the light of day. She thought of Vauxhall for several days thereafter, when she might have expected Richard to call, and he did not.

In her heart she believed he had lied to her. In order

to protect Lady Wilmington, he lied. It would be much safer for everyone concerned that way. More circumspect. Richard prided himself on his discretion. She reasoned that he regretted having said anything at all—a slip of the tongue, and he was not wont to slip. Indeed, on more than one occasion she had held her own tongue on some untimely remark, beset by the thought, "What would Richard say in such a situation?"

And now he avoided her, no longer brightening her mornings with calls that had become quite regular—even predictable.

"Wherever has the lad gotten to?" her mother asked when the third morning passed without his making an appearance. "Used to be able to set my watch on his appearances, so punctual was he. Did you in some way annoy him in your last outing?"

Patience shook her head and said very logically, "Richard has work to do, Mother, in managing his brother's properties and investments. We must not rely on him always being able to come to us as often as he has."

And yet she did rely on him, and missed his company greatly, most especially his conversation.

But it was not Richard, in the end, who came knocking at their door—it was Pip.

Her mother sputtered in her tea when the footman announced the Earl of Royston. "Goodness!" she said. "Can it be?"

Patience jumped up from her chair and ran to meet him in the doorway to the sitting room.

"Pip! At last you come to us."

"Just as I promised," he said, and, taking both her hands in his, he gave her fingers a much-appreciated squeeze.

"Philip!" Her mother rose. "How long has it been? Can it be I have not seen you since the funeral? Such a shock it was to lose your father so young."

"Yes." Philip looked momentarily uncomfortable. For the briefest instant he seemed but a lad again.

"But I hear we have reason to rejoice in this meeting."

Her mother was quick to fill the silence. "Patience tells me you are soon to be married?"

Patience sighed. For a moment she had allowed herself to forget, to imagine Pip might still be hers.

Pip recovered, the look of the lad gone as quickly as it had appeared. "Do you know the Defoes?"

"Only by reputation, which is much respected, but I do know"—mama wagged her finger at him with coy amusement—"that Patience's plans are all thrown to pieces by your commitment."

"Whatever do you mean?" Pip asked, his gaze fixing on Patience, who looked back at him with an equally baffled expression.

The baroness laughed. "She told me once—how old were you at the time, Patience, my dear? No more than seven, if memory serves me . . ."

Patience cringed, a sudden sinking sensation in the pit of her stomach.

". . . that she meant to marry you."

Patience fell back a step, face flushed.

Pip, her beloved Pip, was laughing. "Is this true?" He chortled. "Dear Patience. Why did you never declare yourself to me, pet?"

"That was a very long time ago, Mama." Patience forced a laugh, her cheeks burning. "I am surprised you recall such a thing, for it had quite slipped my memory."

"I was proud of you, my dear. Determined to land a peer of the realm at such a young age."

Patience wished she might sink into the floor.

"You wound me." Pip held a hand to his heart. "Is it so long ago that I fell out of favor?"

Patience laughed and tapped the back of his hand. "I cannot mark the exact day. But you've no business being wounded, you know, now that you are promised to another."

He winked. "No business doing all sorts of things, and yet I indulge myself anyway. I suppose you will tell me next that I had no business procuring you and your mother guest vouchers to Almack's."

"Oh, have you really?" Patience crowed. "What a dear you are. Who has granted you such a favor, Pip?"

"Lord Sefton of the Four-in-Hand club, whose wife is one of the patronesses. He tells me to warn you to beware Mrs. Drummond Burrell, who is quick to condemn young women whose behavior is in any way perceived reprehensible."

"Oh, dear, yes," her mother agreed. "If anyone might find your high spirits objectionable it would be Mrs. Burrell."

"And Miss Defoe? Will she be there? Shall I have a chance to meet her at last?"

"Highly likely," he said. "But if you find you do not care for her, there is always the card room to escape to. Sophie does not care for cards."

"I dislike her already," Patience said at once.

"Patience!" her mother exclaimed.

"Because she will not play cards with you?" Pip asked.

"No." She shot a sly look in her mother's direction. "Because she cannot possibly make you happy if she refuses to play cards with you."

"She does play backgammon. And I am teaching her to enjoy the game of chess."

"Ah. Then perhaps I condemn her prematurely."

Pip grinned, the white flash of his teeth setting Patience's heart aflutter. "I must admit," he confided, "she has not the head for it. You are far better at both than she could ever hope to be."

Spirits buoyed, hope restored, Patience said graciously, "I think I shall have to like her then after all."

Chapter Thirteen

Patience was in heaven. Her feet no longer touched earth. Her heart beat to a new rhythm, a wilder, more ecstatic rhythm that left her giddy and breathless and perched on the edge of the carriage seat.

First she had been promised a night at Almack's, and now Pip wanted to show her the pony he meant to buy. Her mother had agreed to the outing. And so it was just the two of them, facing one another in the open-topped landau, flanked by two buff-liveried footmen, the coachman snapping his whip smartly as they set out for Tattersall's.

The auction house was tucked down a narrow lane near Hyde Park, opposite a tavern called the Turf. No question they were getting close. The smell of hay, and manure, and horse soon outdid the aroma of roast beef, sausages, and fermenting ale. Dogs barked, with an accompaniment of neighs and whinnies to give them the stable's direction.

It touched her deeply that Pip wished to spend time with her in spite of his promised state, that he valued her opinion with regard to his purchase. She wondered why he did not include his fiancée on such an outing, but dared not ask—in fact, did not want to ask, for in many ways the less she knew of Sophie Defoe the easier it was to pretend she would not, in the end, steal Pip away from her.

"Have you seen the woman from the gardens?" Pip asked as they stepped from the carriage.

Pip tried to sound casual in the question. He was so transparent at times. Again she longed to laugh at him—and with him—to tell him at once how he sought the intriguing woman in all the wrong places.

Every morning, she wanted to say. *In the mirror.*

"Do you mean the woman with red hair, or the one who wore red?" she asked coyly, and wanted to laugh, to cry out, *Can't you see? She stands before you.*

"Of course I mean the woman in red. Woman with red hair? Cannot imagine who you mean."

"And I cannot imagine how you could forget her. She was strikingly pretty, with Titian hair. You stood talking to her before we ate. I asked Lady Wilmington who she was, and she would not tell me. Said I must ask you myself."

Pip tugged at his neckcloth. "Saw that, did she? Was she miffed?"

"Who? Lady Wilmington? Why should she be miffed?"

Pip took a deep breath, straightened his shoulders, and said, "Never mind all that. We were discussing the young lady in red."

"Still set on meeting her?" Patience could skirt questions as nimbly as he. She felt a twinge of guilt when he laughed and flung wide his hands in a gesture of frustration.

"I must. You see, no matter how often I tell myself this fixation is quite foolish, I cannot purge her from my mind."

Cannot purge her? But what about me?

Patience strangled her impatience, a wrenching sadness squelching her earlier sense of glee.

"Fixations are foolish indeed," she said, her condemnation meant more for herself than him.

He did not understand.

"It is unkind of you to tease me," he muttered snidely.

Through a gateway they turned, past an enclosed grass ring with a single tree in the middle along a gravel path. In the ring, a sleek bay riding mare was being led through its paces by a stable lad.

Patience, who felt she goaded Pip through a different set of paces, made up her mind that it was time to explain the game she played on him, for while it was quite flattering that he had become so attached to the woman in red, there was also a crushing insult to be found in his lack of recognition, his assumption that a stranger must be more interesting, better suited to his idea of attractive femininity than she. Patience tired, too, of maintaining the stupid, tiresome lie. She did not care for lies, certainly not between friends.

But before she could speak, Pip nodded toward the ring and said, "Viewing day."

The words did not make sense in the context of her thoughts. She stared at him blankly.

"Mondays are the auctions," he went on. "That's when Tat's truly comes to life. You would not believe the crowds, the noise, the smell of horse."

She hated to interrupt, so animatedly did he speak, hands gesturing, as if he would conjure up a vision of it. She did not want to watch the light in his eyes fade, the smile to fail her.

But she must tell him. Today, at an appropriate moment. *Yes.* When the timing was perfect, she would find just the right words before the day was out.

For now she would enjoy their outing, and his company, and the infatuated look in his eyes when he mentioned the woman in red. She must learn to accept the hard truth that it was not an expression she had any hope of stirring in him for her own sake.

How it pained her to face that reality. Even more, it would pain her to put all her cards on the table, to watch his face fall in defeat, for she stood to lose as much as he, perhaps more. The woman in red was but the dream of a few days' time for him. For her, Pip had been the dream of a lifetime. No need to rush the moment. Was there?

They had the grounds largely to themselves. There were any number of stable lads carrying buckets of water, bags of feed, boxes of currycombs and hoof picks. There were lads leading horses, and walking dogs, and mounted on horses they meant to show to visiting clients. But these were few. They were among the only visitors. No more than a handful of fellows crunched along the graveled walkway before and behind them, come to view the horses.

It was wonderful—just the two of them walking side by side, talking and laughing, his hand brushing hers on occasion, his fingers like lightning, sending jolts of humming excitement through her—just like in her dreams. Rather odd, really. She could not remember another time when it had been just the two of them on an excursion. Nothing seemed quite real.

"That's the subscription room." Pip pointed. "The courtyard there is where the auctioneer calls the bid, and here"—he guided her into a pungently odoriferous lane of stalls—"the horses and dogs are kept."

He braced her elbow and nudged her out of the way of a pile of dung with a sharply voiced, "Have a care!"

So like Richard was such a gesture that she asked, "Have you seen Richard of late?"

Too fast the words blurted from her mouth. Richard was not at all what she wanted to talk about with Pip. Too often he played third wheel in person without her raising thought of him on the one occasion he did not stand between them. What was this game her mind and mouth played? What possessed her?

Pip seemed unfazed by the question. "Richard? Not since the gardens. Why?"

She pretended interest in a roan that swung its nose out over the stall door as they passed, stopping to stroke the silky neck. "No reason, really. He was in the habit of calling on us every other morning, but we have not seen him of late."

Pip shrugged. "Likely it's something to do with Chase losing a great deal of money at cards, or the horses, or the latest prizefight. He has had a devilish bad run of luck lately."

"Has he?" His words troubled her far more than she liked to let on, and suddenly she was glad she had asked about Richard, for here was her chance to discover what she dared not ask of Richard himself. "Is Chase as much of a drain on the estate's resources as Mother claims?"

Pip bent to polish away a smear on his boot tip with the paisley belcher she had seen him use as a blindfold. "More so. Keeps Richard in a dither, rearranging the finances." He rose and eyed the gleaming boot with satisfaction. "Bets on everything, Chase does, and loses more often than not—I know half a dozen gentlemen who seem just as determined to run through their inheritances as Richard's elder brother, but none who seem set on flinging themselves into the fray with such abandon, as if it were but a great game with no penalties."

"How foolish of him. How dreadful for Richard."

"Yes. Not much he can do about it, except give his brother the occasional tongue-lashing—to which Chase pays no mind at all."

"And pick up the pieces," she said.

"Eh?"

"Financially," she clarified. This she knew all too well. Her mother had mentioned more than once Richard's clever handling of his brother's estate. "Richard will sell something and make things right again. I wonder if Chase will ever recognize what it is Richard actually does for him and his progeny, should he ever settle down enough to have children."

Pip stopped before one of the stall doors and, leaning in over the edge of it, said, "Here is the pony. What do you think of him?"

Patience peered in. Hock-deep in clean straw stood the tiniest pony she had ever set eyes on, regarding her through a thick blond forelock, its mane and tail and long eyelashes all the same pale blond, while the body of the pony itself was a rich, tawny brown.

"Oh, Pip!" she said under her breath. "It looks like a toy. A beautiful little toy! I'd no idea ponies could be so small."

"Isn't he wonderful? Comes all the way from the isle of Shetland, funny little thing." Pip held out a bite of carrot to the pony, who stepped hesitantly forward to snatch it from his fingers. "Can you not see him fitted out with a cunning little saddle for my new tiger, Tom Thumb? Have you met him? He's a bandy-legged, odd-voiced, dwarfish little man just the right size for this pony. We shall need baskets on the back of the saddle—or better yet, a tiny little wagon to carry my game boards."

Patience had no idea what he was talking about.

"What's become of Mr. Trumps?"

Pip waved his hands airily. "Tired of the lad. And that screeching bird, always squawking in my ear. They had lost their panache. I found myself in need of a fresh spectacle to keep my players entertained, and was sure I had found it in Tom Thumb, but a miniature man on a miniature horse is far better. Do you not agree?"

Patience felt she had been left behind in the conversation. She floundered in his logic and, knowing Pip would one day tire of the pony just as swiftly, could not begin to match Pip's enthusiasm for its purchase. How lovingly he stroked and crooned to the animal as he fed it more carrot. And yet the words, his emotion, rang hollow—even callous. She had never known anyone who threw away pets and people as easily as old shoes.

"But what has become of the boy? The bird?"

"Now, do not fret," Pip soothed. "Or I shall accuse you of sounding just like Richard, who, as you have just said, makes things right. Quite slipped my mind. He was here at Tat's on the day I first caught sight of the pony."

"Here?"

Pip stroked the pony's velvety nose. "Arranging the sale of one of Chase's horses. Said he was in need of the money, which is why I had it in mind Chase had lost a recent bet. Tapped out, as I recall, but nothing unusual in that. Chase gets far more than his money's worth out of the miserly allowance he pays Richard to manage his effects."

"Why did you allow him to pay for the food and wine at Vauxhall if Richard is so strapped?"

Pip's elegant brows rose. "Dickey-boy paid? I'd no idea."

"Yes, I offered him my purse but he refused."

Pip shook his head, golden curls drifting across his forehead. "How very Richard. Foolish fellow. He should have said something. Wilmington has deep pockets. I thought he had seen to it. Speaking of Wilmi, he and Melanie will be at Almack's." He laughed.

"Melanie?"

"Lady Wilmington."

"Oh, Pip . . ." Perhaps now was the time to tell him, after all.

He rubbed his hands together gleefully. "I am convinced we shall find my lady in red there. Don't ask me why, but I have this deeply rooted sense of certainty that I am meant to meet her, to dance with her, perhaps to win her heart."

Patience wanted to laugh and cry at the same time. "Perhaps you shall," she said as the stable lad came to lead the pony into the ring.

Together they followed the swaying blond tail to the ring—just as she must follow her tale of the woman in red, Patience thought, a swaying tale that grew longer and curlier with every day that passed, and always at the back end of the horse. She must tell Pip the truth of the matter. It was stupid, really, not telling him. She could no longer remember why it had seemed so important that Pip not know it was she who had beaten him at games.

She leaned against the pole fence as the pony was urged to go from a walk to a trot, and eyed Pip's perfect profile, the breeze riffling his hair, the sun creating a glowing nimbus about his head. Her angel. How she loved him. How wonderful this moment, the two of them alone.

She realized with a guilty start that the time had come—the perfect time for the truth to be revealed. She took a deep breath, gathered her courage, and opened her mouth to explain.

But again Pip beat her back from the moment of revelation with a cheerful suggestion, his gaze fixed on the pony, his smile of satisfaction in anticipation of his purchase. "You must see to engaging Wilmi in a game of whist, if he is not already encamped in the card room," he said.

"Pip. There is something—"

"He's keen for whist." His tone was persuasive, the twinkle in the quick sideways glance he shot her way meant to sway her. She had seen him use it on others. Especially women: Lady Wilmington—Melanie. Her mother.

"Artful at it," he said.

And indeed he was. She frowned at him, frowned at the sun, directly in her eyes now; it left her squinting. She was much struck by the image of what he proposed, unhappily so, for it did not sound in the least entertaining. "You would relegate me to the card room at a society ball? How can you ask it of me, Pip?"

"I do not mean you should spend the whole evening there."

"I would much rather dance than play cards."

"Yes, but you promised to look for her." He leaned closer, wielding the words deftly, his hand covering hers on the middle bar of the pole fence. "It is logical to assume that a gamester good enough to foil me twice would be in the card room."

"Unless she would rather dance," she said petulantly, and pulled away. It was all so topsy-turvy. She really must tell him. "You see, Pip—"

"I shall have to entertain my fiancée, of course, and your mama."

The pony was chirruped into a leg-churning gallop, his gait smooth, seemingly effortless. Why must it prove so difficult to set right the truth? Why did her little lie charge along with great clodhopping feet of its own? Why must Pip always look elsewhere for the right woman? Her heart ached every time he looked at her without seeing who she really was—and how she felt for him.

"Will Miss Defoe not find it odd that I come to talk to you about another woman?"

"Oh!" He flung up his hands. The pony shied. "You

must make up some frippery excuse. Tell me you wish to dance."

"I do wish to dance."

"Patience!"

He was not so handsome when he frowned at her, when he grew impatient and did not get his way.

"And do you mean to dance with this woman in red?" she pressed. "Under the nose of your fiancée? I do not think it at all kind of you, Pip."

He took her by the shoulders and gave her an urgent little shake, the sun blinding her in flashes, his silhouette throwing a welcome shadow. "You would not have me marry her, not knowing for sure if she is the one, would you?" How intently he looked into her eyes as he spoke. How tight his fingers' clasp upon her arm. "Do you not wish me to know if there is someone I am better suited to?"

Was there hope for her in the way he looked at her? In the very fact that he asked?

She could not say no. It would be hypocritical to say no. What she wanted was for him to realize that she herself was better suited to him than Miss Defoe.

With a sigh she agreed to go to the card room, agreed to inform him if the woman in red was present. After all, she could not say him nay if she wished to take advantage of every opportunity to change his mind about marrying another, and yet she did not like what he asked of her, nor did she like herself for agreeing.

Chapter Fourteen

Patience fretted over her promise as soon as it was made. False promise. Futile promise. It felt dishonest. It felt wrong.

Pip waved to the stable lad. The pony was brought running.

"Let me lead him," Pip suggested. "He must be willing to follow my lead to suit my needs."

The lad handed over the reins.

"I'll be back to bid on him," Pip said when the pony walked to its stall without protest.

"Very good," the lad said.

They turned to go, only to find the doorway, the light pouring into the stalls, blocked by a walleyed bay. The horse seemed more interested in kicking down the doorway than in entering.

A large horse, it reared high, lifting the stable lad who held its halter completely off his feet, and then shaking him off with a vigorous toss of his head. With several swift jabs behind it, the animal cleared the opening of those who followed, and with a disgruntled whinny it charged toward Pip and Patience, the whites of its eyes clearly visible.

Patience froze, but Pip responded at once, and quite heroically, stepping in front of her, his arms encircling her for a moment as he shoved her out of the way. Indeed, her heart, already racing, sped a little faster to see the fleeting look of concern in his eyes as he whirled to face the oncoming animal.

It seemed to fill up much more of the run between the stalls as it skittishly cavorted and buck-hopped toward them, mane flying, hooves crashing, fore and aft, into the stall doors along the way, sending all of the horses who leaned heads from their boxes snorting back inside.

Pip stepped fearlessly into the center of the run, pulling the paisley belcher from his coat pocket in a silken flutter. Patience gasped. The bay reared, head tossing, the muscles of haunch and rump rippling, his height suddenly doubled, hooves striking air. The clarion call of his whinny was unbearably loud, as much a threat as his flashing yellow teeth. The enormous hooves seemed destined to cut Pip down. Designed for it.

Patience tensed, legs poised to run, and yet she could not go. She must be there to distract the animal if Pip went down.

As though he and the animal danced, Pip moved in swiftly, gracefully, pressing himself to the bay's satiny neck, reaching high for the halter's cheek strap as the horse came down. In a swift, almost magical movement he slid the blindfold over the horse's eyes, all the while crooning, "There, there now. No need for histrionics."

Nostrils flaring, head bobbing, the bay halfheartedly reared a second time, swinging his head round in an uncertain jerk. Pip had firm hold of the halter.

"Ho, now," he murmured. "None of that." He ran his free hand in a calming manner along the animal's lathered back and shoulder. The horse made no more attempt to kick or rear, merely stood trembling, head down.

The stable lad squeezed past the horse's sweat-stained rump, while Pip murmured, "No need to be alarmed, old boy. What you need is a quiet corner and a nice rubdown."

The stable lad, hat in hand, apologized profusely to Pip for "letting go the beast," as he led the horse away.

"Pip!" Patience knew better than to startle the horse with a loud cry, but she could not stop herself. She threw herself into his arms. "You might have been killed!"

Pip held her close but a moment in the warmest, most

cherished of embraces, his heart beating so hard she could feel the thump of it against her breast, where her own heart thudded in memory of their close call and his brave rescue of her.

"You are all right?" he said softly into her hair, and his hands ran along her arms as he asked, "He did not catch you in any way with those flashing hooves, now, did he?"

"No. No. I am quite all right," she said, and lifted her face to the sweet radiance of his concern.

"A lucky thing," he said, and clasped her close in a sudden rib-straining embrace before he put her from him with a lively exuberance that spoke of his appreciation for his own strength, for the power of their moment of survival.

She did not want to let go of his coat lapel. Did not want him to make light of this incredibly stirring moment. "You saved my life."

His eyes met hers at last in a heated moment of mutual understanding of how close they had come to real danger. In his unswerving, gleeful gaze she watched his affection for her surface in a manner she had never before observed, saw the warmth in his eyes bloom, as if he saw her afresh.

The cant of his head changed, the tilt of his chin, and he tilted forward on the balls of his feet as if he meant to kiss her. She was sure he meant to kiss her. She could feel the inevitability of it all the way to her toes.

"Yes. Nicely done, Pip."

Richard's voice.

It stopped them, turned their heads, made them fall away from each other self-consciously.

Richard stood calm and quiet, as was his way—and yet shockingly pale—in the same spot where the horse had reared, with the look of a man who had been kicked. He seemed, Patience thought, more rattled than Pip. Indeed, his coat was rumpled, his stock askew, and his hair far more tousled than she could ever remember having seen it.

"Are you all right?" she asked, and went to him, Pip right beside her, equally curious.

Richard's concerned gaze flitted from her to Pip and back again. "I should be asking you. Your situation looked a bit dicey from what I could see on the rump side of the beast. Poor animal. I did warn the lad. He has been frightfully skittish since the accident."

"Accident?" Patience blurted. Had Richard been in an accident?

"One of Chase's team, is he not?" Pip asked.

Richard's lips pursed. He gave a curt nod, a dark lock of hair drifting between bloodshot eyes. He looked tired, poor Richard, tired and defeated. "Ruined the team, actually. The other horse had to be shot."

Patience gasped.

"The race?" Pip asked.

What race?

Richard frowned. "You knew?"

Pip nodded. "Heard mention of it at my club a few days ago. Hampstead Heath, was it not?"

Richard nodded. "Begged him not to. Told him more than once . . ." He sighed and flung up his hands to rake them through already tousled locks.

"Is he injured?" Patience feared the worst. She could see by the pinched lines about Richard's mouth that something was wrong, terribly wrong.

He rubbed at the bridge of his nose, and for a moment his mouth twisted in a way she had never seen before. He cleared his throat, then said gruffly, "Chase overturned the phaeton. He may never walk again."

"Oh, dear!" How inadequate the words, how ineffectual the hand with which she reached out to him. What did one say or do in the face of such a declaration?

"Anything we can do?" Pip offered.

Richard's mouth twisted again. He shook his head. "A prayer might help. Other than that, I do not know that Chase would accept anything. He is all out of sorts. Refuses the maid's entry, has ordered the last two physicians out after they told him what he refuses to hear, and he has no patience with the pity his friends come to offer."

How dark the circles under Richard's eyes. How fragile and windblown his great, unshakable frame.

"Would he care to play cards, or a game of backgammon?" she ventured. It seemed a silly thing, really, to offer cards at such a moment, and yet she must say something, must let him know she wished to help.

Richard gave the idea more thought than Patience believed it merited. He said at last, rather hesitantly, "I think it is a splendid idea, though he might toss you out on your ear as soon as thank you."

Patience smiled. Dear Richard—he was looking more himself again.

"Chase has always been rather brusque," she reminded him.

Pip snorted. "That's putting it mildly."

Patience shot him a warning frown. It seemed most ill-timed of Pip to mention Chase's failings now. She gave Richard's shoulder an affectionate squeeze. "I will not take it too much to heart if he orders me gone."

Richard clasped her hand a moment. His eyes warmed, the worried look easing ever so slightly. "Then do come. Please. Time passes hard for him." He stood a little straighter and clapped Pip on the shoulder, saying, "And now I must see to the horse Chase blames for all his ills. He insisted I shoot it. It did not seem fair, or fiscally prudent. I'm hoping the poor beast will find a happier fate at auction."

They watched him walk away.

And as Pip took Patience's hand in his and led her out of the stables, he said, "Chase never was one to be fair or fiscally prudent. I cannot think what possessed you, Patience, to offer to spend time with him."

"I did not do it for Chase's sake," she said quietly.

"No. I did not suppose you did. Are you in love with him?"

His word caught her completely off guard. With a bit of a choking noise she said, "Who? Richard?"

"Of course, Richard, unless you harbor an inconceivable affection for Chase."

How could he be so thickheaded? So blind to her feelings for him—him!—not Richard.

"Whatever possessed you of such a notion?" she asked.

"Is it so far-fetched?" he asked in a teasing fashion, and playfully tweaked one of her curls. "Melanie has half convinced me you are in love with our childhood friend."

"Has she?" Patience stopped abruptly, stopping his progress as well. She tilted her head to glance at him speculatively, thinking of the moment in which he had almost kissed her, wondering if they would ever recapture such a moment. "Has she, indeed? How interesting."

"How so?

Patience shrugged, miffed that in this moment, too, Richard stood between them. "Perhaps it is jealousy speaking."

"Jealousy?"

"Yes," she snapped. "I am half-convinced Lady Wilmington is in love with Richard, herself."

Pip laughed, giving her arm a playful shove, as he had when they were children. "Preposterous!" he said merrily. "On that score I am convinced you are entirely mistaken."

Chapter Fifteen

The ill-fated race to Hampstead Heath was the talk of the town.

Patience pitied poor Chase. She pitied Richard. They filled her mind, made her heart ache.

This was love, as Pip had insisted, just not the sort of love he believed it to be.

The arrival of Pip's exquisite crested coach on Wednesday evening proved a welcome diversion. If anyone could make her forget, it was Pip. This carefully orchestrated excursion to Almack's—the thought of dancing with him before the evening was out—brightened her spirits immeasurably. Dear Pip. Handsome Pip, standing nonchalantly at the foot of the stairs, in formal white knee breeches, a crisp white neckcloth, and a beautifully tailored, midnight black jacket with tails. He was distracting indeed! He had but to smile and her heart turned somersaults.

"You are splendid!" she blurted, winning a flash of even, white teeth as he turned to look up at her, dimples winking.

"Not half so splendid as you!"

He sounded surprised—looked surprised, too, his eyes lighting up at the sight of her.

She preened, thrilled with his words, for she was feeling splendid in her new ball gown with its white flounces and white quilling, and cherry ribbons and rosettes, with her hair dressed high, much like Lady Wilmington's— Melanie's—had been at the gardens. The style made her look years older, and she had practiced using her new white silk, mother-of-pearl fan to advantage, so that she might reveal only her eyes above it if she wanted, hiding her mouth, which gave away so much of her emotion at moments when she did not want it to.

As she came down the stairs he said, "Lord! You are a vision! Your skirt looks like a windblown white rose." He grinned impishly. "Makes me long to throw myself under it."

Her cheeks flushed warmly. "You remember that?"

He chuckled. "How could I forget?"

Her blushes deepened, which, had she but known it, made her look all the prettier, and gave fresh sparkle to her eyes as she fanned away the heat in her cheeks.

"Will not your fiancée think it strange if I arrive on your arm this evening?" she asked.

"Not at all." He winked at her. "She knows nothing of my having been beneath your skirts."

His gaze still gratified her every vanity in roving over her from head to toe, but she flung up her hand in warning, and said, "Shhh! Pip! Mama will hear."

"Hear what?" her mother asked as she came rustling down the stairs, looking quite marvelous in her best blue flounced silk.

Patience was struck speechless by the timing of her arrival.

Not Pip. He answered at once, completely unruffled, "Miss Sophie Defoe will be there tonight. She always goes to Almack's with one of her brothers."

"Ah! Miss Sophie Defoe. How does your fiancée? Her name is forever on Patience's lips. But what is there in that, that I must not hear?"

Patience quailed, but again Pip replied with aplomb. "I have made a point of telling her all about your arrival here in London, and how very long we have been friends. She begs to meet both of you. Patience wished it to be a surprise."

"I see. I am sorry to have spoiled your surprise, my dear."

Patience plied her fan rather vigorously and tried not to laugh at Pip's sudden grin. "Shall we go then?" she asked.

"By all means." Pip threw open the door for them, and insisted on helping Patience into the carriage. And as he took her elbow he leaned close enough to whisper, "Just what have you had to say about my fiancée, dear Patience?"

There was no time to answer, no way to explain once the three of them had crowded into the carriage, and Patience was hard put not to grin too broadly at Pip's teasing sideways glances.

Traffic was heavy. The line of carriages waiting in King Street seemed to stretch on forever. Movement forward was necessarily at a snail's pace as each carriage carefully deposited its ball gown–draped treasures before the staid pedimented doorway. Patience craned her neck to look upward at the second story of six tall arched windows, where candlelight glowed golden, and the flash of gracefully whirling gowns and coattails gave promise of the evening's entertainments.

For a moment, most disconcertingly, she was reminded of the flash of horse's hooves, the look of defeat in Richard's eyes. He had seen them, seen it all, knew Pip had been about to kiss her.

"Shall we not get out and walk?" she asked, anxious to participate in that giddy whirl, anxious to forget the look in his eyes.

"You wear white, my dear!" her mother objected. "I have every concern you may soil the hem of your gown if we climb down now."

Pip endeared himself to her mother in saying, "I must agree, Patience. Only demonstrate a little of that for which you are named and we shall be there in no time."

Lady Ballard favored him with a rare smile.

Patience made a face at him behind her mother's back, and Pip was hard put not to burst out laughing.

Patience did not feel like laughing. Richard would have agreed with her. She knew he would. No sense languishing in the carriage when they all had perfectly healthy legs in good walking order. *Legs!* Oh, dear, how inappropriate to think of healthy legs when Richard's brother Chase no longer had the use of his. Bared legs under a tree in a public park no longer seemed worthy of her thoughts. No. How changed the world seemed in considering an absence of legs—or at the very least, the use of them. How precious the very act of stepping from the carriage. Much more so the idea of dancing—an evening of dancing. Chase would never again have the pleasure.

Nose pressed to the pane, she gazed longingly out the window as they inched forward another coach length, and said, "Imagine if we should be unable to dance."

"The doors close precisely at eleven, my dear." Her mother checked the little watch pin she wore low on her shoulder. "It is only now just gone a quarter past eight. I do not think it will take so very long for us to arrive."

Patience sighed. "No, Mama. I meant never. Only imagine how dreadful it must be *never* to dance again."

"Dreadful thought," her mother scolded.

Pip understood. "Mmm," he muttered. "Dreadful fate."

"Do you think there is any chance we shall see Richard tonight?" she asked him, and again she thought of the moment Pip had almost kissed her, of the sound of Richard's voice as he had interrupted them.

"Dear boy," her mother said. "I do begin to pine for a glimpse of him."

"I doubt it," Pip said.

"Does he not care for dancing?" her mother asked.

Pip frowned. "He has . . ." His frown deepened. He looked away. ". . . always been turned down for vouchers in the past."

"What?" Patience was astounded.

"Whatever for?" Her mother bristled. "Surely there is nothing objectionable in Richard's behavior or social standing."

Pip pressed his lips together in a grim line. "Not Richard. His brother. Chase has been blackballed, you see, for . . . numerous reasons."

"Yes, but what has that to do with Richard?"

Pip shrugged. "The patronesses use any excuse to eliminate those whom they consider unworthy. Chase's scandalous behavior has always given them reason enough to refuse Richard, who, as his younger brother, has been dispossessed of both his good name and any chance of an inheritance—until now."

"How unfortunate," Patience cried, "if his brother's ill fortune should be the making of his."

"I have tried to reason with them," Pip said. "Lord knows Sefton has had his share of bad luck in placing bets." He threw up his hands.

"I do not know if I wish to patronize an establishment that will not allow Richard entry," Patience said.

"Too late, my dear," her mother announced. "We have at last arrived."

And with that Pip threw open the door and helped them down, and Patience allowed herself to be led past an immaculately clad gentleman Pip identified as the owner, Mr. Willis.

They ascended the stairway, music from the ballrooms leading them upward, and again Patience thought of poor Chase, who would never climb stairs again.

Patience asked Pip, "Would you care to go with me to Cavendish Manor on Friday?"

"All the way to the manor? Whatever for? Is this for the games you promised Richard you would entertain Chase with?"

She nodded.

He laughed. "No, thank you. I've not the slightest desire to have my head bitten off by the rudest, most thoughtless, stingy, and uncaring gentleman of my acquaintance."

"Pip!" She was shocked by his hard-hearted honesty.

"It's true." He laughed, and she halfheartedly joined in. It was Pip's way to laugh at everything.

"Not even for Richard's sake?" she persisted.

Pip shook his head vehemently, golden curls catching the light, teeth gleaming as he teased, "No, my dear. This is your errant move, and now you must play through to the end. Chase is completely undeserving of my sympathy, and I will never give it."

And in your steadfast refusal you begin to resemble

him, Patience thought, though to think such a thing seemed disloyal, and cruel, and surely far too harsh.

Pip, her dear Pip, was nothing like Chase Cavendish. Was he?

Melanie—Lady Wilmington insisted Patience call her that—leaned close to whisper, fan spread, "Sophie Defoe has arrived with her stepbrother, Will."

"Where?" Patience asked at once.

They stood at the far end of the dance floor, backs to the dining room and the card rooms. They faced the raised dais for the musicians, a crowded if elegant little affair uplifted on five slender white columns, with a white trellis edging that half hid the musicians and their music stands so that the dance floor might not be interrupted, and so that a row of lyre-backed chairs might be arranged beneath its overhang for the resting of dance-wearied feet and the clustering of tittering wallflowers.

The painted and gilded ballroom was ablaze with candles: reflected in tiered crystal chandeliers, the light glittering from the many facets of cut glass, and in mirrored sconces all along the walls, and from the bright eyes, flashing smiles, and winking jewelry of a roomful of beautiful women.

Patience had never felt so intimidated, so doubtful of her chances with Pip, who circulated about the room with a smile, a bow, a tip of the head for every one of those pretty faces. Would he behave any differently, she wondered, now that Sophie Defoe had arrived?

"There." Melanie closed her fan with a snap. "By the door. She wears jonquil yellow, and he looks bored beyond words."

Patience gazed upon her nemesis and her bored companion, fear and anticipation seizing her, squeezing the breath from her.

Silhouetted as she was against the darkness of the doorway, Sophie Defoe's fair hair, pulled into dangling knots of curls above each ear, gleamed bright as aged brass. Her skin glowed with the pale luminescence of a pearl. She had stately posture and perfect teeth. Her demeanor was remote, perhaps more than a little proud, as if most of the people in the room did not interest her, indeed met with her disdain, and yet, when Pip moved in her direction a marked fixedness possessed her sky blue eyes, and her lower lip pinched in a little.

She reminded Patience at once of her sister's childhood spaniel, a dog that had eyes for none but her mistress. There was in Miss Defoe's dangling curls some semblance of silken ears that trembled as Pip drew near.

She wondered if Pip had ever noticed the likeness, wondered if she dared mention it to him. He was sure to laugh, and yet she could not bring herself to voice the idea to Lady Wilmington. *Too cruel,* she could almost hear Richard scold.

And with the thought came a pang of anguish that Richard, usually so dependable, was not here with them—with her—in this, her moment of greatest need, for she did not want Sophie Defoe to bring out the worst in her, as Chase's hardship had just demonstrated the worst in Pip. She did, in fact, pity the young woman a little, for she was not convinced Pip loved her. In fact, she wondered if he married her for any reasons other than her title, reputation, and dowry. It seemed a very cruel game he played if that was true.

"Is Pip really to marry her?" she asked Lady Wilmington in an undervoice, her skepticism too unvarnished for such polite company. Heat flared in her cheeks. She amended her tone. "The truth of it still sinks in."

"Life is full of surprises, my dear—disappointments, dashed dreams. Expectations unmet." So smooth Melanie's voice, Patience thought, so pleasant the smile that lifted her lips, and yet there was a spark of kinship in her eyes, an understanding.

Had Lady Wilmington's marriage proven just such a surprise, disappointment, and dashed dream? As if in answer to her thoughts, Melanie's gaze drifted toward her husband, who sat beneath the orchestra dais, jowls swaying as he talked to Pip—golden, glorious Pip, who had turned toward the doorway, toward Sophie, as a flower turns to the sun.

Melanie sighed and eyed the pair in the doorway, the

neat coil of her hair no less glossy or golden, the graceful arch of her neck no less youthful than Sophie Defoe's.

"Sometimes what we think we want," she said wistfully, "what we long for above all else, ends up ours, and proves the greatest surprise of all, for it does not match expectation." She took a deep breath and tilted her head, the deep honey gold of her hair, the dark emerald of her eyes catching the light. "What we women have most control over is how we choose to meet such moments. I have made a game of it, you know. If I can find something pleasant and wonderful even in my deepest disappointments, why, then, I have won. Care to play?"

Patience laughed and linked arms with her new friend, perhaps the most remarkable young woman she had ever met, and longed to blurt out to her that she knew who it was Melanie longed for. There was something pleasant and wonderful to be found in knowing that dear Richard's feelings matched her friend's, and yet it was not her place to interfere.

"Take me to her," she said instead. "I promise to look for all that is pleasant and wonderful in our meeting one another."

"You are a fine player, my dear." Lady Wilmington gave her hand a pat. "I lay odds that in the end, no matter what luck the game of life throws your way, you will come out ahead."

Patience, who was not so certain, given the person she was about to meet, yet felt bolstered by Lady Wilmington's words. She must arm herself with just such an attitude, she decided.

Sophie Defoe turned a flat blue gaze in her direction as she was introduced, her eyes focusing more keenly as Patience made her curtsy, as if she had just been handed new cards and must sort them out.

"But we have met," Miss Defoe said when given her name, the words uttered with such certainty that for a moment Patience was convinced. And yet she knew it was impossible. She would remember those raspberry-stained lips, the sweep of golden-ringleted hair, the proud angle of her tip-tilted nose.

"I'm sure of it," Sophie stated emphatically.

Patience had no notion how to reply. She could not call Pip's fiancée an out-and-out liar, nor could she think of any instance since her arrival in London that they might have met, even so much as to have cast eyes upon one another.

"You have been to Surrey?" she asked.

"Never," Sophie Defoe said with the faintest curl of her lips, as if Surrey bore no reason for her exalted presence. "But we have met," she insisted, her voice on the edge of laughter. The golden ringlets bobbed with her decisive nod, and a look that Patience could define as nothing short of crafty flickered across her features. "Do you not recall seeing Miss Ballard somewhere recently, Will?"

William Defoe, a gentleman as handsome as his stepsister was pretty, barring a certain crudeness to the turn of his nose and a thickness of lower lip and brow that added harshness to his features, turned from the discussion he was having with another young man to glance, first with disinterest, and then with growing attention, at Patience.

"Hmm." He tapped at his teeth with the end of a manicured nail, his gaze sharpening. "Indeed. I never forget a face. Where was it?"

Patience shook her head, baffled. "I've no recollection."

Sophie chuckled. "You shall remember eventually," she insisted.

William smiled at her, as if he were accustomed to charming women with the turn of his lips, and yet Patience was not charmed. Intrigued, yes. But not charmed. She could not pin down exactly why.

Chapter Sixteen

Patience had no opportunity to question Miss Defoe further.

She forgot all about their odd introduction as Pip took her hand in his. Indeed, the noise of the room and everyone in it fell away to the magic of the music, and her anticipation of bodies moving as one to the high, sweet keening of the violins. He squeezed her fingers and looked into her eyes, the blue of his completely mesmerizing. Forget-me-not. And she did not—could not.

His lips were moving then, the lips Miss Sophie Defoe would steal away from her forever, and she mourned the loss of them and celebrated his hand in hers all in the same moment, for Miss Defoe was watching their exchange with . . . was it envy or suspicion in her eyes?

"You wanted to play cards, did you not?" Pip asked.

Patience stared at him blankly a moment. *Oh, Lord!* He really did mean to confine her to the card room looking for a phantom woman.

She smiled up at him as he led her toward the column-framed doorway to oblivion. Perhaps she could wheedle her way out of this stupid plan. "I would prefer to continue my conversation with your fiancée, unless, of course, you mean to ask me to dance," she teased.

"You like her?" he asked.

She could not tell him no. "She intrigues me," she said in all honesty. "As does her brother."

"Really?" His brows shot upward. His gaze flitted from her to Will Defoe and back again.

Could it be he felt some pang of jealousy, she wondered, to match the pangs she suffered whenever she looked at, or spoke of, or so much as thought of Sophie Defoe? "Will you ask me to dance, Pip?" she asked hopefully, and gazed into his eyes, looking for some sign of the heat, the concern, the affection she had witnessed there when he had saved her from Chase's charging horse.

"Later," he agreed, giving her gloved hand a pat, his gaze flickering from the dancers to his fiancée, finally settling briefly on Patience with a look of surprise to find her watching him so intently. "I promise."

Disappointed, she did not argue further, and allowed herself to be led away from the music, for it was Pip's hand that did the leading, his gloved fingers clasping hers, and that in itself was something to treasure despite the fact that Sophie's stepbrother Will eyed them rather intently as they skirted the ballroom.

The card room, designated the blue room by reason of the deep blue damask that had been applied to large areas within the painted and gilded framework molding, matched the eyes Pip turned upon her, the pleading look in them heart wrenching.

It was a shame, really, that she had promised—a most stupid promise—to look for a woman who did not exist. The woman in red. It was not she. Pip was not looking for her. If he were, he might have seen her by now. No. He was looking for something and someone else entirely, a woman more mysterious, elegant, attractive, and clever.

She wanted to shout at him as he found her a place at one of the tables, *Look at me. Please just look at me. See me for all that I can be. All of my potential.*

But she did not shout. She did not explain that she was playing him for a fool as much as she played one herself. She followed where he led, and walked into the quiet murmur of tables big enough to accommodate eight to twelve players, and sat herself down to play. Every table was crowded with dedicated players, well-coiffed heads bent intently over colorful fans of pasteboard cards. She felt the novice here, which seemed odd, for at home she was often touted as the best card player in the area.

This was different, however. An aura of intensity hung above the bowed heads of this quiet group, sure sign that the play went as deep as it was steady.

Pip found her a free chair, introduced her to two of the players, and turned his attention back to the ballroom. Bereft, she settled into the chair and allowed herself to be dealt a hand of cards—stupid cards: whist and Ambigu, Hearts and Bluff. She found meager satisfaction only in that the placement of her chair gave view of the ballroom, of Pip, who came to poke his golden head in now and again, brows raised, blue eyes questioning.

Patience pretended interest in her cards—indeed, she focused well enough to win a hand or two—but all the while, feet tapping, body fidgeting, she kept darting looks toward the dancing, her mind on the music and the odd fascination Will Defoe seemed to have taken in her. Every time she glanced up he was peering in the doorway at her, sometimes from across the room, once from the edge of the doorway itself. And each time it looked as if he wanted to laugh, but refrained. The look in his eyes unnerved her, as if he knew something she did not, something he found vastly amusing, something she was fairly certain she would not.

Pip had promised her a dance—a waltz—and three waltzes had struck up without sign of him.

"Care to dance?"

It was not Pip who asked.

She threw down her cards and started up out of her chair with a cry of, "Richard! What are you doing here?"

He drew her aside, looking quite dapper in tails, dapper despite the shadows beneath his eyes.

"Lady Wilmington talked me into coming," he said, and she knew at once that what he meant was that Melanie had talked him into coming away from tending his brother.

"But I thought . . . Pip said . . ." She looked about her and could not blurt out the truth, not in this crowded room, where she was sure to be overheard—that she knew his brother was refused entry to Almack's, that Richard had been deemed equally unworthy. "He said you did not come here."

Richard led her away from the table and leaned close to murmur, "You mean he told you I had been blackballed?"

She nodded, unable to meet his eyes.

"Chase's injury has changed all that," he said, his emotions masked, his voice flat, and yet she read a hint of bleak regret in the depths of his gaze. "I have been deemed a rising possibility." His smile was rueful, and his voice fell in saying, "Odds have it he will not live out the year."

"Dear Lord!" She caught at his hand. "People bet on such things?"

He nodded, and a small, rather tragic smile twisted his lips. "Chase used to bet on such things. Life's a game, he would say."

"Dreadful." She shook her head. "Dreadful, too, that his injury should be the criteria by which you gain entry here."

He shrugged. "I never would have bothered had not Lady Wilmington talked me into it."

Lady Wilmington, Patience thought. *Poor Richard.* He could not even bring himself to call her Melanie in public. How torturous to love from a distance, to avoid all mention of one's true feelings—as she did—to wait for old age to offer—what had he called it?—rising possibilities.

"I shall have to thank Melanie for insisting." She tucked her hand into the crook of his arm.

"Oh?" Mention of Lady Wilmington seemed to have arrested his attention.

"Yes." She gave his arm a sympathetic squeeze. "I am very glad you have come."

"Are you?" He sounded surprised. "I would have thought you preferred spending an evening with Pip all to yourself."

"With his fiancée here? And his fiancée's stepbrother, who keeps a watchful eye on me, as if . . . as if . . ."

"Afraid you might snatch Pip away from under his sister's nose?"

She frowned, "No. Not that. It is something else. Only see how he watches us even now, with that odd smirk upon his lips."

"Does he?"

"Yes."

He might have turned to look had she not given his arm a squeeze. "Do not look, or he will know that we speak of him, which will only add to the intrigue, when what I really wish to do is dance. Pip has promised me a waltz, but instead I have been forced to sit here looking for a woman who does not exist. . . ."

"Forced?" he murmured. "That is not entirely correct, now, is it? When are you going to tell Pip the truth about your lady in red?" He looked and sounded disappointed in her, and she could not bear it that he should be disappointed.

"Soon," she promised. "But for now I would dance."

"As you will," he said, his hand at her waist familiar, entirely comfortable as he led her onto the floor in a graceful whirl of skirt and tails. "I see what you mean about William Defoe," he said. "He watches your every move."

"Does he?" She gasped, and might have turned to stare had he not reminded her, "Do not look, or he will know that we speak of him."

She laughed to hear him repeat her every word so precisely.

"Perhaps he is taken with your charms," he suggested.

"If that is the case, I wish he were not," she admitted. "There is something in the way he looks at me that . . ." She wrinkled her nose.

"What?"

"Makes me feel most uncomfortable. As if he knows a dreadful secret about me, and would not be above telling." She slid a glance across the room. Will Defoe stood waiting, watching. He nodded ever so slightly at her, and smiled an unwanted smile.

"Do you think he could have been there the night we went to Vauxhall? Perhaps recognized me?"

"Ah!" Richard shot a look over her shoulder. "Quite possible. I do not know that I would recognize him masked."

"Even Sophie claims to have met me, and I've never set eyes on her before this evening."

"Sophie Defoe at Vauxhall? I cannot picture it."

She remembered that Lady Wilmington had said much the same thing.

"Would not soil her slippers," she murmured.

"What's that?"

"Nothing," she said. "Perhaps it is all nothing."

He seemed willing enough to drop the subject, though his gaze drifted calmly over her shoulder on more than one occasion, and she knew he continued to watch Defoe watching her.

They danced well together, she and Richard, their movements comfortable and smooth, nothing awkward or self-conscious in her. Their conversation, broken only by the movements of the dance, went almost as smoothly.

With Pip it would be different. She had been looking forward to—and dreading—the moment dear Pip would ask her to dance. The very idea made her nervous. Fear of stepping on toes and tripping over her hem troubled her no end.

She wondered, as the music came to a close and they walked away from the dance floor, if such fears ever troubled Richard. "Do you mean to dance with Mela-nie?" she asked.

"Perhaps," he said. "Though I had thought to stand talking with you over a cup of lemonade first. Why do you ask?"

She led the way to the tables in the dining room, where punch bowls full of orgeat and lemonade offered pale refreshment.

"It occurs to me," she said carefully, as she dished up cups for both of them, "it must be difficult in some ways for a beautiful young woman to be married to a gentle-man of advancing years who suffers from the gout."

"Yes," he agreed as he turned to study the dance floor. "She does not lack for partners, though. I believe Pip has the pleasure at the moment."

"Do you ever suffer pangs of jealousy, dear Richard?" she asked.

He blinked, as if startled by the question. "I suppose I do—on occasion. What prompts the question? Are you troubled by jealousy, Patience?"

"Me? Whomever should I be jealous of?"

"Why, Miss Sophie Defoe."

She was dancing, Miss Sophie Defoe, with a gentleman Richard identified as Lord Sumner. She was an elegant dancer, her posture proud, her head held high, each step taken with confidence and grace, and yet she did not display complete decorum in her circuit of the dance floor, for her gaze did not fix on her partner, as was considered proper. Instead she watched Pip and Lady Wilmington. Her attention remained so distracted that in the end Patience said emphatically, though it was not entirely true, "I am not at all jealous of Miss Sophie Defoe. I do in fact pity her."

When Richard's eyes narrowed quizzically, she went on, saying, "He does not love her, you know."

"Who? Pip?" His voice was gentle. "No, I don't sup-pose he does, but I must admit that I am surprised—and pleased, Patience—to hear that you find room in your heart to pity her."

She frowned at this, and said, "Would you not pity her, if you were me?"

He swallowed the last of his lemonade and took her empty cup, and before he walked away with them, said enigmatically, "I would. I do, for I've reason to believe she will never snare our friend in marriage. He has given his heart to another."

Never snare him? Given his heart? Whatever did he mean by that?

She had no opportunity to ask him, for though she whirled to follow him, the music ended then, and someone tapped her on the shoulder, and when she turned, it was Pip, handsome Pip, glorious Pip, his face flushed with youth and beauty and the exertions of dancing.

"Shall we dance?" he asked.

Chapter Seventeen

Patience stepped into her dreams.

To dance with Pip seemed a bit of magic unfolding, especially with the faint glimmer of hope in her heart that what Richard said was true.

Could it be true?

That Pip loved another?

Could it be . . . oh, please let it be . . . her.

As if the speed of time itself had been suspended, the world whirled by in a great hurry as she slowed, finding focus in forget-me-not blue, in the satin fullness of smiling lips, in the sweet, swirling, heart-pounding enchantment of tandem movement: hand to waist, hand to gloved hand, gazes wedding.

To dance with Pip had so long been her goal, her dream, that all else slipped away on a rushing tide of music and gliding, bouncing, heart-stirring movement. Nothing else mattered. No one else in this golden moment.

They two became the center of the universe, everything else revolving around them, the stars at Almack's glittering with envy, as stunned as she that the golden, glorious, much sought-after sun, Philip Yorke, Earl of Royston, heir to the Yorke fortune, had asked plain Patience Ballard to orbit the room.

In the periphery of her vision she saw heads turn: moons caught in Pip's gravitational pull, Sophie Defoe, Sophie's stepbrother, then Lord and Lady Wilmington, his lordship smiling, her ladyship with a pleasant, if not a pleased expression. Of course, Mama looked up from her conversation with Richard and beamed at her, while Richard—dear, dependable Richard—held out his arm and asked Mama if she would like to dance.

Patience smiled, her heart full, her view of the world gone all rose and gold and whirling, the music sweeter than before. The thrill of Pip's touch sang in her fingertips; it raced the length of her arm. The hair at the nape of her neck prickled.

Her skirt belled, pale petals touched with red, dizzy as her pulse. She felt caught up in a cloud of importance— an aura of social glitter. Pip was important and desirable, and by association, by his attentions to her, she took on a temporary glow. The power of it rose within her, left her giddy, drunk with it.

"I suppose she is not coming," he said.

Who is not coming? she thought, her concern for an answer a distant thing. His hand was at her waist, and the sound of strings flowed around them like water. Her limbs felt limber and agile and graceful as Pip, dear Pip, led her in the dance.

She tipped back her head and laughed as the answer came to her. "The woman in red?" she asked smoothly, her voice self-assured, throatier than usual, in keeping with the moment.

He nodded and glanced about, as if he would spot her himself. His every move, the pressure of his hand at her waist, guided her, anticipating her every move. Their gliding progress was perfect, just as she had imagined— better than she had imagined.

"You are wrong," she said lightly, as lightly as her feet upon the floor. She was ready now; the timing was perfect. Her dress twirled about her like a fallen rose. It was time to tell him. The words came easily. "She is here after all, has been here all along. You have only to open your eyes and she is right in front of you."

He laughed, his laughter turning heads, his hair glinting golden beneath the chandeliers, his teeth and dimples flashing. He narrowed his eyes in amused confusion—a teasing glance, a flirtatious look. "Here all along? What do you mean?"

She smiled, the room spinning, their bodies moving in perfect tandem. His eyes glittered with curiosity. She waited for the truth to sink in, anticipating it. The music rose to a crescendo. Realization dawned in his eyes.

"Of course," he said. "I should have known. She gave herself away when she laughed."

Patience laughed, the sound of it more sensuous than ever before. It had given her away, that laugh. Even as she smugly thought so, her amusement faded, her steps faltered along with her thoughts.

When had she laughed? That night in the park. She did not remember laughing. She played the moment again in her mind. There had been laughter. Not hers.

"Melanie!" Pip said, triumphant. "I should have known it had to be her. Always playing games. Teasing me. Why did you not tell me before? Did she swear you to secrecy?"

She did not tell him after all—did not disabuse him of the notion that Lady Wilmington was the lady in red. Did not remind him Richard loved her. There seemed no point to it, really. He could not see it—could not see her as she wished to be seen. His disinterest squeezed at her heart most painfully.

The music faded.

His hand fell away.

Her spirits sank.

In that flattened moment William Defoe stepped forward to ask her to dance.

She looked at him without true comprehension. The words made no sense. Dance with him?

Pip turned in that instant to smile—not at her—at Lady Wilmington, a look in his eyes she had never seen him turn on her.

Out of pique she said, "Yes."

She would make him take notice, she thought, by dancing with every eligible gentleman in the room, even William Defoe.

It was a stupid game to play, a foolish ploy destined for failure, but she was not thinking clearly at the time. Her heart took over her head. And William Defoe took her hand and led her onto the floor.

He made no conversation for the first half of the dance, which was not wholly unusual, for the steps took them apart and together again.

"Just how well do you know my stepsister's future husband?" he asked, the question voiced in such a way that it took on a suggestive, even vaguely unseemly connotation.

She did not rush to answer, for again the dance forced them apart, and Patience was unsure of herself, of her words, with this stranger. She could not be sure how he would interpret—or possibly misinterpret—anything she told him. His gaze remained fixed on her in a most intimidating stare, as if he would read the answer in her eyes. She wondered why he asked, if he feared she might prove competition for Pip's affections.

She was tempted to blurt out that he need not worry. Instead she said, "I know Pip the child better than Pip the man. We have been apart for six years and more."

"Pip." Again that assessing gaze, the smile that spoke more of sarcasm than humor. "Sophie said you called him by a pet name."

Patience made no reply. She could not remember having addressed Pip as Pip within Sophie Defoe's hearing.

"What manner of boy was Pip, then?" he asked.

"Much the same as he is now."

And when his brows rose, she said, "Playful. Handsome. Always laughing. Good at games."

"Not so good as he thinks he is. I have seen him lose. More than once." He threw back his head, the noise issuing from his throat more snort than laugh. "One might describe Sophie in much the same terms."

"The perfect match, then," she suggested with forced enthusiasm.

"Absolutely perfect," he said with the same amused sarcasm that had troubled her earlier.

Their dance ended, but not Defoe's inclination for conversation. As he led her to the dining room for refreshment he asked in silken tones, "Do you mean to marry him?"

She feared she gave herself away. Her gaze strayed across the room, where Pip stood chatting in a relaxed fashion with Lady Wilmington. *Him? Who?* she wondered, but what she said, making great effort to keep her tone nonchalant, was, "I've no plans to be married."

"A childhood friend of yours as well, was he not?" He nodded toward Richard, who looked up from the conversation he made with Sophie Defoe, smiling pleasantly, and just as pleasantly disengaged himself that he might come and rescue her from Defoe's delving curiosity.

Chapter Eighteen

Patience reconsidered her words later in Pip's carriage, on the way home again, lamplight guiding them through darkened streets, candlelight golden in the windows they passed, gilding Pip's hair, gilding his cheek, his lips, his lashes. Little golden glances of all that she dreamed of.

"I've no plans to be married. . . ."

How boldly she had laid claim to the lie. She did have plans to be married, had envisioned it in her mind from the time she was a child. She had pictured her wedding day, her wedding dress, a wedding cake, and flowers. She had dreamed of the fair gentleman who would stand at her side.

The golden dream was promised to another. Pip. She had planned to marry Pip. She had imagined every aspect of the day.

The problem was, he did not plan to marry her.

"Why so quiet?" Pip's concerned voice broke into her reverie. "Did you not enjoy yourself?"

It pleased Patience that he cared enough to notice, that he cared enough to ask. In that concern the slimmest golden thread of possibility still held her attached to him, to an impossible dream.

"Not enjoy herself? Of course she did." Her mother roused herself from the dozing state most carriages immediately inflicted upon her to voice opinion. "How could a young woman not enjoy herself in her first visit to Almack's? And so very kind of you to provide escort,

Philip. Was it not kind?" She gave Patience a weak whack with her fan.

"Most kind, I'm sure," Patience murmured obediently, though it was not true, really. Pip had not asked her out of kindness. He had asked her because he wanted her to do something for him, because he needed her. And she had not really enjoyed herself as much as she had expected. Not really.

"The dancing was nice," she said. She would always remember the dancing. "And I was pleased to meet your fiancée at last." But most of all, she thought, she had been pleased to see Richard there. Richard, who had rescued her from the card room and from Will Defoe; Richard, who knew at once how much she wanted to dance; Richard, who had been banned, and now was not. She could not imagine enjoying any place terribly much that had ever intended to stop Richard's entrance.

"Do you mean to come with us tomorrow?" her mother asked Pip. "To Cavendish Manor. I so look forward to a wonderful coze with Lady Cavendish. It will be like old times."

"Not quite like old times," Pip said, and shot a glance at Patience.

"No," her mother agreed sadly. "Poor Chase. I wonder how long he can survive in his current state? The manor is not the same without his father."

"Not without games of hide-and-seek." Pip winked at her, and gave her skirt a covert yank.

His words sent a thrill of the forbidden down her spine. This secret, this most intimate of secrets only they two shared, reminded her of all that she felt for him, of all she had wished for. That he mentioned it, and winked at her, with such an intimate look of mischief, twisted the thin thread of hope, tugged hard. Could it be she might win him still? Could it be he was still interested in her despite his promised state?

"I suppose it cannot be too long before Richard is in charge—dear Richard," her mother said.

Richard.

How did he manage to step between them, even at a distance?

Richard would have frowned at Pip's suggestive remark. He would have frowned had he known how much Patience's body reacted to the yank on her skirt. He would have, in some subtle way, managed to remind her of Sophie Defoe.

It seemed entirely inappropriate at the moment, even shameful, that Pip should tease her with bawdy remarks, given the subject they discussed. *Poor Chase.* Patience was glad when they reached the familiar doorstep of their London home, glad in many ways that Pip was not to go with them to Cavendish Manor.

Chapter Nineteen

A surprise met Patience at the door to the manor.

They were welcomed by none other than Mr. Trumps, Pip's former tiger. Dressed far more soberly than when last she had seen him, in the deep blue livery of the Cavendish household, he wore a bagwig rather than a turban, but the flash of his cheeky grin at sight of her was unmistakably the same.

"Good morning!" He suppressed the smile, bowing flawlessly.

Patience laughed and held her hands out to him, saying, "Mr. Trumps! Do you remember me? I'd no idea you were here."

"My real name is Smith," the lad said, as though sharing a secret. "Toby Smith. Master Richard took me in when my lord Yorke had no more use for me. Did you ever tell my lord it was you who beat him at chess?"

"Chess?" Her mother frowned. She did not care to be left out of conversations. She did not care to be kept waiting just inside the doorway. "Who have you beaten at chess, Patience?"

"Pip, Mama, though he does not know it." She turned her head in such a way that she might wink at the lad without her mama observing. "This is Mr.—Toby. He used to be Pip's tiger."

Toby bowed again and urged them, "This way, Mrs. Ballard. My lady has a new rose to show you in the garden."

Patience was to be delivered to the yellow drawing room.

"The gentlemen will join you momentarily," Toby told her as he quietly drew the doors shut behind him.

The songbirds had yet to be released from their damask cages. The same clock ticked and spun upon the mantel. The view alone seemed lusher, more verdant than she remembered. As if someone had known she would need them, two decks of cards sat squarely in the middle of the tufted leather cushion in the window seat.

Richard, Patience thought. Did he know her that well?

With a smile she shuffled the decks together as she watched her mother and Lady Cavendish through the open window. A cool, floral-scented breeze teased her nose. She absently dealt a hand of Patience onto the Italian inlay table at her elbow, and pretended not to hear Chase's raised voice as Richard wheeled him through the adjacent gallery, where row upon row of the Cavendish family had been painted and framed for posterity's sake, and row upon row of windows stood open to the same breeze she enjoyed.

As a result, every fretful word that the two uttered drifted in by way of her window, as did the screeching noise of the wheeled chair Richard had purchased for Chase's transportation about the house.

Pippet, the cockatoo, stirred in the large wire cage that graced one corner of the drawing room. Like Mr. Trumps—no, she must remember to think of him as Smith now, Toby Smith—the bird had been taken into Richard's care. Tilting its head it gave a whistle that sounded remarkably like the screeching wheels of Chase's chair.

Patience might have laughed at this had not Chase muttered drunkenly, "Can't shtand visitors, Rich. Why torment me?"

In dappled sunlight the exposed kings and queens upon the table seemed to wink and wave scepters. The zigzagged backs of the facedown cards shimmered with imagined movement. Patience squinted at them, found a red ten to play upon a black knave, uncovered a red eight, and unearthed a black nine from her stockpile.

"I am in constant pain," Chase complained.

Her hands stilled. The clock ticked and clucked.

". . . must pretend that I am not. Imp'lite, otherwise. You've no idea what it's like."

Crisp and calm and orderly came Richard's reply, like the steady ticking of the clock, like the careful placement of her cards. "I understand far more than you give me credit for, Chase."

The bird twisted its head to listen, feathers rustling as it hopped from seed bowl to perch.

"They talk of all I can no longer do: horshes, racing, dancing, drinking, women, the clubs."

A little squawk, before the cockatoo tapped at the bell tied to the side of the cage, as if trying to drown out Chase's unhappy voice.

"Tell whoever it is . . ."

Ding. Ding.

"Go 'way!"

Ding, ding.

Patience sat back in the ringing silence, wondering if she made a mistake in coming, in her hand a red queen, sad-looking woman.

Richard asked, his voice so low as to be almost imperceptible, "Drinking, Chase? After the doctor told you it destroys your liver?"

Chase laughed harshly. "Not enough. Give a dying man a brandy, Rishi. Better yet, a bottle. What can it hurt?"

She uncovered the king of hearts, sword through his head. He did not look as if it bothered him too much.

Richard's reply was lost in the cockatoo's frantic *ding-ding-ding.*

"Your friend, not mine."

Ding-ding-ding-ding-ding.

"*You* play with her."

Her play seemed stalemated, no more cards to turn.

Richard's voice, quieter, more soothing, was not easy to make out. Patience heard only snatches.

"No need to be rude."

She gathered up the cards.

"No need to be anything anymore," Chase said.

Pippet screeched happily, "Dickey-boy."

"Legless!" Chase sounded angry—hopeless. "Without issue."

She gave the deck a listless shuffle.

"Dickey-boy." *Ding, ding.*

"You shall evenshually inherit."

So melancholy his voice. Resigned. The cards felt heavy in her hand.

"Dickey-lad."

"They will fall over themselves currying favor; just you watch."

Ding-ding-ding.

Patience saw no point in dealing a fresh hand. She sat holding the cards indecisively.

"Not Patience." Richard's voice was calm, unflappable, absolutely certain of himself—of her.

Dear Richard. His voice calmed her. She shuffled the decks again, a bit jumpy—afraid she would say the wrong thing to Chase, afraid she would be as shaken as the bird's bell by sight of him, that he would see disgust or pity or shock in her reaction to him.

"Do you remember Patience?" Richard asked. "She used to come here when we were children."

Slap, slap, slap. She dealt herself another hand.

"Idolized Pip, dinnshe?"

She stopped, a card hovering.

"Impressed by a pretty face and certain title."

What!

Slap. Slap! She dealt with increased vigor, offended. That was not why she loved Pip!

"Followed after him . . ."

Ding-ding-ding. Slap. Slap.

". . . bish in heat."

She inhaled sharply, almost dropped the cards, caught them just in time.

They were nearing the door.

Tick, tick.

Her cheeks burned. The cards were all out of order. They made no sense to her.

"You will watch your language, Chase. She is a well-bred young lady who does you a great kindness in this visit."

"I do not think any young lady comes to see me these days for my own sake, Dickey. She comes 'cause of you."

The door swung wide, then, and Patience schooled her features into blank welcome, wiping all feeling from her heart for a moment—just a moment, please God. No flinching. No shock. No fear. No pique. *Bitch in heat, indeed!*

She almost dropped the cards.

He looked yellow! Almost as yellow as the faded birds trapped in the damasked walls. Caged in his chair. Flightless.

Patience could not completely control her surprise, but she could control the shaking of her hands, with the cards, familiar faces, the motion of her hands a comfort.

She dealt a king of hearts, faceup, blade sunk deep.

Richard frowned as he entered, his gaze—and his brother's—fixed on her immediately: his one of concern, while Chase, chin up, bloodshot eyes at once bleak and defiant, looked as if he were anything but happy to see her.

Patience abandoned her game and stepped forward, hand out. She took his limp, yellowed fingers in hers, unable to harbor resentment toward this once brash and brawny young man. She looked him in the eye and saw some hint of the overwhelmingly masculine energy that had once frightened her, and mourned its complete destruction. "How do you do, Chase?"

Chase glared at her. "How do I do? Cannot move. Skin the color of mustard, and you ask how I do? Is it not clear? I do demned awful."

He drew himself up in the chair, his legs motionless, so completely motionless beneath the lap blanket. "But let not my impending demise deprive me of all manners. How do you do, Miss Patience? Have you yet learned the meaning of your name?"

Richard made an abrupt, unsettled movement, as if ready to defend her, to rescue her again from this broken canary.

Patience would not allow it. "I am sorry to admit I am no more patient than I was as a child." She spoke firmly, her eyes meeting Chase's without flinching, without once looking down at the lap blanket.

Chase nodded, head swinging a little wildly, as if he were not in complete control of it. His eyelids seemed too heavy to keep firmly open. She could smell the rum and laudanum on his breath from where she stood. The vocal slur returned. "I alwaysh thought you mose ill-named."

"I suppose my name has been a bit of a cross to bear," she said crisply. "Just as yours may now prove."

Her words caught him off guard. He shook his head, confused. "Don't follow."

"A legless Chase, and an impatient Patience?"

He choked out a laugh. Eyes brightening, he regarded her with something akin to respect. "Cruel irony, that. I see you have not lost your direct ways."

"No. Much to my mother's chagrin."

"Mussen mind." He wagged a finger at her. "Rishard admires it. 'Mires you."

She glanced at Richard, brows rising. "Does he, indeed?"

"He does," Richard said calmly, smiling as he turned away to offer Pippet a slice of carrot.

"So you've come to play cards with the gimp?" Chase's voice acquired renewed vigor and vitriol. Before she could respond he went on. "Don't care for cards. Never have. So go away now. Done your charitable deed for the day." Chase grabbed the arms of the chair and barked at Richard, "Back to my room, Dickey. We're done here."

Patience eyed him a moment, lips pursed. She bit back a snide retort and slid a look at Richard.

Richard glanced back sadly, as if to apologize. When he made a move toward his brother, Patience gave the slightest shake of her head.

"We need not play cards," she said. "What games do you prefer?"

Chase said nothing for a moment. He glared at her again, as if confused as to why she refused to be gone. Then he pursed his lips and said, his words a challenge, "I like dice. Do you know Hazard or Chuck-a-luck?"

Is life a game, she thought, *and I am Patience, and Chase is Chuck-a-luck?*

"No. I have never played at dice," she said. "Will you teach me?"

They rattled and clicked away the afternoon, as Chase taught them Hazard, and Help-Your-Neighbor, and Chuck-a-luck at penny ante, the same inlaid Italian table she had long ago played Patience upon for casting, and a cunning little brass birdcage tosser for their throws.

It was evident Chase enjoyed his superior skill. Patience made no great effort to win, preferring to watch poor, maimed Chase caught up in the rattle and fall of the dice, his bloodshot eyes lighting when he won the pot, his crowing noises growing louder as their play progressed. The cockatoo grew excited, and spread his wings, and arched his crest, and squawked so loudly he had to be moved to another room.

Toby Smith came in to carry the bird away, and as he walked out, the bird perched on his shoulder, Patience could not help but think of Vauxhall, and how like Chase Pip was in his profound enjoyment of games.

Unlike Pip, Chase was completely ungracious both at winning and at losing, and he fussed when the limitations of his body made it imperative he be handed the dice cage rather than reaching for it. It did not matter to Patience, for after an awkward first game, in which he insulted her every ineptitude, he seemed to relax, to forget his legs' immobility beneath the paisley shawl that draped his knees. He seemed to regain better control of both thought and speech.

More than once, Richard's gaze met hers—exceptionally warm glances in which his mouth and jaw softened, and she realized how very rigid his features had become since the accident, how stiff the set of his shoulders, how dark the shadows smudging his eyes. These visual exchanges smoothed over any ruffled feelings she might have harbored when Chase rubbed her the wrong way.

Chase tired after the third game of Chuck-a-luck.

"Last game," he said. "Let it be Hazard. I'm all done in."

He won. It was his favorite game, and yet he did not crow or laugh as he had before, said only, "Well, then. It's a good day if I go out a winner."

She thought it an odd comment as he wished her goodday, far more formal and polite than before. He could not bow, but he tipped his head, and when Richard stood to wheel him away, he said with an irritable gesture, "Stay! You've Patience to see to, and I have none."

She thought it a witty barb, an indication of his growing weariness, drunkenly loosed, for Chase was definitely intoxicated, and had asked for a glass of brandy while they sat playing.

Richard had not refused the spirits; neither had he been free with them. He showed no change of feeling or emotion by way of expression or gesture in response to Chase's unending barbs, and yet she knew his brother's attitude pained him as much as did his brother's situation.

"As you wish," he said calmly, and rang the bellpull.

When they were alone together, the sound of the wheelchair grown distant, the chime of the mantel clock suddenly sweet and fragile in the ensuing silence, Richard said, "Well, that went rather better than anticipated, don't you agree?"

"I do." Patience voiced her reply a trifle too fervently. She wished it had gone better, for Richard's sake, wished she might ease the lines from his forehead and the tension from his stance, wished she might do anything at all to halt the inevitable, for while she would not wish upon herself a brother like Chase, she, with no brothers at all, could fully comprehend what Richard stood to lose. "We must do it again sometime," she suggested. "Soon."

"Would you?" Richard sounded surprised, amused, even faintly desperate. "That would be very kind."

"His friends . . ." she began.

"They've no idea how to be with him." He gathered together the dice, his hands careful and meticulous in stacking them, sixes up. "They come on rare occasions. All awkward and inappropriate and gruffly well-meaning. Taxes his nerves, really. He is never so sapped and disheartened as when they visit. Today was different. To hear him laugh again . . ." He took a deep breath, and looked on her with such warmth and appreciation it made her wonder, if life was a game, what game Richard was.

"It is really rather wonderful of you and your mother to come."

She smiled at him, glad their visit had been help rather than hindrance. "What of you, Richard?"

"Me?" He rose from the table abruptly, his tone dismissive as he crumpled the page on which they kept score. He busied himself clearing the table, something the servants would have done. She wondered if he meant to avoid her question.

She swiveled on her chair, watching him. "You have the look about you of a weary man."

He laughed ruefully as he absently turned the empty dice cage with a rattle and squeak. "Kind of you to mention it."

She took up the cards again, gave them a fresh shuffle. "I do not mean to tease you."

"No, of course. Thank you for asking." He rubbed the flat of his palm across his forehead, a gesture he had used often the day of his father's funeral.

"How do you manage?" she pressed ever so gently, and dealt two hands of eight, turning up the seventeenth card, a nine of hearts.

He shrugged, sighed, made a dismissive gesture, seemed not to know what to do with his cards once he looked at them.

"Is he always like that?"

Richard chuckled wryly. "You manage to bring out the most obnoxious in him."

She smiled. Waited. Set the stock cards in the center of the table where they might both reach them.

He spoke slowly, as if unsure whether she still listened. "I keep asking myself, What would Father have done?"

She nodded, made a noise of understanding.

He sighed. "I do my best not to fall apart in front of Mother, or lose temper with Chase when he is unreasonable, or divert my anger and sorrow onto the servants."

How tall he looked perched beside her on the edge of the old leather cushion. How capable. Bowed but not broken. He reminded her of the oak tree they had climbed so many years ago. She could see it behind him, through the window, just beyond the garden.

"You were made for this, you know."

"What?" He cast a sardonic look from beneath dark brows. "Death and misery?"

"No. No." She must make him understand. She did not jest. Not now. "It is just . . . your personality is perfect for such a crisis. As if you've prepared all your life."

He shook his head. "What? Fate? Destiny? No. I will not have it." For the first time he allowed anger to surface. He tossed his cards facedown upon the table, and looked at her with the intensity he had so often displayed, but this time when he frowned his features pulled into lines of anguish. He shook his head. "As for being prepared, I have fooled you. I feel completely unprepared. I do not know what game we play, what moves to make."

She had no idea what to say, how she might help. This was a Richard she did not know, had never imagined. His unexpected vulnerability moved her, struck her to the heart, in a way she had never anticipated. She got the strangest feeling that his words in some way applied to her. A silly conceit. He had far more important things to think about than her.

She sorted her cards, paired off a queen of diamonds and a king of hearts, and said, "Any marriages?"

He gave her a confused look, "Marriage? Who would you have me marry?"

Such a desperate look in his eyes—as if she had the answer.

She smiled, reached out toward his cards, was surprised when he grabbed her hand.

"Tell me, Patience. Who do you see me marrying?"

She stared at him, felt the fast beat of his pulse in the wrist he pressed to the back of her hand, a bit too warm. Something in the moment reminded her of a day long ago in this same room—when Pip had hidden beneath her skirts, his hand too hot upon her ankle—when Richard, flustered, had reached out to touch her sleeve.

He seemed flustered now, his fingers clinging to her hand, his gaze clingy, too. It unnerved her.

She moved her hand, tapped the cards.

"I meant the cards, silly. We play bezique. Hearts are trump."

"But of course they are." He sounded disappointed, as if he knew before he looked that he had few hearts in his hand.

Birds chittered in the garden as he sorted his cards. Her mother and Lady Cavendish murmured. In the distance a horse neighed, familiar sounds, and yet the world seemed changed. In her neck a tension rose, the sense of impending disaster, of loss. Marriage would mean losing Richard just as she was losing Pip.

"I would not have you marry anyone at the moment," she admitted quietly.

"No?" He looked up.

"No. Not unless you are in love, and perfectly suited."

"But I would marry." He eyed her over the fan of his cards, blackbird-wing brows taking flight.

"Oh?" The air weighed heavy in each breath she took. The ticking sound of the clock seemed slowed.

"Yes. To someone perfectly suited."

"Is anyone perfectly suited?"

"I am convinced of it."

But that could not be Lady Wilmington. A married woman. Who did he mean?

"You surprise me." Her chest felt suddenly too pinched by her stays.

"Will you wish me happy?" he asked. "Or will you miss our cards and conversation?"

"Of course," she said a trifle irritably. "To both. Now play your hand."

He laid down the king and queen of spades.

"A royal marriage," she said. "A perfect pair of the same suit. Were you talking cards all along?"

He smiled enigmatically. "Was I?"

Chapter Twenty

"Bezique," Patience said triumphantly, and added the knave of diamonds and queen of spades to the royal pairs already littering the table.

"That's forty points." Richard jotted the number on a bit of paper already busy with scores. "But you will have to do better than that to beat me."

"And so I shall," she said, her eyes on the marriages of red and black. How easy to pair cards in a game, she thought. How difficult to pair people in real life. She looked up to find he watched her, head cocked.

"If only it were that easy," he murmured, as if he read her mind.

"Winning, or marriage?" she asked.

He smiled and set aside his cards. "Either. Oh. Almost forgot again." He stretched out his legs that he might pull from his pocket a jingling handful of coins, which he stacked carefully on the table beside her hand. "These are for you."

She eyed the silver in confusion. "What's this, then? We do not play for money in earnest, do we?"

He laughed and made his discard, and, plucking up another card, declared a seven of trumps for ten points. He waved his cards at the pile of silver. "Long due repayment of a favor."

"Favor? It is generally you doing me favors."

"You loaned me money at Vauxhall."

"Ah," she said, "I remember now." She drew a knave of hearts with a little frown of impatience, and discarded an eight. "I also remember you promised on that evening to reveal to me the name of a gentleman you thought suitable as a match for me."

Tossing down his unplayed cards as if tiring of the game, he ran a hand through his hair, and rose abruptly to look out another of the windows. "I suppose I did."

She straightened the coupled cards that his movement had separated, and thought of their childhood, of Pip's hand at her ankle while Richard stood looking down at her staggered cards. She could see his face clearly in her mind's eye, the expression in his eyes as he stood before her like a blackbird, head cocked.

And as clearly as if he had spoken, she recognized the truth.

"You knew!" she whispered, amazed, eyes gone wide. "You knew!"

"Knew what?" he asked from the window, his voice gentle.

"That day I played Patience here at this table."

"What, that Pip hid underneath?"

She inhaled sharply.

He turned, dark hair catching the light, green eyes amused. "I knew," he agreed.

She pretended to return her attention to the cards, but she saw them not—saw only, in her mind's eye, the staggered configuration of the old deck. She felt the heat of the hand at her ankle, the breath at her knee. She blushed. She knew she blushed; she could feel the rising heat in her neck and face. So many years ago, and still she blushed. She had convinced herself he had not known—could not have stood talking to her so calmly.

"All those years, and you never said a word!" Anger welled in her, fired by her embarrassment. "Not so much as a suggestive remark! Pip would have . . ."

"Teased you unmercifully?"

She glared at the matched pairs on the table. The kings and queens stared back at her, unblinking. It was true. Pip would have teased her no end.

He shrugged, not the type to tease. "I am not Pip."

No. He was not Pip. No one but Pip was Pip. No one

but Pip would do, and she might not have him, might never have him. A queen never paired? She did not like the idea.

Were they happy matches? she wondered. Did the king of hearts understand the queen of hearts' moods? Did he tease her? Or did he refrain? And what had the knave of diamonds done to so impress the queen of spades that she ran away with him?

"You never told me who he was," she said.

He turned once again from the window.

"Who?"

"The gentleman you once considered as a match for me."

He cocked his head, the blackbird revived, just as he had when they were children.

"Is he any closer to being in a position to consider such a match? You mentioned obstacles."

He turned back to the window, straightening his shoulders, clasping his hands in the small of his back, blackbird's wings folded. "It is very nearly time for me to introduce you, I suppose."

"No hurry." She rose quietly from the window seat and went to stand beside him, wondering what she might do to relieve some of the emotional burden he carried. For a long moment they just stood there together, staring out at the garden, glancing now and again at each other's faded reflections, drawing strength from the silence, from the sight of Lady Cavendish weeping on her mother's shoulder among the roses.

"It is far better he rails at you," he said, voice low, "than that he sink into dark, silent moping where he bellows for drink, and threatens the household with violence he no longer has the strength to carry out."

"The gentleman whom you would introduce me to?" She deliberately played the fool.

"No. I meant—"

She stopped him with a light touch. "I know."

"Of course." He started to laugh, but the sound failed him, falling off on a mournful note.

She could not hide her pity. "Is there nothing to be done?"

He shook his head and took a deep breath. "There is little anyone can do, least of all me." His voice cracked under the strain of his words. "He resents . . ." He sighed, shrugged. "We have never been close."

"And yet you love him," she said with certainty, her hand seeking the warm perch of the inner crook of his elbow. "It is evident in your every word and gesture."

Head bowed, his gaze still on the distant horizon, he tilted his head her way. "He does not see it that way. I feel destined—or is it cursed?—to love those who cannot see how much I care."

"*I* see," she protested, and gave his arm a heartfelt squeeze.

"Do you?" he asked wearily, his eyes so filled with sadness when he turned to face her that she wondered if she did, indeed, understand the depth of his despair.

"Of course I do." She gave his arm another squeeze. How could he doubt the depth of her empathy? They had known one another since childhood. He was her closest, her dearest friend. He had kept her secret all that time.

He stepped away, her hand sliding from its nest. She regretted he took no comfort in her clasp.

He bent to lift a stray card from the floor, a worthless seven he placed carefully upon the table's edge.

"I do not think you understand," he said. "Not really."

She was surprised to find, as he turned in to the light from the windows, that his eyes sparkled, bright with unshed tears.

She thought of Lady Wilmington. Surely he knew how much she cared for him.

"Does she trifle with your affections?" she dared ask.

He looked up suddenly, as if the question surprised him.

"The one you love. The one you have yet to express your affections to."

He closed his eyes, as if he could no longer bear to look at the world, and said with a weary nod, "Without knowing. She does. Yes."

Chapter Twenty-one

Patience listened to the sound of footsteps approaching through the neighboring gallery, and assuming they were to be interrupted, she begged, "Tell me who she is?"

"Someday, perhaps."

She gazed at him with a feeling of frustration—dear Richard, clever Richard. Why would he not confide in her? "She would be quite foolish, and completely unworthy of you, if she did not recognize how wonderful a person you are."

He seemed surprised by her compliment. He stared at her intently a moment with a pleased expression. "She is wonderful in her own way. I do not think she understands just how wonderful."

Patience felt a pang of jealousy that he should speak of a woman so ardently. She could not imagine Pip using such words to describe her.

"You will tell me how she responds?"

He nodded, his gaze very serious. "You will be the first."

"Promise?" she teased.

"Promise," he said in all seriousness.

"Beg pardon, sir." Toby Smith stood in the doorway.

"Yes, what is it?" Richard asked.

"A moment of your time, sir?"

Richard rose. "You will excuse me?"

"Of course." Patience watched them pause in the doorway, curious what the boy needed. How urgent the movement of the lad's hands, the wide-eyed look.

Richard frowned, and bit off quick questions.

She rose, concerned, arriving at the doorway just in time to watch the two of them stride off through the gallery, heels ringing, rows of painted Cavendishes blankly observing their haste.

She paced the drawing room thereafter, going often to the doorway to gaze into the gallery.

A maid scurried by, arms bundled with soiled linens; another passed her going the opposite direction carrying a steaming pitcher. A footman headed across the garden in the direction of the stables.

The ticking of the clock seemed suddenly very loud.

Patience wandered the room, uneasy, her face anxiously staring back when she passed the swan-topped mirrors.

She remembered thinking this drawing room quite splendid when she was a child. It had, with the years, grown dowdy with neglect, the carpets thin, the upholstery worn.

A large drawing room, it spanned the width of the house, windows looking out on three sides, so that one might view both garden and park. Upon the mantel sat the familiar ormolu clock. Above her head caged birds still sang, but the canary yellow damask wall fabric, upholstery, and draperies had faded to a frayed, buttery yellow. Melting—the room seemed to be melting away, no improvements made since she was a child, since the death of Richard's father.

As heir, Chase had spent his money on horses, a new carriage, hunting boxes in Surrey, Sussex, Kent, and Oxfordshire, a huge London town house, three packs of hounds.

No need for any of it now.

How much money had slipped through Chase's fingers? In lost bets? In upkeep of a series of expensive mistresses?

Patience wondered if things would have been different if Chase had found himself a wife. She had heard he preferred singers, dancers, and actresses. It was quite scandalous—and always mentioned in hushed voice—like Pip's Titian-haired songbird.

No sign of such women here. She wondered if they knew of Chase's injuries—if they cared. She wondered if Richard would be responsible for sending them packing now that Chase had no more use for them, tried to imagine it—what a task!

Richard, so careful of the finances. Had he issued banknotes for the upkeep of such women in his role as his brother's bookkeeper? He had never mentioned detail of his responsibilities, certainly none so tawdry.

Footsteps drew her gaze. It seemed appropriate in that moment that two footmen walked by the doorway, a hip bath between them.

Who meant to take a bath at this hour of the day? Would the earl still be in possession of servants and bathtubs had Richard not seen to its upkeep?

So much she did not know about dear Richard. She had never thought to ask.

The clock mocked her, its hands seemed permanently fixed at half past three. Still no sign of Richard, no sign of anyone but her mother and Lady Cavendish strolling peacefully among the flowers, Lady Cavendish bending now and then to clip a handful of blooms to add to the basket full of cheerful color at her hip. The drone of their voices echoed the drone of the bees.

Such a peaceful scene, Patience thought, so at odds with the race of footsteps now, plunging along the corridor, agitated voices rising, a cry for "Fresh linens to his lordship's room!"

Gravel crunched as a horse was led into the drive, its tail flicking flies.

And there went Richard, his hand upon the shoulder of the lad, Toby, a stream of urgent words voiced too low for her to hear. A stable lad gave the boy a leg up, flung him into the saddle.

"Quickly now," Richard called, pulling a coin purse from his pocket, handing the lad a flash of silver. "Tell Moore he must come at once!"

Moore, the physician!

The boy dug in his heels. The horse kicked up gravel in a spray, and Richard stood watching him go a moment, shoulders sagging like the coin purse in hand, a coin purse that stirred memory in her. She could not quite place it, had no time to place it before he turned on his heel to find her waiting for him in the doorway.

"Chase has taken a turn for the worse?" she suggested.

"Chase," he said harshly, his voice low, anger brilliant in his eyes, "grows impatient with death."

Chapter Twenty-two

Patience stood stunned.

Richard turned his back abruptly on the drive, and with a crunch of gravel took the pathway that led around the house, his long-legged stride too fast for her, too furious. She had to take two steps for his every one.

"What do you mean?" Breathlessly she ran to catch up, her heart racing, trying to make sense of it.

"I mean," he said curtly, coming to a halt, looking about him as if afraid he might be overheard, his every movement abrupt and angry—most unlike the Richard she knew so well. He lowered his voice and spoke with a simmering sort of rage that frightened her. "Chase has swallowed an entire vial of laudanum. After casting up accounts all over the bed he has fallen into a senseless stupor he well nigh may never wake from."

He set off again, every line of him angry.

What? Suicide? She could not believe it. "But he will not be laid to rest on hallowed ground! His estate reverts to the Crown if—"

"I know." Richard turned the corner of the house, the gardens stretching before them in a sudden wash of color.

He closed his eyes and bowed his head, as if to shut out the beauty. Jaw clenched, he shook his head.

Patience had read an account in last week's paper detailing the ritual suicide burial of a Captain Peters at a crossroads in Surrey, a stake driven through his body that his spirit might not wander. Such an ignominious end to her son would break Lady Cavendish's heart.

"Mother has yet to be told," Richard said abruptly, as though he read her mind. His gaze sought out the movement of both their mothers at the far end of the garden.

"No!" she said, and grabbed at his arm. "You cannot tell her he attempts to take his own life. Must not tell her. It will break her heart."

He shook her off and set off, grim-faced, among the rows of flowers, butterflies rising in dancing clouds before him.

She did not follow him this time. She did not think it appropriate. Richard looked so tall and straight-backed, his features set in hard lines as he approached his mother, as he took her hand in his and spoke. Lady Cavendish dropped her pruning shears, dropped the basket of flowers, fragile blooms exploding color and petals as it hit the grass.

She turned at once and ran to the house, skirts held high, her manner wild-eyed and windblown as she charged up the garden steps and along the walk. Richard followed, his face a picture of concern.

He did not look her way. It pained her that he did not so much as spare her a glance.

Her mama bent to gather up the basket, the flowers, the garden shears. Patience went to help, tears scalding her eyes, tears she would not allow to fall.

"You have heard?" her mother asked as her shadow fell upon the flowers.

Patience nodded. She could not speak, knew she would burst into tears if she made the attempt.

She knelt, her hands seeking the fallen blooms, plucking up the few resilient survivors, her gaze drawn to the house.

"He told you first?" her mother murmured, brows arching, as if that were in some way remarkable. "Before his own mother?"

She nodded again, more flowers in her hands, most of

them ruined, bent, or scattered by the fall. So fragile life was. So beautiful. So violent. So unexpected.

"Is Richard Cavendish in love with you, my dear?"

That brought her head up with a gasp, the flowers forgotten, gripped too tightly, their perfume suddenly overwhelming.

"What?"

Chapter Twenty-three

For a moment Patience was struck speechless. Then in a rush she blurted, "Richard and I are no more than friends."

It had sounded so very silly—Richard in love with her. "To be sure, the very best of friends," she went on, and then the idea began to sink in, to tumble about in her mind with substance and force. Could it be true?

"I see," Mama said, her emphasis on those two words such that it sounded as though she saw something far deeper, far more intriguing. It made Patience want to protest even more vehemently, *We are only friends!*

"We must leave at once," her mother said as they walked back toward the house. "Unless they require our assistance in some way."

Preoccupied by her mother's question, by the very suggestion that Richard loved her, Patience murmured agreement. "Of course."

They were not needed.

There were more than enough helping hands to set the world in order at Cavendish Manor. And as their carriage was brought round, as a footman opened the door for their leave-taking Richard hurried out to play the good host in saying farewell.

He walked them to the carriage, his eyes on the drive, on the road down which he had sent a lad racing. "Thank you for coming," he said absently as he helped her with the step. "Both of you," he said fervently, and at last he glanced at her, and by way of the step they stood eye-to-eye, so tall was he.

In the instant that their eyes met, Patience wondered about her mother's outlandish suggestion. Was Richard in love with her?

He looked away again, such tension in his jaw, in the pucker of his brow, such a glimpse of near panic in his eyes that, struck by a sudden impulse, she kissed his cheek.

He blinked, surprised, and turned his head, and she, meaning to kiss his cheek a second time, bussed him swiftly on the mouth—a glancing kiss, no more than a brush of the lips, and yet it startled her, startled him; she saw his eyes widen, his brows unknit themselves a moment to rise.

She could not look at him then, could not reconcile the sudden yearning within her to kiss him yet again. Were these the kisses of good friends?

Words tumbled from her mouth to ease the moment, to bridge the gap between them that her eyes could not vault.

"I am so very sorry," she said.

He mistook the reason for her apology, said at once, hurriedly, "Not at all."

"It started out such a good day," she went on.

"It did, didn't it?" He spoke as swiftly as she, their words stumbling over one another, and then she was in the coach, and he shut the door, and all the while his gaze was fixed on her, curiosity there, a question, and she had no answers, only surprise and a sense of disbelief, and an odd, disjointed wonder that seemed all wrong for the moment.

"What happened today?" her mother asked as the horses were clucked into motion and Richard lifted a hand to wave. "I thought the three of you meant to play games."

"We did," Patience said, her gaze finding Richard's once again, dear, dependable Richard, whom she saw as if for the first time as he turned away to deal with his brother's dreadful choices. "We played Hazard."

Chapter Twenty-four

Patience met the news, when it came two days later, without dismay.

Never revived from his stupor, Chase had gotten his final wish, achieved his final end. The physician pronounced his death an inflammation of the liver, a condition prompted by recent injuries in the fall from his carriage.

Patience knew better. She had asked her mother if a person might die from drinking too much laudanum. Mama had looked at her astounded, as if to ask why in the world she would ask such a question, but then she had closed her mouth, biting down on her lower lip a moment before saying, "Yes. Especially when one is not in prime health to begin with."

The funeral followed at Cavendish Manor almost immediately thereafter. The body, carefully painted a color somewhat less yellow in hue, was displayed in state for three days, the house shrouded in black crepe, the body attended by a member of the family at all times. Distant cousins, long-forgotten drinking mates, and absolutely everyone in the neighborhood traipsed in and out of the house to pay respect, all clad in mourning blacks, all ready with a tale of the last time they had encountered the deceased.

Pip told Patience about it the day he came in his carriage to take her, her mother, and her elder sister, Prudence, to the memorial service.

"An admirable turnout," Pip said as they followed the

nodding plumes of the hearse to the chapel and found themselves delayed by a long line of crepe-draped carriages that had arrived before them.

"I did not know Chase was such a well-liked fellow," Patience's mother remarked.

"He was not," Pip said flatly as he peered out the window, and when he turned to find his party eyeing him with some surprise, he explained away his callousness, saying, "To be sure, we shall see a good many of his racing, gambling, and drinking cronies, but there will come those, too, who mean to ingratiate themselves with the new earl by way of an excessive show of sorrow."

"They will fall over themselves currying favor. Just you watch." Chase's voice sounded in Patience's head. He had known! Of course, he had thought she meant to curry favor with his brother. A bit of nonsense. She viewed Richard no differently now that he was a mon-eyed earl, did she? He was still her dear, dependable Richard, just as he had always been.

He greeted them with solemn politeness, looking no different than before, except for the drawn lines of his face, the dark circles under his eyes. He took her hand in a firm grip when she followed her mother through the door.

"Patience. A moment, if you please."

"Of course," she agreed.

Cupping her cheek in a black-gloved palm, a gesture so gentle and unexpected it took her breath away, he said, "Dear Patience." He drew from his pocket a jeweler's box.

Something in his eyes gave her the impression he meant to kiss her, which startled her so much she fell back a step. Panic and fascination warred within her breast. She did not know what to do if Richard should kiss her here, in front of Pip and everyone.

She had imagined kisses, of course, all kinds of kisses, especially since her lips had brushed his at Cavendish Manor, but in her imaginings it was always Pip she was kissing, not Richard. Pip, who stood watching them now.

She did not know what to do with her feelings, did

not know how to respond to Richard if he wished to, in a moment, transform their lifelong relationship. The moment terrified her.

She need not have worried.

Richard kissed her in a brotherly fashion, his lips pressed to her forehead, his hand cupped beneath her chin. Such warmth, such comfort in the gesture. A brotherly kind of kiss—short, sweet, no unnecessary lingering. She was relieved, and touched, and at the same time a little disappointed—she could not have said why.

He pressed the jeweler's box into the palm of her hand and stepped back with an expectant look, waiting for her to open it.

Inside nested a mourning ring, a pretty little pearl that gleamed like a fat tear against her lusterless black chamois gloves.

An unexpected honor. Mourning rings were usually given only to family members or lifelong friends. And so she was—if not to the deceased, to Richard.

"Did not think you knew Chase that well," Pip said, surprised, as Richard lifted her hand and placed it on her gloved finger.

She and Richard shared a look.

"You knew him at his worst," Richard said. "And managed to make him laugh when I thought him beyond all laughter. You allowed him to cheat at dice without complaint, to insult you to your face with what he considered his wittiest barbs, and thus he had a good day, his last day. He would have wanted you to have this. And if he did not, I do."

How chill his black-gloved hands in slipping on the ring. She longed to warm them. "I am deeply honored," she said.

As Pip waved her ahead of him into the pew, brows raised, she said, "You should have been there that day, Pip."

"You know how I felt about Chase," he said under his breath.

"Not for Chase," she chided. "For Richard!"

* * *

The service was short, but well delivered. A group of angel-voiced, ruddy-cheeked choirboys sang the coffin and pallbearers out to the hearse.

Pip gave her a nudge. "Richard's brats have come all the way from London to sing for more suppers."

"What do you mean?" She frowned at him. He seemed to have little understanding of how to comport himself at a funeral.

"Richard's lambs, I should call them. He always refers to them as such when wheedling alms for them. Convinced Chase to send them Christmas turkeys every year." He chuckled. "He has strong-armed me into sending them mincemeat pies and a goose or two, and of course there are the paintings we have had to buy."

"Paintings? Pies? What are you talking about?" she insisted, more confused than ever. Richard had never said anything of this to her.

"Lost lambs. Orphan lambs. Coram's Foundlings. Has he never taken you to see the paintings at the hospital? Raises money for the little ones annually, our Richard does, assisting them with their Christmas concert, and morning teas, and an artwork auction. He must think kindly of you, indeed, if he has not begged a contribution or two."

She had no idea what he was talking about, no idea just who her dear friend Richard really was, it seemed.

Only family and close friends followed the hearse to the cemetery after the service.

They stood waiting in line to offer condolences to the family, Pip restless to be done with the thing, fretting under his breath with acid sarcasm, as if to laugh at death, "What can one say about the death of someone one despised? It is a shame his life was cut short? Oh, how I shall miss him? What a fine fellow he was? Lies, all lies. A game of grief and commiseration I will not play."

Patience lost patience with him, snapping out, voice low, "You could say you are sorry for their loss, for the lost potential of a loved one's life cut short. You need not have loved him, but without a doubt his family saw something in him to admire, if only the memory of what he once was as a lad, and the dreams they had for him."

Pip eyed her askance a moment. It was not often she spoke thus to him.

"Calm down, my dear," he said. "You are quite right. I do thank you for precisely the right phrase. I can honestly make such utterances with complete conviction." He then practiced how he would say the words, altering his emphasis on different parts of the sentence before deciding on exactly the proper inflection.

Still put out with him, Patience studied the crowd of mourners, looking for familiar faces. "I must say I am surprised Lord and Lady Wilmington are not here today," she remarked when Pip had flawlessly delivered his line to Lady Cavendish.

He cast a startled look her way. "Have you not heard?"

"Heard what?"

With a troubled expression he pulled her aside and said in lowered voice, "Wilmi has suffered a bad bout of heart palpitations."

"No!"

He nodded, sadness in his eyes. "The day after Chase popped off. He ate a bowl of fruit as he and I were playing a game of billiards. He remarked on how very good the cherries were, said that his aim was off, and without another word dropped like a sack of potatoes. I was certain from the gray look of him that he was stone-cold dead."

"You were there!"

"Indeed. It was a dreadful moment, as you may well imagine. His heart, the quacks say, must have spasmed mightily. Melanie will not leave his side."

"How awful!"

"Yes. He is weak as a kitten. I fear we may be attending another funeral all too soon."

"What a comfort it must have been to Melanie that you were there."

He nodded. "I did my best to calm her, to arrange

that Wilmi be made comfortable in his bed, and saw to it the local physician was called—even sent for the vicar. In case . . . well, just in case."

Like Richard, she thought. How very like the day she had spent with Richard.

"It has been, I think," he said haltingly, "a week of events most odd and terrible and wonderful all at once."

"Wonderful? In what way wonderful?"

"I do not mean to sound unfeeling, but would you not agree it timely that fate should see to removing impediments to the future happiness of two whom I love most dearly before I commit myself to marriage?"

"Whatever do you mean?"

"I mean I know that Melanie, as much as she loves her husband, loves another more, and now that Richard is Earl of Cavendish he need no longer hesitate to declare himself to the one he loves. We may all be happy now."

Patience pursed her lips. "I do not think a funeral the appropriate time or place to speak of such happiness," she said glumly.

She found nothing to cheer her in the prospect of losing both of her childhood companions to marriage. She had no marital prospects in her own foreseeable future— a future that seemed foreshortened and trivialized in the face of death.

"Will you do me a very great favor?" she asked Pip.

"Depends on the favor." He nudged her playfully in the ribs.

"Will you take me to see Richard's lambs?"

He blinked at her, amazed, and with a frown of distaste asked, "Whatever for?"

Chapter Twenty-five

Patience was reminded of the evening Richard had taken her to Vauxhall as Pip handed her down from his coach in front of a small, whitewashed gatehouse. Before the gate hung a large cast-iron bell. It was ironic and appropriate somehow; there was resonance in the moment, a ringing echo of that other illicit coach ride in which Richard had transported her into Pip's private world.

Now Pip carried her into Richard's.

As her fingers slid from the hand she had so long yearned to clasp Patience stared for a moment at the neat stitching that shaped the soft, lemon-colored kid of her gloves, at the diminutive pearl mourning ring that still graced her finger. Not for Chase's sake did she wear the thing, but for Richard's, and every time it moved on her finger, every time she caught glimpse of her hand, there was the wink of it, and with it thought of an afternoon at Cavendish Manor playing Hazard and Chuck-a-luck.

The edge of the gold band bit into her finger when Pip clasped her hand—her dream come true. How long had she yearned for her hand to be treasured in Pip's good-sized grasp? How many times had she imagined a clandestine carriage ride alone, his attention all for her? And yet any pleasure she might have taken in spending time alone with him was overshadowed by the intensity of her curiosity in seeing what Richard kept secret from her—here, at a foundling hospital.

The gate, the bell, the brick pile beyond, a group of

lads playing—nothing seemed too objectionable. As an area for dwelling, Bloomsbury was highly regarded, a favorite haunt of writers and poets. Recent construction marked a number of desirable squares of attractive houses.

The foundling home itself was surrounded by open fields full of butterflies and daisies, sheep and cattle grazing. A pub from Queen Anne's day squatted on the corner, the sign above its door batted by the wind. The coach driver looked as if he prepared to doze. The footman at the back of the carriage wore a bored look, and yet Patience felt as if they stepped into the forbidden—into potential scandal—she and Pip.

She knew why most young women came here. There was inherent in a home for unwanted children a private, tucked-away sense of shame and scandal. Pip felt it, too. He looked about, head high, a trifle too high. He had thought it wisest to tell her mother that he took her to the museum collection in nearby Montagu House, and Patience had not bothered to contradict him.

She hesitated to approach the gate.

"Are we to ring this?" she asked, reaching for the bell's sturdy chain.

"Not unless you mean to leave a baby with the gate-keeper," Pip said with an awkward laugh. He held wide the squealing, wrought-iron gate, frowning at the noise it made—or was it the thought of babies that troubled him?

Leave a baby! With the gatekeeper?

It took a moment for the enormity of such an idea to register, a moment in which her shoes carried Patience through the gate, and a warbler winged past, twittering sweetly, and ahead of them came the sound of children laughing, none of it sounding quite real, quite right, for how could unwanted children laugh?

How does a mother bring herself to do such a thing? Patience wondered. She looked about her with fresh eyes. The smell of the breeze that batted at her careful curls seemed changed; the cry of the bird had gone plaintive.

A young woman brushed past them, rushing out of the squealing gate as Pip drew it closed, his head turning, to follow her progress, his eyes fixing on her face as if in recognition. She wore the deep green livery of a familiar household, and yet Patience could not, in that moment, place whose. The young woman's eyes were swollen and red, her shoulders racked by sobs, and in her arms she clutched a bundle from which a thin arm stretched, baby fingers reaching up to grab the wind-flung green velvet ribbon that tied the end of her braid.

She had not the heart to leave the little one, Patience surmised as the gate clanged shut behind them. There was something triumphant in the thought, for surely it was better for a child to remain in its mother's care than in the hands of strangers.

"Blackballed," Pip said flatly with a shake of his head, regret darkening his eyes. "They've not enough room for it, there are so many. Come along now."

On they went while Patience mulled the word about in her head. *Blackballed?*

Little boys in brown wool uniforms with peaked caps and starched white collars played with sticks and hoops in the courtyard between the widespread arms of the redbrick building that was the foundling hospital.

"What do you mean, blackballed?"

Pip shrugged, as if it were no great thing. "The women draw little balls from a bin to see if their babies get in. White balls, the child stays. Black ball, the child must go."

She could not quite fathom his meaning, so matter-of-factly did he put it.

"Unwanted even by the foundling hospital?" she asked.

"Yes. Not enough money. Never enough, if you listen to Richard."

"And why do their mothers not want them in the first place? Their own children? Are they ill?"

He looked at her, astounded. "A few. For the most part it's unwed mothers, servants left with child by the hands of a master—and thus no father, no food, no money."

Hoydens, she thought, and for the first time truly understood her mother's lifelong concern with matters of ladylike behavior. "Oh!" she said quietly.

"I cannot think why you should wish to come here."

She looked about them, at the boys who glanced their way in the midst of their game with curious eyes.

"I wanted to see . . ."

The brick building loomed.

"What?"

Through the windows, rows of little girls in matching brown pinafores and starched white caps bent over bits of needlework. Patience thought of the woman who had been turned away, of the baby.

"What will become of it? The baby?"

He shrugged. "She may take it home again, struggle to feed it. Then again, she may go to the Thames with it."

She gasped. "Throw it in?"

He nodded grimly. "Like a bag of unwanted kittens. Those who haven't the heart to drown their young leave them bundled up along the bank. Wait for the weather to take them."

Patience had no words. She stared at the laughing lads as they scampered across the yard.

"Why did you come here, Patience?" Pip asked again.

"I wanted to see—"

"A bit of scandal?"

She made a face at him. Did he truly think so little of her? "No!" She shook her head vehemently. "I wanted to see what so impassioned Richard that he would enmesh you all in it so completely."

Pip shrugged, paused a moment, watching the lads, as she did. "I think he hoped to sway us . . ." He shook his head impatiently. "Sway Chase, in any event, from his wild ways with women. Show him the sad outcome of his wickedness." He turned and trotted up the little flight of steps leading to the pedimented doorway.

"Was Chase wicked?" she asked from the bottom of the steps.

Pip paused in reaching for the door latch. He waggled his brows suggestively. "Extremely wicked."

"And did it work?" Her breath came fast in mounting the steps, as urgent as her question. "Was he deterred?"

Pip stepped back from the doorway. He studied his

shoes a moment before answering, "Not Chase. Not enough that anyone would notice, in any event, but for the Christmas turkeys."

"And you?" she dared ask, coming alongside him. "Did Richard persuade you to give up your Titian-haired dancer?"

The golden curls that kissed his forehead bobbed violently, so suddenly did he turn to look at her. "He told you?" he demanded, blue eyes flashing.

She shook her head and took a step back, startled by the heat of his anger.

"Who then?"

"You."

"What?"

"Just now."

His eyes narrowed, golden lashes framing a hard glitter of sapphire and obsidian. "Explain."

She tugged at her gloves—new gloves, and the young woman with the baby had had none. "I guessed. You see, Melanie would not tell me who you were talking to at Vauxhall. Nor would Richard explain your relationship with her."

"She saw?"

"Melanie?" They spoke as one.

"Yes."

He looked worried, contrite.

"She told me I must ask you who she was, that it was not her business to sully an innocent mind."

"She would leave it to me, would she?" he muttered as he held open the door for her.

With a sudden yell from the lads a runaway hoop crashed into the bottom of the steps, bounded halfway up the flight, following them, and then fell back down again with a rattle.

As if it brought with it the truth, Patience knew, suddenly, where she had seen the green livery before, the green livery that the young woman with the baby had been wearing.

She had seen it at Vauxhall, under a tree.

*   *   *

Patience was given a complete tour of the foundling home, a trek through dark hallways that smelled of beeswax, shoe leather, and chalk, hallways that filled with children of all ages when bells were rung between classes that taught the rudiments of trade: sewing and wait skills for the girls, wait skills and the figuring of money for the lads.

She tried to imagine the world bereft of these well-dressed, rosy-cheeked children, given to the Thames. It was too horrible to comprehend. She thought of her own childhood, of climbing trees, and hide-and-seek, and beating Pip at backgammon. She could see, in her mind's eye, with fresh appreciation, the bounty of her life—of Richard's, of Pip's.

She thought of Chase as he had once been, older than they, but still a child—a precocious, rambunctious prankster of a child, blessed with loving parents and the privileges of wealth. Even as a child he had taken joy in pinching the cook's buttocks and undoing apron strings, and in kissing the scullery maid under the mistletoe. How many maids had he brought to such a place? How many to the Thames?

How much it must have pained Richard. How much she understood his need to do something.

"You mentioned teas?" she reminded Pip when at last she had seen the whole, and he wondered if she were not ready to go.

"Yes." He rubbed his hands together enthusiastically. "Hungry, are you? I know just the place for fresh scones and clotted cream."

"I did not mean tea for me, although that sounds lovely," she said. "It is more a matter of wishing to take part in raising money for the orphans."

"Oh! Those teas. Well, you must ask Melanie."

"Lady Wilmington?" She was for a moment surprised, and then it all fell into place. *Of course.* "Let me guess," she said. "Richard talked her into it."

Chapter Twenty-six

Patience attended Lord Wilmington's funeral less than a fortnight later, and in the days following went alone to call upon the widow Wilmington, arriving at a house swathed in black ribbons and plumes, a dark wreath upon the door. Inside, the ceiling was tented in black, the mirrors covered, the drapes drawn.

Surrounded by such reminders, Patience recalled the kindness of Lord Wilmington at Vauxhall, how readily he had welcomed her to his box, to the spot beside his chair, how jovially he had introduced her to his friends and included her in the conversation. She felt a pang of regret that she had not had a chance to know him better.

Melanie saw her in the little drawing room, the blue drawing room, whose dark, damask-lined walls had not been draped in black. The draperies at the window, which faced onto the garden, had been parted, and in the bright swath of green-tinted light, the widow looked out at a blue sky and nodding flowers.

"Thank you for seeing me," Patience said, and with a guilty start Lady Wilmington allowed the draperies to fall back into place, hiding once again the world that strictest mourning dictated she must ignore. "I know that this time is generally reserved for visits from only the closest of friends."

Melanie smiled at her, a brilliant flash of a smile. Like the light from the window it poured over her.

"And that is exactly what we are," she exclaimed, descending upon her in a quiet abundance of black fabric.

"We must be. You and I and Richard and Pip." She led her to a little table set for two. "I mean to feed you cucumber sandwiches. And pineapple and melon from Wilmi's beloved hothouses. And poppy-seed cake, and tea. And you must feed me news from the outside world. Tell me everything. Simply everything. I am starved for attention."

Black suited the widow. She had never looked more endearing, Patience thought as she was graciously offered sandwiches and fruit at a table draped in crisp white linen, where a fine portrait of Lord Wilmington smiled down at them.

Lady Wilmington confided over lemon-scented Darjeeling and poppy-seed cakes, "It is dreadfully dull, this mourning business, with only an occasional peak at the garden. No perfume, no silks, no curls, no jewelry. I may not even occupy myself with needlework. Wilmi would laugh to see me suffer so for him, who lived only to bring me pleasure. 'You must go dancing, or to the theater, my love. Lift your spirits.' I can hear his voice counsel me as clearly as if he were standing in the room. He would not want me to mope or pine, not my dear Wilmi. From his deathbed he bade me not to fall into a state of melancholy, insisted I must remarry at once. I hear him laugh, for he knows it is not allowed, none of the things I like best in the world, not for another six months."

"The time will pass more quickly than you think," Patience assured her.

"So everyone says." Lady Wilmington sighed. "But I find the hours drag most tediously."

"I hope you will not mind that I've a favor to ask of you."

"A favor?"

"Yes. Pip has taken me to the foundling home."

"Pip?" She sounded vastly surprised. "He hates to go there."

"Yes, well, I begged him. The boys sang at Chase's funeral."

"Did they? I am sorry to have missed that."

"They were quite moving; they had voices like angels.

Pip tells me you are active in the monthly teas that are held to raise money for the children, and I wish to help. It occurred to me I might take over some part of your duties while you are confined to mourning.''

"Oh, my dear.'' Lady Wilmington leaned forward to clasp her hands, and tears glittered in the corners of her eyes. "No wonder Pip agreed to go. You are an answer to my prayers.''

It was six months later, at one of the foundling hospital garden teas that Patience next saw Richard, fresh out of mourning. Or rather, he saw her. She speculated later how long he had stood propped against the trunk of the oak, watching her, a look of wonder in his eyes, a wonder so strong it made her turn, the hair at the base of her neck prickling, with the feeling that she was watched.

And someone *was* watching—two someones, as it turned out. The first who caught her eye was not Richard at all, but Sophie Defoe's stepbrother, Will. He was staring at her over the rim of a cup of tea, steam rising about his nostrils. She was reminded of the tales of dragons her father had fabricated for her as a child.

"Miss Ballard!'' he said, approaching the table where she was directing several of the older orphan girls in the arrangement of cake plates and tart trays, punch bowls, tea urns, and an array of napkins and silverware. "I must say I did not expect to see you here.''

"Nor I you.''

"I lend use of my footmen and stable lads to these teas on occasion, in token contribution, for the directing of the carriages, and carrying the paintings, which tend to be too heavy for the children.'' He waved toward a trio of tall footmen, who were at that moment carrying a canvas-wrapped painting through the trees toward the display area in the walnut-paneled great hall of the hospital.

"How very kind of you,'' she said, and could not take her eyes off of the footmen, something familiar in them, something she could not quite place.

"I see I have been looking for you in all the wrong places."

He meant the remark to be suggestive, even provocative, and he did not know her well enough, she thought, to take such liberties. Indeed, his suggestive tone, and the idea of looking in the wrong places, made her think of Vauxhall. And she did not want to think of that night, or what she had seen there.

"And where did you hope to find me other than in the country with my family?" She tried to sound dismissive.

"Why, Almack's, of course, and Astley's. Even"—his brows rose suggestively—"Vauxhall."

Vauxhall? Why the gardens? Unless . . .

He seemed to be waiting for her to make the connection. He eyed her most keenly, something sly in the manner of his gaze.

"And why did you look for me?" she asked, while in her mind the thought ran—*He saw me at Vauxhall! That long-ago night of the masquerade. He must have!*

"You intrigue me, Miss Ballard. Indeed, I am quite drawn to you."

Her eyes were drawn again to the backs of the retreating footmen, the dark bottle green of their uniforms. She was certain he had been there, certain he had seen her, and something in his knowing frightened her.

In that moment of fear she was beset by the notion that someone watched them. The hair prickled at the back of her neck, and she turned to find a gentleman in gray, a black armband at his shoulder, leaning against one of the larger oaks, his gaze fixed on them.

A smile lifted his lips as her eyes met his. He raised his teacup in salute.

"Richard!" she cried, and without so much as a word of farewell to Will Defoe, behaving the hoyden once more, skirts flying, she ran to him, arms wide.

"Has it been six months?" she asked into his coat lapel, grasping at his armband, giving his shoulder a squeeze. "Oh, how I have missed you!"

A moment's juggling, and he tossed the spilling teacup

into the grass, and then he wrapped his arms around her in a great bear hug, such as he used to give her as a child, and said, muffled, into her hair, his voice mocking, "Who are you, my dear?"

She looked up at him, surprised. "I am Patience."

"Are you? Here? I never thought to see it." He chuckled. "You do not look it, running to see me in such a fashion."

She boxed his shoulder. "I have been impatient to see you again."

"And I you." He smiled, holding her at arm's length, that he might look at her, that she might look into his eyes—those eyes gazed back at her with such warmth and kindness and affection it made a shiver run the length of her spine. "I did not think to find you here, of all places. Was that Sophie Defoe's stepbrother?" he asked.

"Will?"

His brows rose in the much-missed manner they were wont to. "You know him well enough to call him by his given name?"

She shrugged. "Not really. It is just that Pip always refers to him as Will. Do you think it was terribly rude of me to run away from him like that?"

"Incredibly rude," he agreed with a familiar teasing twist of his lips. Light fingered his hair, dappled his cheeks, kissed the tip of his nose. How new his face seemed to her, how beloved its expressions, discovered afresh.

"Tell me, what do you think of him?" she said.

His brow furrowed. "In what capacity would you have me consider the question?" When she turned a confused look upon him, he went on hastily, "More to the point, what do you think of him?"

She smiled and shrugged. "I am not entirely sure. That is why I asked you. You tend to be a good judge of character."

He looked surprised and pleased that she should say so.

"I think—" she said, then stopped herself.

"What?"

Patience wrinkled her nose and pressed her lips together a moment before admitting, "Perhaps I ought not say what I think, for it is not a fully formed opinion."

He looked profoundly surprised to hear her say such a thing. "You have never scrupled to tell me anything in the past."

"No. But perhaps I should have. I would learn to be discriminate rather than blurting out my every thought and feeling, especially with you."

His brows rose. "Why me?"

She nodded sheepishly. "My tongue knows no bounds with you. I tell you everything that flies through my head. I am not quite so forthcoming with everyone else—indeed, with anyone else."

"Not even Pip?"

She laughed. "I cannot tell Pip my every thought. He does not listen as you do."

He smiled—the slightest inclination of his lips. "I am profoundly flattered. Perhaps you are right not to tell me. I must trust in your heart, and intellect's truest inclination."

His words made a smile bloom upon her lips. No one else spoke to her like this. No one else reminded her of her heart and mind's truest inclinations. "I have missed you," she said.

"And I you. And now you must unburden your heart with regard to Will Defoe, if that is still your desire."

She sighed and blurted out, "I think he must have seen us at Vauxhall last year. In fact, I am sure of it."

"I've no memory of seeing him there."

She bit into her lower lip and said, "I think he saw us run beneath the trees. You and I."

"And why do you think this?"

"He has referred to it indirectly, and—"

"Has he?"

"Sophie insisted she had seen me before. Do you remember? The first time we met, at Almack's."

"You think Sophie was there as well?"

"Yes. Well, perhaps."

"Go on."

"I saw their servants' livery there, beneath the trees, attached to a set of legs."

"Legs?"

"Yes. Naked legs."

Chapter Twenty-seven

Patience divulged the whole, words flowing from her mouth in a quiet, halting stream.

Richard listened, head bowed, a pucker forming between his brows. He stood close, that she might keep her voice low, until she had finished her explanation, and then he paced away from her a few steps, the trees throwing splashes of light and shadow across his brow. He blinked, squinting into the sun—or did he glare in Will Defoe's direction?—as he said angrily, "I never should have taken you there, to the gardens. It was foolish of me. Most irresponsible."

"You must not blame yourself, Richard," she protested. "You cannot. I insisted we must go to see Pip. Remember?"

He paced back and forth before her. "But I need not have answered your wishes, taken you there. Put you in harm's way."

"You brought me here, too."

"What?" He stopped his pensive motion, turned to look at her with ageless eyes, his gaze dark with doubt and self-recrimination.

"Are you not surprised to see me here?"

The pucker at his brow twitched. "Yes. Whatever gave you the idea?"

"You did."

"Me. How do you figure?"

"Pip told me about your orphans."

"Ah."

"I made him bring me to see for myself."

"Pip brought you?"

"Yes. He told me of turkeys and Lady Wilmington's teas. And, oh, I almost did forget—the Defoe livery again. We saw it when we first arrived here, a young woman weeping, with a baby, wearing the same green livery I saw in the park."

He considered this a long moment, his expression thoughtful before he asked her, unexpectedly, "Pip spends time with you, then?"

"Since the funeral he has been ever so attentive. I think Chase's death, and Wilmi's following right behind, have made him rethink some of the pursuits to which he has devoted much of his life."

"And Sophie Defoe?"

"I have not heard him mention her of late. And I have not asked."

"And so you may get your wish after all."

"What? That he will not marry her? I earnestly hope so, for I am convinced neither she nor her stepbrother are quite what they appear to be, and Pip openly admits he does not love her. He deserves far more in marriage, dear Pip."

"Are you still in love with him?" He asked lightly, as if he assumed she would say yes, and yet there bloomed a look of mingled hope and sadness in his eyes that gave her the impression he considered her affections a hopeless cause.

Resistant to any pity he might feel for her, and yet no longer certain what it was she felt for Pip, Patience said only, "I wish him happy. Myself as well." And when it looked as if he meant to say something more, she blurted, "You said once you knew someone you wished to introduce me to."

He paused, mouth half-open, as if she had caught him completely off guard. "Given up on childhood dreams, then?"

She gave it thought. Had she? "Dreams change," she said.

He dropped his head, chin to chest, as if this saddened him. "Some do," he admitted.

She said, her voice low, "What of you? Do you still depend on childhood dreams?"

He lifted his head to look at her with ageless agate eyes. "One."

His answer surprised her. She had never imagined practical, sensible, dependable Richard to be the type to dream.

But before she could ask him what that dream was, they were interrupted by two of the female guests who frequented the teas, a Lady Harwood and her daughter Judith. They wished to speak to Richard, whom they had not seen since the funeral, and whom they were certain must know how they might go about making a sizable donation to the poor cherubs at the foundling home, for while they had drunk their fill of tea, they did not care for any of the paintings, and yet they wished to do something.

"We shall speak again later?" he suggested to Patience.

"But of course," she agreed, and watched them drift away. She went back to overseeing the tea tables, and every time she looked up Richard was surrounded by guests, women who had never shown much interest in him before. Women with daughters of marriageable age.

It was strange to view Richard as a grand catch, but that was what he had become with Chase's death, no denying it. It bothered her to think some pushing young miss might come between them, might turn his head. She had come to depend on Richard always being there, her closest friend and confidant, her dear, dependable Richard.

He made a point to speak to her once more before he was swept away again by a flock of females all vying for his attention, smiling and fluttering their lashes and making a great competitive chatter, like the sparrows that swept down to compete for the cake crumbs in the grass.

"The gentleman we spoke of . . ." he said. "Shall I arrange a meeting?"

She hesitated a moment; then, with a feeling of finality, a feeling that matched the empty cake plates, the dregs of tea leaves, the drift of visitors away from the trees, she nodded. "Yes, please do."

It was not Richard who arrived upon the doorstep two days later, breathless with news. It was Pip.

"I have broken it off," he announced, his eyes alight with an unusual fire, his words tumbling out in a rush. "I am on my way to see Lady Wilmington and wondered if you wished to come along."

"Broken off what?"

"My engagement to Sophie."

"What?" She was stunned, shaken to her very core. He was not to marry Sophie Defoe? He was free to marry another?

"Come. I've the landau waiting. Ask your mother if you may go. I will tell you everything on the way."

Patience's mother was quite happy to have her go, given such auspicious news. "Broken it off, has he?" Her eyes sparkled mischievously. "Well, my dear, hope springs eternal. Go and change your dress. The blue or the wine-colored wool look very nice on you. You will need something warmer for an open carriage."

Patience dressed herself in the warmth of wool and hope that day, a reserved level of hope. News that would have once thrilled her did not send her heart to the flights of fancy she might once have expected. She was not the same young woman who had come to London so many months ago. Her real thoughts and feelings for Pip did not match those she had conjured from childhood dreams. He was not the man she had imagined.

That he would break off his engagement to Sophie Defoe was a dream become shocking reality. It did not seem real or possible that Pip might now marry another, certainly not her. She had little enough time to consider the matter, though, for Pip was impatient with her delay in changing clothes, and swept her into the landau as soon as she reappeared downstairs.

What amazed her the most, however, was the fact that

Pip insisted she make room for him beside her on the seat rather than plopping down across from her, as was his habit.

"Something I must talk to you about," he said when she raised her brows. "Something I would prefer was not overheard." He dipped his chin in the direction of the coachman's back.

Her heart thumping with the sudden, unexpected potential of the moment, Patience slid into the corner, arranging her skirts so he would not be obliged to sit upon them.

With the landau in motion, the great rumbling of its wheels on the street precluding their being overheard, Pip turned to face her. Earnestly taking her hands in his, he said, "Do you remember the first time we went to Richard's foundling home?"

The words took a moment to sink in. This question, of all questions, was not at all what she had expected him to ask.

"The young woman with the baby?" he pressed.

"I remember."

"More important to my story . . ." He gave her hands a squeeze, his eyes alight again with the banked embers of emotion this story kindled in him. "She"—he leaned forward—"wore Defoe livery."

Patience tried to stay focused on what he said rather than the heat and pressure of his hands. "What has she to do with your jilting Sophie?"

Again he glanced over his shoulder. "Not jilted. At least I would not have her labeled as such. She has chosen not to marry me."

"But—"

"I had a private word with the maid, you see." He turned her hand, palm up. "Lavished her palm with a bit of silver." He demonstrated with imaginary coin, the movement of his gloved fingers against her gloved palm dizzying her. "I mistakenly assumed she would be in dire need of it, and then I begged her to tell me who the father was."

He released his hold on her, brow furrowed. "Told her

I had my suspicions, and that I would make the fellow regret having abandoned the child."

He stopped, sighed, watched the passing houses with a frown.

"Was it Will Defoe's child?" Patience demanded.

He rubbed at his forehead, impatiently. "No. No, I've still no notion who the father is. She surprised me—the maid. Said I had better ask who was the mother."

Patience sat silent a moment, confused, and then she gasped. "No!"

He nodded, eyes squeezed shut, his face set in lines of regret. "Of course I could not credit such a claim without confirmation. To take the word of a maidservant who might bear a grudge against the Defoes—who might have reason to lie—went against the grain."

Patience sat frozen, unspeaking, hands clasped tightly in her lap, knowing what must come next, dreading it, for poor Sophie Defoe's sake.

"But then I considered all that I knew, and realized that Sophie had gone away to the country at the time the babe would have been born, and her father has been most anxious to sign paperwork for the betrothal, the settlements, and her stepbrother . . . the way he looked at me, as if he were ready to laugh out loud, ready to laugh at me. I cringe to think of it now, to think how close I came to great unhappiness. And you have saved me!"

He beamed at her with deepest affection, both his claim and the loving focus of his smiles completely unexpected.

"*I* saved you? How have I done this?"

He laughed, and gleefully clasped her by the shoulders, and said breathlessly, "Because, after much deliberation, I took my suspicions to Richard, and he told me what you had seen at Vauxhall."

"Oh, dear. I am sorry, Pip."

"No need to be sorry, my dear. You have saved me from a match destined to fail. And for that I must kiss you."

And with no more warning than that, he leaned forward abruptly and smacked his lips to her forehead, and Patience did well not to gasp.

As quickly as he had leaned forward, Pip leaned back, blue eyes shining with affection, and all of it for her. "Such dear friends I have been blessed with," he said, and gave her hand a quick squeeze.

They sat in silence the rest of the way to Wilmington's estate, and she basked in the memory of his lips to her forehead, and his words rang again and again in her ears: "You have saved me from a match destined to fail. And for that I must kiss you . . . kiss you . . ."

When they arrived at their destination, and Pip helped her down with no abatement to his smiles, his hands seeking hers for a companionable squeeze as they walked to the door, they discovered Melanie already had a visitor.

It was Richard.

Chapter Twenty-eight

"He is in love with you, you know," Patience said.

She and Melanie sat beneath the trees, at a little table beside the trout stream that had kept Lord Wilmington occupied many a languid hour. At water's edge, Richard and Pip were skimming stones across a still pool in the bend of the stream.

Such a peaceful setting. It lent itself to confidences, to the unburdening of secrets.

Melanie stared at her a moment without speaking. "Is it so very obvious?" she said at last, rather wistfully.

And so she knows, Patience thought, *and would not have the world privy to their feelings.* A turtledove sailed through the trees toward the water, with a flash of banded tail and a throaty call. "I have known him all my life," Patience said. "Perhaps it is easier for me to recognize."

Melanie sighed. "You must be right. I thought we had been most discreet."

They squinted at the backs of the two young men skipping stones, one dark, one fair, the sun bright in their eyes, hands raised to shield their gazes.

"Wilmi knew, of course," she murmured.

"Did he?" Patience was shocked.

Melanie did not look at her. She seemed to know such a revelation required a moment's contemplation.

"Oh, dear, yes," she said evenly. "I could not carry on behind his back. Never that. He even approved. You might say that in his own way he fostered the relation-

ship—contrived opportunities that we should find our-
selves alone together."

"He didn't!"

"Oh, but yes. A prince among men, my Wilmi. He was
not unaware of the vast difference in our ages, you see,
and he wanted a son. In name if not in fact. He knew
his health was hateful, that he could never outlast me,
that his current heirs would take everything, and cast me
out of the house."

Patience looked toward the great, winged Georgian
pile that Melanie referred to. It was no longer the widow's. She would soon be asked to vacate, if she had not
been asked already.

Melanie sighed, waving her hand in the direction of the
stone throwers. "From the start he allowed me certain
freedoms, always with the understanding that he did not
want to endure gossip, or public censure."

Patience felt herself unused to the ways of the world,
uncomfortable with such careful arrangements. It seemed
so very improper, so completely at odds with all she
knew of dear, dependable Richard. She could not fathom
such an arrangement, could not picture it, any more than
she could reconcile the idea of a baby, or bare legs under
the trees at Vauxhall, with Sophie Defoe. "Did Richard
know Wilmi knew?"

"Richard?" Melanie seemed surprised by the question.
"I do not think so."

"Indeed, I think he might be quite shocked," Patience
allowed her thoughts voice. Once said, the words
sounded foolish and naive.

But Melanie met them without censure. "Such a fine
young man, our Richard. Such exemplary sensibilities. I
would prefer he did not know." She reached out to touch
Patience's wrist. A butterfly touch, there and gone.

"Of course. I quite see why."

"I can depend upon your discretion, then?"

"Absolutely."

Melanie regarded the gentlemen again. One in particular, Patience was quite sure.

"I knew I might. He is so very fond of you. I just knew you could do nothing to hurt him."

Patience studied Richard's tall silhouette, watched the strain of bone-colored buckskin across buttocks, thigh, and calf as Richard bent to fetch up another stone. Fabric strained in a similar fashion across the shoulders of his coat as he swiveled and threw another skipping stone. He laughed—how good to hear the sound. "He has suffered too much already."

"Yes, of course. Poor Chase. Richard will find himself the object of much soothing attention now—a great deal of female attention."

Patience thought of the women at the foundling home.

"Chase warned him of it," she said.

"Did he? Poor man. How difficult it must have been to face the consequences of his impending demise."

"Difficult indeed."

"I am so very glad Wilmi went the way he did— quickly, no suffering, no real curtailment of the joys of his life, no lasting debilitation." She touched a single elegant fingertip to the corner of her eye. "But enough of that. I will grow maudlin if I continue in this vein. We were speaking of Richard, and women."

"Were we?"

"Oh, yes, Pip and I were discussing the change in his circumstances only yesterday."

"Were you?"

Two days in a row Pip had visited Lady Wilmington? How good of him to comfort her. How kind.

"Oh, yes. We spoke of many things." A shout from the water's edge drew their attention.

"Seven skips!" Pip crowed in admiration, clapping Richard on the back. "A fine throw!"

"He is in love with you, you know," Lady Wilmington said with a smile, her graceful head inclined toward the pair.

And thus her words were echoed back to her exactly, Patience thought. She stared a moment in disbelief at Pip, her fair Pip, who had kissed her in the carriage. "And for that I must kiss you," he had said. Her throat tightened, choking off her reply. Could it be true? Her dream come true? "Did he tell you so?" she asked hopefully.

Melanie tipped her head, to look at her with a coy smile. "Not in so many words, no. But one has only to catch him looking at you in odd moments. His affections are quite clear. Do not tell me you were not aware?"

"Not at all," she said breathlessly, heart thundering.

"Pip said he had yet to tell you—said he had been afraid to tell you these many years."

Pip afraid! Of her? Tears sprang to her eyes.

"Oh, my dear Melanie! You've no idea how happy this news makes me. I thought there was no hope. I never dreamed he felt for me what I have so long felt for him."

"You mean to say you harbor feeling as well?" Melanie said gleefully. "I would never have guessed it."

"I do."

Richard returned at that moment. He smiled in response to her smiles. "What do you?" he asked brightly.

"Love you," Lady Wilmington said.

Patience was happy enough to agree. "In this moment," she said with happy spirit, "I love the world." And when he tilted his head and narrowed his eyes, puzzled, she leaned forward and kissed him on the cheek, and said, "We may all be happy now."

"I have been meaning to tell you," he said with a mischievous smile, "I have arranged a meeting with the gentleman we last spoke of."

"Your mysterious friend?" She smiled back at him and shook her head. "No need."

He frowned. "But?"

She gave his cheek a pat, shared a conspiratorial chuckle with Melanie, and told him, "You were right. Dreams do come true."

He shot a confused look between the two of them, and his brows rose as they were wont to do, and he asked hopefully, "Do they really?"

Chapter Twenty-nine

Patience was sure Pip must say something on the way home. She waited patiently through his perfectly unobjectionable chitchat recounting how lovely had been their visit, how well Lady Wilmington looked, how timely that they should visit in the same instant Richard should have come to call, how wonderful the garden party Melanie was planning sounded.

"You do mean to be there?" he asked.

"Yes. I would not miss such a gathering."

"Melanie mentioned there is to be an announcement."

"Yes. She is soon to be ousted by her cousin, is she not?" Patience sighed. She did not want to talk about the garden party. She did not want to discuss Lady Wilmington's proposed announcement—although she did wonder if Richard's name might figure into it—wondered, too, why he had looked so baffled when she had turned down the offer to meet his mysterious friend. Did he simply hope to see her married to someone he knew and cared for, that they might more easily remain friends?

A logical conclusion, certainly a practical one, and yet it left her testy; she did not know why. But of course the real reason was because Pip would seem to address any topic but that which most interested her—his feelings for her, the feelings he had kept hidden from her for years, the feelings Melanie had informed her he was afraid to divulge.

"Who am I?" she asked him suddenly.

"Who are you?" he repeated the question, his features

a picture of confusion. "What do you mean, who are you? Do you not recall? Are you feeling faint, m'dear?"

She sighed in her impatience. "No, I am not faint. And of course I recall, but I wish to know from your perspective who I am."

"Oh, a game, is it? All right, then." He sat back to regard her through narrowed eyes. "You are Patience Ballard. . . ."

"Am I?"

"Last time I checked."

"Patience. Am I Patience?"

"Not at the moment. You seem very impatient with me, and it is not fair, as you have not informed me just what game it is we play."

"What does Patience mean to you?"

"Patience? Why it means to wait, quietly, calmly, unruffled—precisely the opposite of the mannerisms and expression you are displaying right now. In fact, quite the opposite of the mannerisms you typically display. Why do you ask?"

"I am tired of being Patience."

"But who then do you hope to be?" he asked, much confused.

"I am tired of waiting." She stirred restlessly in her seat, ready to fling herself at him. "Of hoping. Of dreaming. I do not want to be Patience anymore." She wondered if he would admit his feelings at last if she threw herself into his arms. "I should like to be impetuous, and daring, and noisy, as you are." She gathered herself for a move, given the slightest sign.

"Me?" He flung up his hands, as if to ward her off. "But you are wrong, my dear friend. I am the soul of patience. Have been for years."

"Are you?" She was surprised, hopeful, breathless, now ready to be patient a little longer.

"Without question, and so you shall see at Melanie's garden party, for I mean it to be a night of revelation for myself as much as her."

Patience quieted, puzzling over his words. Did he mean to declare his love for her at this garden party?

"All right." She sat back to consider the dilemma of what she must wear to the garden party, for it promised to be an evening when all eyes might turn in her direction, and she had given away the better part of her clothing allowance to Richard's foundlings.

"Do you know . . ." Pip paused.

Well, of course she didn't. "What?"

"Richard said . . ." He stopped, gave her an odd look, and took note of the street where they were turning. With a frown he went on, "Richard said the strangest thing today."

"Richard, strange? How unlike him."

"Yes." He seemed to be puzzling it still.

They came to a halt in front of her parents' town house. "What did he say?"

Pip glanced at the back of the driver's head. "Too much to go into here. Care to come play a game of battledore tomorrow?"

Battledore? They had not played battledore since they were children, she and Pip. How like him to make her wait till tomorrow with whatever his mystery was.

She tried to sound disinterested as she stepped down, saying, "What time?"

"Early," he said with the sort of smile that always managed to melt her heart. "While it is cool." Then he winked at her. "But not so early there is still heavy dew on the grass."

Patience arrived with her battledore racket at a quarter past ten. Pip, to her amazement, had already set up the net, an ancient thing that had stiffened with age and gone paunchy in the middle.

Patience had grown nervous about Pip's unusual request. What could Richard have said? Why go to such lengths to tell her?

She allowed herself to suppose Pip wanted a moment alone with her, a very private moment to ask a most private question of her, nothing to do with Richard at all, and it made her hands sweat a bit on the racket handle as she knocked at the door. Her voice faltered in asking the butler for Pip.

Her knees even went a bit soft as she was led through the house to the back garden.

Pip made it all right again.

He met her with a sour expression, a battered shuttlecock in his hand. Sadly lopsided, it was missing three feathers.

"Only one I could find," he apologized.

She laughed, relieved. He did not look as if he meant to ask her anything at all important. "Oh, dear. Silly thing will have no sense of direction whatsoever." Like her mind, she thought, wandering off on stupid tangents.

"Well, I'm game if you are." His grin stirred a flight of shuttlecocks in her stomach as he bounced the cork end of his wounded bird against his strings.

One could not call it a game. It was more rightly dubbed the shuttlecock chase. The featherless cock insisted on flying into the wooded copse bordering their playing area far more often than it should. No matter which way one hit the thing it whirled off in unexpected directions. Their pursuit of it was an exercise that had them both laughing and whooping from the start.

On their third foray into the wood to retrieve the "blasted thing," as Pip kept referring to it, Patience asked, "What was it Richard said to you yesterday that you found so strange?"

"Here's the tricky devil!" Pip bent to pick up the pitiful shuttlecock. He responded as if he had not heard her question as he gave it another thwack against catgut. "I thoroughly enjoyed our visit to see Melanie yesterday. Did you?"

"Of course." She dodged in the direction she was sure the shuttlecock must go, and miscalculated entirely.

As she set off into the wood again, she asked, "Did it have something to do with Melanie?"

"Do you like her?" Pip asked as he followed, racquet batting at the grass and ferns into which the shuttlecock might have flown.

"I do. She has been very kind to me."

"And you to her."

He said it carefully, as if he had given the matter thought.

"Have I?"

"But of course. You were so good in listening to Wilmi as you did, all of his old stories."

"They were new to me."

"And in visiting her while she was in mourning."

"Richard's idea."

"Here it is," he called, and bent to ferret their wayward cock out from under a juniper bush. And as he rose, he looked up at her, laughter in his eyes, and asked, "Was helping out with her teas at the foundling home Richard's idea?"

"No. Mine. You tried to talk me out of it, as I recall."

He held the shuttlecock out, as if he meant her to take it, but when she reached for it, he moved his hand as he had when they were children, teasing her, dangling it just out of reach. "I thought you too unspoiled." He waggled his brows, eyes sparkling with a familiar teasing light. "Too unwise to the ways of the world to get involved."

She reached for the shuttlecock again, and again he moved it just out of reach, so that she leaned in closer, reaching high, her rib cage brushing his, their arms bumping as she laughed, and grabbed at his hand.

And suddenly he turned his hand, so that hers met with his, and between their palms the mangled shuttlecock was pressed. When, in her surprise, she would have snatched it away, triumphant, he clasped his fingers to hers, that she might not.

Her eyes went wide.

"Perhaps I was wrong." The light in his eyes, the throaty tone of his voice proved unexpectedly provocative, as he released his hold on both her fingers and the shuttlecock, in a way that led her to suppose he meant to flirt with her.

Her heart beat a little faster; her breath came short in asking, "And Lady Wilmington? Did you try to dissuade her as well?"

He laughed, and politely held back a branch that blocked their way. "No. Melanie is very wise to the ways of the world. It is one of the reasons I mean to marry her."

"Marry her?" She did not for a moment take him seriously. "Do not tease me, Pip. You cannot marry her. Must not."

He frowned. "Why so?"

"Because . . ." She twisted the shuttlecock between her fingers, eyeing with pursed lips feathers gone awry. "Because Richard is in love with her, and she with him, and I would not have you spoil that."

"Richard?" He gave a great guffaw, and swung his racquet at a violet, decapitating it. "Whatever gave you such a preposterous idea?"

"Melanie."

"What?" He looked momentarily stunned, indeed the arc of his racquet froze in midair, and then he laughed again, and swung the racquet again, scything through the grass. "She plays a game with you if she has said such a thing."

"She was in earnest."

He shook his head. "Impossible."

"Why impossible?"

"Richard is in love with . . ." He smiled an impish smile, and twirled the racquet like a ballet dancer, just above a row of nodding daisies. ". . . someone else entirely."

"You are wrong."

He made an exasperated noise. "If anyone would know these two, it would be me. I cannot believe you suggest such a match. They are completely unsuited to one another."

"I happen to agree, but love is not always wise, or sensible, or well matched."

"This truly is preposterous!" His voice rose, impatient, a little doubtful. "If Richard were in love with her he would have said something to me yesterday, when he told me . . ."

"Yes, what did he tell you?"

When he did not at once reply, she drew breath sharply. "Did he admit that he has been having an affair with her?"

He ducked under the net. "Something equally preposterous."

"I tell you he is in love with her, and if you are as good a friend as you claim, you will not break his heart in stealing her away from him."

He turned at that, and looked at her incredulously through the net, his gaze so intense she took a step backward. Jaw set, anger flashing in his eyes, he whirled the racquet twice in his hand, as if he wanted very much to strike down her remark before he spat out, "Are you sure it is I who would be thief?"

She did not know how to respond to such a question, and with an exasperated sigh he banged the palm of his hand against the catgut of his racket. "C'mon. Let's play."

"What did Richard say?" she called out rather irritably as she managed to get the shuttlecock airborne, its flight a corkscrewing nightmare of misdirection.

He bashed the spiraling cock with undue energy. "I will tell you if you promise to tell me if what he said is true."

She frowned as she scampered back from the net, and missed the direction of the shuttlecock completely. "All right. I promise."

"Bloody hell!"

"How unlike Richard. He is not given to blasphemy."

He ducked under the net again. "No. It is the damnable shuttlecock. Flown into the woods again. Did you not see it sail past?"

"Sorry. I was certain it would go hither, instead of yon. Which way?"

He parted the trees for her. "Into that ocean of ferns."

"Oh, dear."

"Yes. Confound the thing. Onto your hands and knees."

"I shall get dirt on my gown."

He pulled her down beside him, shoulders bumping,

hips bumping, his manner playful and teasing, an unusual light in his eyes. "You never used to fuss."

She elbowed him with a trace of irritation. "I used to have more of a dress allowance."

He threw back his head to laugh, and caught at the hem of her skirt as she passed, giving it a tug as she bent to look among the fronds of ferns.

"Now, please tell me what it was Richard said that was so important you would ask me here to play battledore with a vexingly featherless cock."

He laughed, waggled his brows at her, and jumped up from where he knelt. "Oh, that."

"Yes, that." She waggled her eyebrows back at him, the muscles of his thighs catching her attention as she bent again in search.

He caught the drift of her attention, winking at her with such a devilish gleam in his eyes she blinked in dismay. Never, since he had spoken to her at Vauxhall Gardens as the mysterious woman in red, had Pip turned the full power of his charms upon her. And his smile, the rakish gleam in his eyes could be dizzying indeed.

Blushing, she rose at once to her feet, saying, "Why, there it is. Not in the ferns at all."

He turned, looked in the direction she pointed, and laughed. "Up a tree, is it?"

"And too high to reach," she warned him.

"Do you mean to make me climb?"

"You never used to fuss," she mocked him, giving his hip a bump as he walked beside her. She could tease, too. Indeed, she could be quite coy when she wanted to. "I think I can get at it." She threw a coquettish glance over her shoulder. "If you will be so good as to give me a boost."

"A boost, is it, my little hoyden?" He laughed again, his every glance and gesture as changeable as the leaf-filtered light that dappled his cheek. "Still hoist your skirts to climb trees now and again, do you?"

Her thoughts went all muddled to have him smile at her as he did, shadows deepening the blue of his eyes, sunlight winking golden in his hair.

"Whenever the opportunity presents itself," she said with a nervous laugh.

"Dress allowance be damned?" Mischief danced elfen in his eyes, in the quirk of his lips.

"Well . . ." She eyed the tree uneasily. Perhaps it had been foolish of her to suggest she could reach so high.

"Turn around," he suggested.

She turned around, for no more reason than that he asked it, letting loose an involuntary gasp as he encircled her waist with his hands, and adjusted her stance so that her back was to the tree trunk.

The unexpected heat of his touch, the firm possessiveness of his grasp made her heart lurch. Shaken and confused, she looked into his eyes.

Laughter looked back at her, his lip curling with it, as if he knew exactly what he was doing to her.

"If you give a good jump, I think I can lift you into the crotch," he said smoothly.

She did not know how to respond to his suggestive tone, and so she pretended to ignore it, glancing over her shoulder even as she relished his closeness, the brush of his breath on her hair, the heady pressure of his thumbs on her ribs.

"Yes," she said breathlessly. "Just might work. On three, then?"

"One," he said with a nod as he leaned closer.

She bent her knees, tensing the muscles in her thighs.

"Two," she said under her breath.

He tightened his grip on her waist.

"Three," they called out together as she leapt, as he lifted, thrusting her high. She grabbed a limb and drew herself a little higher, into the lap of the ash, her bottom banging bark, one hand reaching out to grip what she thought would be his shoulder, and turned out to be hair.

"Gently," he said with a laugh. "Gently now."

Both of them laughing, triumphant, they grinned at one another as she let go, apologizing, grabbing at his shoulder instead for a moment before she found purchase on another branch.

"Quite all right," he said.

She swayed, finding the best spot for balance, and he grabbed at her knees, steadying her.

Their eyes met for a moment, a head-whirling, heart-lurching moment that had nothing to do with the tree and everything to do with the heat of his hands, of his gaze. In her current position his head was on a level with her bosom, his eyes quite naturally drawn to that which was directly before him.

He smiled, the curve of his lips, the appreciative gleam of his teeth almost too much for her, as his brows rose archly, and he said, "Rather better than I expected."

She blinked, licked dry lips, looked away, reaching for the shuttlecock, stretching hard.

"Don't let me fall," she called to him.

He pressed forcefully with one hand upon her knee. With the other, his grip slid lower, maintaining her balance while allowing her to stretch. His fingers circled her ankle—as they had when they were children, and yet not at all the same.

"That's almost got it." She teetered, fearless, breath coming fast. "Just a little farther."

"I've got you," he said.

He had her. She would not fall. She closed her eyes a moment, relishing the truth of it, short though the duration of such possessiveness might be. A little bit of a lunge and she had the shuttlecock at last.

She could feel his every breath as she sat up, waving her prize, exhilarated by her climb, by her triumph, by his grip upon her nether limbs.

"Ta-da!" she crowed.

He did not let go.

His arms encircled her legs. Her knees pressed fast to his chest.

He did not let her go.

She stared at him, eyes widening, fire kindled within her breast, a dangerous fire that ignited heat again between her tightly clasped legs.

He stood staring, hands sliding at last away from her ankles, and yet not in the expected direction. Up her silk-encased legs, and not down, his fingers trailed more fire, hot upon her calves, as he gently squeezed the aching swell of tightened muscle.

She knew she ought not allow him to touch her so, knew it was not proper or ladylike or good, but the hoyden within found nothing but pleasure in his touch, in the question in his eyes.

Pip grinned, teeth flashing, a smile to melt her heart, to make molten the fire he kindled in her. He gazed into her eyes with a forget-me-not blue heat she had never before witnessed.

Speechless, she froze, shuttlecock grasped tight, tree branch grasped tighter still, unable to avoid his eyes, his hands, as they delved deeper beneath her skirts, traveling in an intoxicating manner to the hollow behind her knees.

"Richard tells me you are in love with me," he said.

The words seemed to hush the breath of the breeze-stirred trees, and silence the voice of the birds.

She closed her eyes, breath catching in her throat, as he stirred the wondrous, unbelievable passions she had kept hidden, walled away from him for a lifetime.

He knew! Richard had told him.

She thought of all that Melanie had said, and wanted to weep her joy that at last he meant to voice his feelings for her. She wanted to lean forward, to wrap her arms about his shoulders, to kiss his mouth.

But she might fall if she let go the tree. Worse yet, he might be diverted from the road his hands traveled beneath her skirts. And the hoyden clamored for the journey to continue.

"He tells me you have been in love with me . . ." His fingers trailed higher. His elbows shoved her skirt aside. ". . . since we were children."

She thought of that day in the card room—the heat of a child's touch, no match for a man's, as her leg muscles tensed beneath his roving hands. Her knees instinctively clapped together as he fingered the tops of her stockings, the tapes that bound them. No man had ever dared touch her thus. She trembled and, fearing what might come next, pressed her knees together tighter than before, trapping his hand when he moved to stroke the tender flesh of her inner thigh.

She opened her eyes then and looked into his, startled to find desire unmasked.

"Is it true?" he murmured, his breath coming faster as he leaned in, his hand sliding a little closer to her most private parts despite the desperate clench of her knees.

She gasped, afraid of her own rising desire, and reached out to stop him. "You mustn't," she said.

"Can it be true, dearest Patience?" he whispered. "All this time you wanted me, longed for my affections, and I never saw sign of it, never reached for what was right under my nose?"

He bent to kiss her wrist, the weight of his head, the tumble of golden curls in her lap something out of a dream, as his hand, a trapped bird, fluttered, gliding, seeking her heat. "Can you forgive me such neglect, pretty Patience? I have been a fool to ignore you."

He found answer in her silence, in the slightest quivering of her knees. The hoyden in her wanted to know what came next, ached to know what a man might do between her legs—like the legs in Vauxhall Gardens, spread wide to welcome the rocking thrust of a man's naked buttocks. He loved her. She could see it in his eyes, could feel his desire in the rapid rise and fall of his chest, in the persistent pressure of his hand.

"Do you not want me, Patience?"

She took a deep, shaking breath, breathed the words, "I do."

He smiled, joyous, his face, his voice, the way he touched her, beautiful—so beautiful—all that she had imagined, and more.

"How long have you wanted me, Patience?" he whispered so softly she must lean a little closer to hear, and with that movement he gained unexpected ground, his fingers gently brushing the curled hair at the apex of her thighs, melting the last vestiges of her resolve.

She swayed, wide-eyed, breath caught.

What was this magic? Dared she let it continue?

"Have you wanted this since you let me hide beneath your skirts so long ago, my dear?"

She dared not nod or shake her head, afraid of the implication of even that slightest of movements, unsure just what it was he thought she desired of him.

"Do not stay my hand," he coaxed. "Let me beneath your skirts again, my love."

"I need a place to hide," she heard the distant memory of his voice, felt the distant brush of his fingers at her ankle. The forget-me-not blue of his eyes was not forgotten, the golden fringe of lashes, the spaniel-sweet affection of his gaze.

Life had led her here. Since childhood this moment had been destined. She almost expected Richard to come bursting through the wood, chasing after Pip, interrupting this game, interrupting her thoughts at the most inopportune of moments.

He had reached out to touch the velvet of her sleeve, hand trembling—as she trembled now, afraid as she was afraid.

"Spread your legs, my love," Pip whispered, and she remembered the heat of his breath at her knee, the pinch of his fingers at her ankle. "My fingers would do naught but make sweet love to you," he reassured her, not the boy anymore, not the complaining lad at all. Here was a man of sweet words and coaxing ways. "This is what you have waited for so patiently, my dearest Patience. I vow it is."

He knew, too, the inevitability of this moment. He loved her. He vowed it was so, his voice like velvet, his touch just as soft.

The words reassured her.

Trembling with the power of a lifetime's suppressed desires, she spread her legs for him, ready, wanting.

Pip smiled up at her reassuringly, lovingly. His fingers, very sure of themselves, of what they wanted of her, burrowed, found throbbing, swollen heat.

She started at that, cried out a soft "No!"—made a move to pull away, but he stilled her with a shushing noise, a calming squeeze upon her knee, as the other hand cupped the mound of her hair, the heel of his hand pressing hard against the burning need, rocking there with such exquisite pressure she dropped the shuttlecock and leaned away from the tree into his shoulder, toward his hand, as he stirred to greater heights the ache of a decade's yearning.

His fingertips were quick to press the point, to seek out the liquid depths of her desire. The probing sensation sent shudders the length of her backbone, so that her knees spasmed, her calves flexed about his ribs, and her toes curled within her shoes.

She understood for the first time the moaning noises she had heard beneath the trees in Vauxhall Gardens, as a similar sort of wordless exclamation passed her lips.

He chuckled knowingly, and sought a little deeper the ache that would not be soothed. She longed to fling herself down from the tree into his arms, but contented herself instead with leaning forward, into the delicious prod of his finger, that she might lean her head upon his shoulder and whisper, "You love me! Dearest Pip. You love me! I did not think it possible."

"Possible?" He breathed a low laugh. "I think it very probable I can love you even more deeply if you will only come down from that tree."

"I do not think that wise," she said, even as she slid into his arms, limp with desire.

"No?" he asked, pressing her to the trunk of the tree as he nuzzled her neck, as he lifted her skirt to probe the swollen, throbbing wetness that thrilled to his touch, to the cool caress of the breeze, to the rhythmic motion of his finger that wrenched another desperate moan from her lips.

His lips sought hers then, stifling her cries, his mouth a well of heat to match that between her legs. His tongue prodded her lips, mirroring the motion of his fingers, and she sighed and parted her lips far more readily than she had parted her knees, and pressed her mouth to his with ardent heat, knowing she encouraged him in so doing— wanting to encourage without a word said.

She felt a flash of fear, a moment's self-preservation, remembering words her mother had drummed into her head: "You must not allow a man too much freedom with your person, my dear. They will try to take advantage." In her mind's eye she saw the woman at the foundling home, unwanted babe in her arms.

But his kisses were like honey, a nectar to make her forget a mother's warnings, the folly of another. She could not get enough of him—his hand—dear Lord—his hand had definitely been allowed too much freedom. The hoyden in her wondered, for half of a heartbeat, why it was said that men took advantage, as she moaned her delight and took full advantage of roving fingers and delving tongue.

Dear Pip. Glorious Pip. This was what she had wanted all these years. She had had no idea, of course, just what it was she longed for, no idea of the melting pleasures in store.

His lips, his tongue, left a damp trail along her jaw. His hands fumbled with her skirts, with the flap of his breeches.

"Oh, God, I want you," he said, and she thrilled to the words, wanting to be wanted. How long had she dreamed of him saying just that?

"And I am yours," she whispered, heart aglow, body fired. "We have only to speak to my father."

He laughed against her cheek, pulling her closer, his belly bare and warm against hers. "Your father has no place here, Patience. This is just you and me, and this. . . ."

He stilled her with the heated touch of velvet flesh, with another delving kiss.

"Yes." She sighed as he pressed closer, his hipbone thrusting against hers. "You must ask him for my hand," she said.

"Your hand?" He laughed as he lifted her, kissing her again, pressing her hard against the tree. "It is not your hand I am wanting right now, but something else entirely, and you and I both know he would not appreciate my asking him for it." Her bared buttocks were bitten by the wood, her skirt raised against his chest, his hands busy between her legs, the prod of warmth sliding deliciously in the dampness, pressing heatedly for entry.

And she saw in a single heartbeat, in the blink of an eye, her blood racing, fired, a baby's fingers reaching—reaching for green velvet ribbon tied in a weeping maid's hair.

"Will we make a baby?" she whispered in his ear, a little afraid, and yet happy as she had never been happy before, wantonly wanting warm, probing heat to touch the aching need within her even deeper than before.

Pip flinched as if she had hit him, hands slowing, kisses breaking away. He opened his eyes to look at her—forget-me-not blue, lashes gilded by the sun—beautiful Pip, golden Pip.

She braced her back against the tree, ready to be loved by him, prepared for a magical, life-changing moment, completely unprepared for the sudden flash of irritation, for the wilting probe between her thighs.

"What a question!" he bit out fiercely, allowing her to slide to the ground.

It dawned on her that she had done or said something wrong. She wished that she might take it back, might unsay the words.

"Good God! What a question to pose in such a moment, Patience!"

The breeze cooled her legs, cooled the fiery damp as her dress slid back down again.

He buttoned the flap, tucked himself in, every movement hard and angry—a rejection. "Next you'll tell me you are a virgin."

He shamed her with the word.

Of course she was a virgin! What sort of woman did he take her for?

Confused by such thoughts—embarrassed by all that had passed between them, by her inability to cease the throbbing heat between her legs—she smoothed her skirt with shaking hands, and groped for the top of the stocking that had fallen down about her ankle.

"But of course you are, aren't you?" He grew angrier

by the minute, more distant. "And I almost . . ." He stopped, unable to meet her gaze, then raggedly whispered, "Good God! What am I about?"

He smoothed his hair back out of his eyes with an angry flick of the wrist. "What in heaven's name am I doing? Richard will kill me."

Richard!

In her memory she saw the knowing look in Richard's eyes as he had turned his back on her, on the staggered rows of cards, on the knowledge that Pip lurked beneath the table. She knew in that instant, with a terrible sinking feeling, that she loved an illusion, not the man before her. And she knew she could not bear to see Richard give her such a knowing look again, could not bear that he should turn his back on her as Pip turned his back on her now.

"Do you mean to ruin me, Pip?" she whispered.

He seemed not to hear. His head was turned as he buttoned his waistcoat, as he pushed a tree branch out of his way. He bent for the shuttlecock. "Damned thing!" Arm arcing, he threw it deep into the woods, a tumbling flash of birdlike white. And then, with a single guilty glance in her direction, and a muttering of "I do beg your pardon. Unforgivable really!" he snatched up his racket from the ground and set off for the house, leaving her standing there, back braced against the tree, knees trembling with mortification, legs still spread.

Chapter Thirty

Patience straddled the branch, skirt rucked up, bare legs and bare feet dangling, bare toes waggling in the breeze. Pennies of light and shadow fell lightly on her face, gold and copper on her eyelids. The breeze sighed among the branches, set the leaves to whispering. Above them a squirrel cluck-chucked, and leapt from high branch to high branch, sending a small cascade of broken branches and bruised leaves clattering through the swaying roof of green.

"Patience," she heard a familiar voice murmur.

Pip, she thought. That was Pip's voice, long ago, the voice of the boy she had fallen in love with.

"Are you sleeping, Patience?"

She did not respond, pretending she was asleep, pretending so he would call out her name as sweetly again.

Something tickled the arch of her foot. A leaf? A fly?

"Leave her alone, Pip." Richard's voice this time, an uncertain, broken voice that leapt, like the squirrels, first high and then low.

"It is only a beetle," Pip said, and she remembered— remembered even as her nerves jumped and she sat up too abruptly, and teetered on the branch, on the bed, ready to fall, already tumbling, the bedclothes sliding, her balance gone, Richard's arms steadying her—and his eyes—oh, how he had looked at her from ageless agate eyes!

A dream. No, not a dream—a memory of childhood. She wiped the beaded sweat from her upper lip, and thought of Pip's touch, and the image from childhood rose again, swimming before her eyes, blotting out the afternoon.

Pip had held a handful of leaves, tickling her foot, giggling at her terror—not a beetle, not a bug at all—and she need not be frightened, might still the frantic beating of her heart, for she had not fallen, would not fall, with Richard ready to catch her. Dear, dependable Richard.

She flushed with fresh shame as she recalled how close to falling she had been that afternoon—no Richard to save her—not even her own common sense to the rescue.

Patience pushed back the covers and sat in the middle of her bed, heart thudding, feeling foolish. She closed her eyes and saw him look at her again—that look—so long ago, and still she remembered. She had not wanted to see what his eyes had to say. Not then. She had turned away and slapped at Pip, that she might touch him as he continued to tickle her toes with the leaves, and together they had burst out laughing, falling back against the tree trunk giggling as Pip continued to tickle her toes, and she, jerking her foot at first away, and then back again, had teased him to continue, making a game of it, unable to face Richard, unable to thank him for stopping her fall.

Had she seen that look again? Had she surprised it on occasion in the deep green of his eyes? When she had jumped down from the carriage on the night when he had taken her to see Pip? When she had looked up from spinning the dice cage for Chase? At the foundling house garden party? Did he cast such looks upon Lady Wilmington when she caught his eye?

What was it he had said in the gardens, against a starlit sky? "Love follows desire. If one is lucky."

Did love follow her desires?

Her heart ached to think her dream so hollow, a tin cascade rather than the rush of a rain-fed stream. She thought of the screech of a cockatoo named for a man who no longer marveled at its cleverness. She thought of Toby Smith, who had not come up trumps at all with

Pip as master. She wondered what had become of the beautiful blond-tailed pony. Would Pip cast love aside as cavalierly?

Did love follow her desire? Had it ever?

Heart aching, tears clouding her eyes at thought of facing Pip again so soon, Patience wondered how she might gracefully excuse herself from Melanie's garden party.

How could he? she kept thinking. How could he touch her as he had? Kiss her? Speak of his desire for her— indeed, demonstrate that desire—if he did not love her? If he meant, as he had said, to marry Melanie?

The entire exchange seemed to her completely, absurdly illogical. It pained and exhausted her trying to make sense of it. Even more frustrating, she could speak of it to no one—certainly not her mother. Prudence, the sister older than she and, as wife and mother, wiser in the ways of men, would undoubtedly carry the story back to Mama. She and Patience had never been close enough in years to exchange many confidences. She had always considered Patience her baby sister. It was probable she always would.

Richard came to call. She stood at the top of the stairs and listened to the familiar timbre of his voice below, and sent her maid rushing down to tell her mother she was feeling indisposed, and had no wish to be disturbed.

It occurred to her, as she remained closeted in her room, that she might have found some roundabout way to ask for Richard's opinion and advice, but she was unable to face him—afraid she would burst into tears with the slightest provocation, in front of her mother, who would demand an explanation.

She refused to so much as come down for dinner, so that her father, who rarely asked after her, startled her mother by making inquiry. She went down to tell him she did not feel like eating. Her mother said she was looking quite pale, and though Patience insisted that there was nothing wrong, she simply did not feel like eating and had a touch of the headache—Mama sent for a physician.

Patience dutifully stuck out her tongue for him when he arrived, and repeated to him that there was nothing really wrong.

The physician gave her a powder to put into water before she slept, and informed her mother that he did not think it serious, merely a touch of the melancholy, but that if her spirits did not improve in a few days' time to send for him again.

Patience watched him leave from her bedroom window. She did not want to be fussed over. All she wanted was time in which to ponder her sins, to consider every word, every gesture, every caress and kiss Pip had offered, and she had accepted.

Surely one must begin to understand the incomprehensible before one could begin to set it right.

And if she could not see clear to setting it right, she needed time in which to mourn the death of dreams. It seemed odd that this confusion of feeling should be inspired by that which she had wanted more than anything for as long as she could remember—an afternoon in which she had seen more demonstration of Pip's affections for her than on any other.

That aspect, more than any other, tore at her heart, at her confidence in the very fabric of her world. She seemed trapped in a game in which vital cards had been hidden from her, a game she was not meant to win.

A bouquet of flowers arrived the following morning, roses and nodding bluebells, rare at this time of year, a message of constancy lifting her spirits, allowing her a moment's soaring hope that they were from Pip, that he meant to set her world in proper orbit again. But they were not from Pip. Richard had sent them, hoping she felt more herself today. Dear, dependable Richard.

She must warn him! He stood to lose as much as she if Pip had his way and married Melanie.

Chapter Thirty-one

Patience considered not going to Melanie's garden party. It promised only pain and embarrassment.

Her mother would not allow it.

"I have nothing to wear." She regretted the words as soon as they left her lips.

Her mother laughed and said, "I told you so. You will recall I warned you this would happen."

Patience wished she might retrieve the words—a stupid excuse, not the reason at all. And thus the night of the garden party found her parading downstairs in her mother's perfumed wake, forced to agree that deficiencies in her wardrobe did not offer reason enough not to go to a once anticipated gathering.

"You look lovely in that," her mother insisted as Richard arrived to act as their escort. "Doesn't she look lovely, Richard?"

"She looks . . . tired," Richard said, such concern in his eyes, in his voice, Patience wanted to throw herself upon his shoulder and sob.

She would have loved to have turned and run up the stairs again, to fling herself facedown upon her bed, but Richard waited for them at the foot, hands clasped in the small of his back, blackbird wings folded. His familiar strong-boned face met them with a smile. Something was changed in his features, a special brightness captured there; all of his goodness, the kindness of his heart, shone from the dark green of his eyes. It drew her gaze as never before.

"I have not slept well of late," she said faintly. "Thank you for the flowers, Richard. You are very kind. Most considerate. I cannot imagine where you managed to find bluebells this late in the year. You look happy."

This last came almost as a complaint, for how could he be smiling when, like she, he stood poised to lose love?

"I am happy."

His smile took firmer hold of his chiseled lower lip. Light from the chandelier played softly in the gleaming darkness of his hair.

"I have been looking forward to Melanie's party. New dress, Lady Ballard?" He honored her mother with a formal bow.

Her mother beamed and twirled away from the bottom stairstep, saying, "The very latest mode, dear Richard. So kind of you to notice."

"And Patience." His gaze swept over her, the green eyes narrowing. "I have always had a fondness for the sight of you in those cherry red trimmings."

"Do talk to her, Richard." Her mother took his arm, her voice lowered as if to reveal a shameful secret. "You see before you a young woman who has thrown away a six months' clothing allowance. I tried to talk her out of it, but she will not listen."

"The thing is done, Mother," Patience protested quietly. "And no great hardship."

"Thing?" Richard asked. "What thing have you done, Patience?"

"Nothing, really," Patience muttered, the words a lie. She had done many things since last they had spoken— unmentionable things that made her palms sweat, and hidden parts of her body begin to tingle. Things she would know more of. She had no desire at all to discuss a subject her mother had already belabored ad nauseam.

"Patience allows her heart to rule her head."

Splitting head, Patience thought, as she watched her mother's chin wag, her curls bouncing, feathers bobbing.

Richard turned to tuck Patience's hand into the crook of his arm. "What's this? Trouble in love?"

Patience stared at him a moment, wondering if Pip

had said anything to him, hoping he had not, and at the same time longing to tell him how she suffered, the sad, confused state of her heart. If anyone would understand it would be Richard.

"She has fallen in love most inappropriately," her mother said disapprovingly.

Patience frowned, stunned. Had the dreadful truth of her daughter's disgrace somehow reached her mother's ears?

But no, Mama's head was bobbing again as she scolded Richard. "It's those foundling lads of yours, Richard. Fully half of her clothing allowance has gone to put clothes on their backs rather than her own. And I blame you, in part, for her foolishness."

Winged brows rose. Deep green eyes blinked in dismay.

Patience snapped her mouth closed, took a breath, rearranged her thoughts. They did not know. No one knew. Just she and Pip, to their private shame.

"My going without dresses for a Season seems small price to pay," she said quietly. "Indeed, I considered my purchases quite a bargain. The price of a single ball gown alone provided all of the lads with wool coats."

"My dear Patience!" Richard's sudden smile was so broad, so completely pleased with her that it stirred in her a momentary answering smile. "How very kind."

Oh, but I am not, she thought, smile fading. *I am so very stupid of late.*

" 'Tis nothing but foolishness." Her mother echoed her contempt. "Today she tried to convince me she could not go to this garden party because she had nothing to wear."

Richard met these words with raised brows. "You did not wish to go?"

What would you think of me if you knew the real reason I do not wish to go? Patience thought.

"Oh, dear!" her mother exclaimed as they reached the door. "I must run fetch my shawl. I am sure to need it."

In the silence that followed the flurry of her footsteps upon the stairs, Richard asked again, "You did not wish to go to Melanie's party?"

A thousand thoughts raced through Patience's head as he stood regarding her with an intensity she had so long taken for granted. "I did not want . . . could not face . . ." She stopped, unable to explain.

"What's wrong?" he asked.

"Oh, Richard," she said with a sigh.

"What is it? Did Pip . . . ?"

Her gaze rose to meet his, startled. "Did Pip what?" she whispered, afraid for a moment. Reason returned, and logic. She said, "Did he tell me he means to marry Melanie? Yes."

He held the door wide. The evening's breeze washed her in the scent of his cologne, cedar and lime. A comfort, that scent.

She turned, eye-to-eye with him in the doorway. "Do you want to go?"

"Yes."

She sighed, wondering how he could bear it that Pip should love the woman he had so long waited for. She studied his face, looked deep into his eyes a moment, and thought of Pip's touch, his kiss. Was that how it had been between Richard and Melanie?

He looked back at her most intently, his gaze guarded, questions in his eyes, and she had no answers for him, only more questions. So many she dared not ask.

"Who am I?" she said at last, stepping into the last of the day's sunshine, a golden wash of it, the slanting light momentarily blinding her.

He tucked her gloved hand into the crook of his arm, brilliant light gilding raven black hair, gleaming golden in green eyes. "Is this a riddle?"

"Perhaps it is." She nodded, looked away. "Life's riddle."

He opened the door to the carriage. The footman let down the step.

She gathered her skirt in her free hand as he handed her in.

"You are Patience," he said with gratifying certainty as she sank into the seat, the carriage swaying as she arranged her skirt.

"Am I?" she asked as he darkened the door in following her. "I feel more like heartbreak than patience."

He said nothing until he was settled, dear Richard, reliable Richard. She could count on him to make her feel better. He always did. He knew what she was after with her question.

"You are allowed to be both, my dear, under certain circumstances."

"And you, old friend?"

For a moment his eyes narrowed, his gaze quickened. He seemed to hold his breath.

"Are you impatient with your Patience?"

He cocked his head, gaze guarded, hints of something waiting there, in the shadows that claimed his features, in the stillness that momentarily claimed his limbs. Questions, perhaps, waiting to be answered.

Who held the answers?

His chin rose, light catching the line of his cheek, the tip of his nose. "I am the soul of patience."

She blinked, considering this, and thought of Lady Wilmington and said, "Ah, yes. I suppose you are."

He nodded. "Oh, these many years."

She sighed again, envying him, envying Melanie to have aroused the lasting passions of such a man. She forced a smile. "Do you enjoy being the soul of patience? You are rather good at it, I think. So good, few notice your Patience."

He smiled, relishing this double-talk. His eyes danced with mischief. "I prefer it that way. There is only one I would have notice."

She puzzled over that a bit before she said, "Of course. And she has been unable to look too much in your direction, distracted by another."

She reached out to give his gloved hand an affectionate pat.

He blinked at her, as if in touching him she startled him. Light flashed in his eyes. His lashes fluttered like dark moths. A hesitant smile lifted the corners of his lips.

She smiled. "Has Melanie not told you?"

"Melanie?" He frowned, and bit his lip, and cocked

his head in the inquisitive way that made her think of crows. "What was she to tell me?"

"She said—"

They were interrupted by her mother's inquisitive, "Did I miss anything?" at the window.

Richard sat staring at Patience, questions bright in his eyes, the smile that had so warmed his features earlier completely disappeared.

"Nothing," Patience said.

Chapter Thirty-two

She stepped through the gate that led into Melanie's garden on Richard's steady arm, her mother in their wake, and was reminded of another night at another garden, so many nights ago—an evening that had felt to her like a beginning, as much as this evening felt like an end. She had longed to see Pip as much then as she longed, now, to avoid him.

It seemed ironic that she wore the same gown she had worn on that long-ago evening, beneath a red domino. Ironic because, while clothed the same, she felt she was a completely different person than she had been then.

"I hear Lord Wilmington's cousin has arrived to take possession of his property," her mother said from behind them.

"Yes." Richard pointed at a handsome gentleman surrounded by a bevy of women. "Fortesque is his name. A nice enough chap."

"I shall just go and see if I can manage an introduction," Lady Ballard said, and abandoned them, fluttering away like a great moth in the growing darkness.

They walked on in silence a moment, Patience moody, trying to imagine what it must be like to be thrust from one's home, in awe of Melanie that she chose to celebrate so publicly her own ousting.

"What of Melanie?" she asked Richard, hoping he would tell her something of his situation in that regard.

He smiled. "Well, she will soon be making her home elsewhere. Won't she? Other gardens to tend."

Pip's gardens.

Poor Richard. What a brave face he wore.

Sadness and a sense of loss swept through Patience with such intensity she felt like weeping. Pip had never really been in love with her. She had been foolish to dream dreams of him so long without encouragement. She began to believe his latest behavior a last desperate bid for freedom from a confirmed bachelor and womanizer—for that was what he was, and always had been. Like Chase, only not too much like Chase, thank God.

But that Melanie, whom she had come to respect, should discard Richard as she had, that she should change strategy in the last stages of their game of love, with such a dear and deserving fellow, seemed the height of cruelty.

Poor Richard. Poor, dependable Richard.

So lost was she in contemplation of her mounting pity for him that the walk was nothing more than an impression of the sweet scent of flowers, of a myriad of flickering lamps. His question startled her.

"Will you wish them well?" he asked.

Ahead loomed the smell of food, the lilt of laughter, the elegant stirrings of a string quartet.

A game of blindman's bluff among the temples and ruins in the garden was already afoot. A female guest wearing a red blindfold stumbled past them laughing as she staggered, arms out. A gentleman teased her into following him.

Could she? Would she? It seemed too much to ask.

She asked. "Have you no intention of pursuing her?"

Richard turned his head to watch the young woman with the blindfold. "One must always wish one's friends lucky in love," he said. "Shall we make our presence known to our hostess before we engage in any games?"

Games? She was in no mood for games. She noticed he avoided answering her question.

"I wish you lucky in love," she said as they went on, past a bubbling fountain and into an alcove where tables and chairs had been arranged for the guests to dine.

Richard turned to look at her, lamplight flaring in his

eyes, the reflections from the huge punch bowl and a tower of glassware captured in his glance. "Thank you, Patience. Perhaps we shall both be lucky."

Laughter turned her head, a familiar sound. Melanie held court at one of the tables, and at her side sat an amused Pip, golden hair glinting in the lamplight, cheeks flushed as a cherub's.

No angel this. She knew all too well the devils that drove him, the unholy desires.

Heat rushed to her cheeks, an unwanted fire quickening in the places he had touched. But she felt no flicker of hope. Only shame, deep and undeniable, and regret that she had not realized sooner that he would never be hers. She steeled herself to meet his gaze, steeled her heart against any last pangs of regret. She must play the hand she had been dealt.

"Here they are!" Melanie rose to greet them with a smile. "We have been waiting for your arrival to make our announcement."

Pip rose as well, his laughter stilled, his smile fading, a wary watchfulness in his eyes. He feared her reaction, what she might say, his fear for Melanie. She might ruin things for him in a moment, and he knew it. Patience felt power over him far greater than that wielded on a chessboard or in backgammon—a power she did not want.

She forced herself to meet his gaze unblinking, emotions guarded. This was the moment she had been dreading, a moment in which the past hung heavy between them, a moment on which their future—had they any—balanced.

What did she want? What did she really want? To give him pain as he had pained her? To seek revenge?

"I understand congratulations are in order."

Richard put out his hand. His smile was genuine, the words unforced.

Patience was stunned by his sense of gentlemanly grace in that moment, by the simple beauty and appropriateness of Richard's unfailing manners.

"Thank you, Richard." A sudden glitter of tears wet Melanie's cheek as she leaned forward for his kiss.

Patience marveled anew at his calm, good-natured acceptance of what this woman had done to him—with his best friend as accomplice.

Partners in crime, she considered them, and wondered as Richard shook Pip's hand and clapped him on the shoulder how one man could be so gracious and giving, another so heartless and grasping.

"Will you wish me happy?" Melanie asked her, a trifle hesitant in the question, her smile a shade too bright.

"One must always wish friends happy in love."

She parroted Richard's words.

Hearing them, he turned to smile at her with a sympathetic twist to his lips that kindled in her an answering smile.

Pip turned as well, his expression guarded, as if he had expected rejection from her, as if he believed he deserved nothing less.

"I believe a toast is in order," Richard said. "Help me fetch the glasses, will you, Pip?"

Pip agreed. Other than a nervous glance in Patience's direction, he seemed glad to be led away.

"I am so relieved." Melanie held out her hands to Patience. "I thought . . . Well." She laughed. "Never mind what I thought."

Patience allowed herself to be swept into Melanie's embrace.

"I thought," Melanie whispered into her hair, "given your feelings for Pip . . ."

Patience jerked back, angry now, unable to resist voicing her feelings now that Pip and Richard were not there to hear. "Pip? Never mind Pip. What about Richard?"

Melanie squinted at her in surprise. "What about Richard?"

Laughter behind them. Patience could think of nothing to laugh about. She lowered her voice.

"How could you hurt him so?"

Melanie stepped back as though she had been struck, looking over her shoulder at the gaggle of guests who made their way through the tables, laughing and talking, teasing the young man who now wore the blindfold, leading him onward with taunts and coaxing.

Melanie leaned forward to ask, as if incensed by the question, "How could I hurt him?"

So puzzled she managed to look, as if she had done nothing wrong, nothing questionable.

Words poured out of Patience. "How could you abandon Richard when he has loved you so long, when he meant to marry you?"

Melanie laughed and shook her head. Leaning close she said, aghast, "Richard was never in love with me. It has always been you. "

Patience stood stunned, disbelief freezing her tongue. And in that confused state she fell prey to the young man in the blindfold. He bumped into her quite by accident. And having first begged her pardon, he then cried, as if amazed, "You're it! I cannot tell you how happy I am to have happened to bump into you. I thought I'd never touch anyone!"

"Should not have touched Patience, lad. She does not play that sort of game."

It was Pip who spoke, his tone apologetic. He had returned in that instant with drinks, Richard at his heels.

"I am not playing," Patience protested weakly, overcome by what Melanie had said, not ready to believe it, not ready for Pip's attempted apology. She had eyes for no one but Richard.

"Oh, but you must play blind man," the young man whined. "I shall just tie it on, shall I?" He held the red scarf before her eyes.

"Come. Come, Patience." Richard set aside the drinks he carried to assist the young man who would blindfold her. "It's just a game."

She said nothing to stop him when he pressed the red scarf to her eyes with hands that shook ever so slightly, when he tied it tight against her head with much care for her curls.

She allowed him to turn her in place three times, until she was dizzy with the turning, and completely disoriented. The hands at her shoulders seemed those of a stranger.

She stood, head whirling, her world spinning, the ground unsteady beneath her feet. She put out her hands to steady herself, to reach for something, anything to stop the world from spinning, the world that seemed determined to turn upside down.

Richard loved her! Could it be true? *"It has always been you."* So completely sure of herself Melanie had sounded. So startled by Patience's assumption that he had been in love with her.

She could not help it. She let slip a few hot tears, the silk catching the moisture, the cloth hiding her eyes, hiding her face as the possibility that this was true welled within her.

Her whole world was already spinning; she did not wish to stumble about making a fool of herself in a blindfold. What she wanted was to run away somewhere and hide, and weep until she could weep no more.

The hands that had spun her fell away. Head still reeling, she stood a moment, unsteady, trying to understand her own folly.

How could she have so completely misunderstood? How could she have supposed Pip's interest turned to her when all along it had been Melanie he loved?

"Patience," came a whispered voice, Pip's voice, and then Pip's stifled laugh.

They expected her to play, did not realize she had been playing all along, stumbling about in the darkness of self-deception, blindfold on, unable to see the truths right before her eyes.

"Patience. You cannot just stand there." Melanie's coaxing. Her party. She did not want the games to fail to entertain her guests.

How entertained had she been, Patience wondered, to know that silly little Patience vied for Pip's attentions as much as she did—had—from the very start? She had had him under her thumb before Patience had ever arrived in London. She could see, looking back.

"She looks like someone in that mask," Pip said quietly from somewhere to her right. "I cannot quite place . . ."

"The lady in red?" Melanie suggested. "The one who bested you at chess?"

"But that was you," Pip said.

Patience laughed at that, a little hysterically, the scarf puffing out away from her mouth.

"Not me," Melanie said with a laugh. "Whatever gave you such a nonsensical idea?"

"Does she mean to stand there all evening?" the young man who had once worn the blindfold said from somewhere behind her.

Patience thought about the night in Vauxhall Gardens, of Richard leading her to Pip, knowing he might lose her. What courage that had taken. She thought about his generosity in spending money he could ill afford on food and wine, on cake she had not eaten. She thought about the way he had chased after her, into the dark wilderness of the trees, ready to save her from harm. Blind. She had been blind.

She thought of Chase, and Pip's castoff cockatoo, and the boy, Toby. Richard loved the unloved, even when they did not acknowledge or appreciate his love—as she had not appreciated it. She thought about tearing the blindfold from her eyes, of running away, deep into the park, beneath the trees. She would fall down in the grass and bemoan her stupidity.

Before she could follow through with the idea his voice turned her head.

"Patience."

Richard. Dear Richard. She turned toward him—the only one among them she wanted to face in this moment. She took a step, held out her hands, suddenly afraid of falling, bewildered by the darkness.

"Patience." Richard again, directly ahead of her, exactly where she had heard his voice before.

She took another step.

"You are supposed to try to get away, my lord," the young man said.

Richard's reply was quiet, but very sure. "You play the game your way; I will play the game mine."

"Oh, ho!" Melanie murmured.

She took another step, another, and then she could hear footsteps in the grass, moving toward her, not away. The scent of him engulfed her, cedar and lime. Richard, dear Richard, always there when she needed him, always looking out for her. Her waving hands found purchase on his sleeve, gripped the arm that had so often been her support.

"And so I am caught," he said.

Chapter Thirty-three

"He is in love with you, you know." Melanie's voice in her memory. She had said as much the last afternoon Patience had come to this garden.

Richard. All along it had been Richard. How long had he harbored feelings for her? How long had she been blind to them?

Melanie had tried to tell her as Pip and Richard stood throwing stones. "Pip said he had yet to tell you—said he had been afraid to tell you these many years." Not Pip who was afraid, but Richard.

What a fool she had been. A blind fool. She tightened her grip on his arm with one hand, with the other wrenched the blindfold from her eyes.

The expression on his face touched her heart, the concern in ageless agate eyes.

"Are you all right, my dear?" he asked and, arms encircling her head, reached to untie the blindfold, hands gentle in her hair, his eyes as gentle in their loving regard. "It is tangled."

He loved her. How clearly it was writ upon his face.

"I have been blind," she said, safe in the haven of his arms, trying to catch his eyes, but his hand, his gaze, were fixed upon her head, tugging at the knot. Another moment and he would step away, and she did not want him to.

They were watched. They were listened to, but it did not matter.

"I have been so very blind," she repeated.

"That is the point of the game," the lad who had foisted this stupid blindfold on her said with a laugh.

She paid him no mind, all her attention on Richard, dear Richard, dependable Richard, whom she saw as if for the first time—his face gilded by lamplight—his dear, beautiful face.

"How long have I been so afflicted?" she whispered, regret in her voice, regret paining her heart.

Something changed in his eyes, a spark of light and warmth and . . . was it hope blooming? His hands fell still. His breath—did it catch in his throat?

"Methinks we tarry here too long," Melanie said softly.

"This game is best left to two players," Pip agreed.

She saw them only peripherally, and did not turn to watch them go. Her gaze was fixed on the pensive set of Richard's mouth, the uncertainty in his eyes.

He busied himself with the knot in her hair again, whispered to her curls, "Since we were children, Patience. I have loved you since we were children."

She lifted her chin that she might see the wonderful truth of it shining in his eyes. "Oh!" she whispered, her voice very small. "Really? All this time, and you said nothing?"

How close to the vest he played his cards, she thought.

He clasped tight her hand, and whispered, "You were in love with my best friend—I had no right to speak, and little to offer."

She laughed as she wept and, tilting her chin higher, standing on tiptoe, kissed his chin. The kiss was infinitely gentle, warm, and salty.

"Little to offer"—she gave a watery chuckle—"other than your constant, beloved companionship, sound advice, and deepest friendship."

"These you were ready to accept of me." His voice was wistful. "I wanted more. I longed for your passion." The scarf fell away, his hands as well. "I know you have always considered me a friend."

He pulled the scarf through his fingers like a magician.

"Yes," she said, her voice weak. Too weak. Her best friend. She could not imagine life without him.

He bowed his head, clumped the scarf in a ball.

"I have always clung to the belief . . . that your fondness for me . . . might deepen."

She leaned closer as his voice dropped, catching one end of the scarf, tugging it from his hold.

He took a deep breath, chin set, lips thinned, consternation weighing heavy in his gaze. "That you might . . ."

She slipped the scarf around his neck.

". . . at last, come to lo—"

She did not allow him to finish. She simply stood on tiptoe, drew him closer, and kissed him on the tip of his nose.

He stood frozen a moment.

She leaned back and looked him in the eyes, and murmured fondly, "Dear Richard. You have been so very patient with your Patience."

He shook his head and stepped back. "No more word games, my dear."

"Oh, but you must, Richard," she insisted, her cry heartfelt.

He sighed, holding up his hands. "Patience. Do not play with me." He opened his mouth as if to say something more, and then, with a shake of his head, walked away, fists knotted in the small of his back.

"But . . ." She ran to stand in front of him, breath coming fast, her pulse racing. "You are the soul of Patience. You cannot give up so easily."

He looked at her in disbelief, and said nothing for so long that tears sprang to her eyes, and she whispered, "Please, Richard."

So still he stood, so dark the pucker of winged brows.

"Speak plainly with me, Patience."

"I have. I do."

"Do you mean it?" His voice was faint. "No game, this?"

She stood on tiptoe then to kiss him on the lips—a sweet kiss, a tender kiss—while he remained frozen, resistant to her, until with an unexpected moan he swept her into his arms and crushed her to him, and endowed their second kiss with all the love this patient man had kept bound within himself over a lifetime's worth of waiting for her to notice him.

It was a kiss that left Patience breathless, weak in the knees—a kiss that stirred within her an unexpected wave of passion, which prompted her to kiss him again and again with such fervor that at last he held her at arm's length and looked into her eyes, and said, "Who are you?"

She laughed. "Impatience."

He threw back his head to loose a heartfelt laugh before he bent his head to dizzy her again with the impatient passion of his kisses.

Signet Regency Romances from **Allison Lane**

"A FORMIDABLE TALENT...
MS. LANE NEVER FAILS TO
DELIVER THE GOODS."
—*ROMANTIC TIMES*

THE NOTORIOUS WIDOW
0-451-20166-3

When a scoundrel tries to tarnish a young widow's reputation, a valiant Earl tries to repair the damage—and mend her broken heart as well...

BIRDS OF A FEATHER
0-451-19825-5

When a plain, bespectacled young woman keeps meeting the handsome Lord Wylie, she feels she is not up to his caliber. A great arbiter of fashion for London society, Lord Wylie was reputed to be more interseted in the cut of his clothes than the feelings of others, as the young woman bore witness to. Degraded by him in public, she could nevertheless forget his dashing demeanor. It will take a public scandal, and a private passion, to bring them together...

To order call: 1-800-788-6262